CW00666510

Our Silent Footsteps

Our Silent Footsteps

RACHEL HEALEY

Copyright © 2024 Rachel Healey

The moral right of the author has been asserted.

Apart from any fair dealing for the purposes of research or private study,
or criticism or review, as permitted under the Copyright, Designs and Patents
Act 1988, this publication may only be reproduced, stored or transmitted, in
any form or by any means, with the prior permission in writing of the
publishers, or in the case of reprographic reproduction in accordance with
the terms of licences issued by the Copyright Licensing Agency. Enquiries
concerning reproduction outside those terms should be sent to the publishers.

This is a work of fiction, based on the personal memories of Mary Beker. Every reasonable
attempt to verify the facts against available documentation and the memories of other
family members has been made. In some cases, names, characters and incidents have been
changed or are the product of the author's own imagination.

Troubador Publishing Ltd
Unit E2 Airfield Business Park,
Harrison Road, Market Harborough,
Leicestershire LE16 7UL
Tel: 0116 279 2299
Email: books@troubador.co.uk
Web: www.troubador.co.uk

ISBN 978 1 80514 244 7

British Library Cataloguing in Publication Data.
A catalogue record for this book is available from the British Library.

Printed and bound in Great Britain by 4edge Limited
Typeset in 11pt Minion Pro by Troubador Publishing Ltd, Leicester, UK

Dedicated to the memory of those whose lives have been shaped by war.

PART ONE

Warsaw, POLAND, 2005

They say that to really know a person you need to understand their past. If that is true, then Mary Beker did not know her husband at all. She did not know him on their wedding day, she did not know him during the fifteen years they were together, and she still did not know him when she buried him in 1960.

His was a past smothered by war. A past he then cocooned in a silence of his own making. She had only asked Jozef about it once, a lifetime ago, in those early days of courtship. They'd been sipping Turkish coffee in a café in Mary's home city of Alexandria, Egypt, savouring the bitter taste despite the searing heat. She'd felt a need, a yearning to know all about him before her heart fell too deeply; before love took over her senses. She asked him about his life in Poland and immediately regretted it. The invisible scars bled anew as Jozef gripped his cup and mentioned a young family he assumed were dead, a wife taken from him in a place far from here. All at once, that wall guarding him from his painful past crumbled and raw anguish haemorrhaged through.

It was so unbearable to see you like that.

She buried her questions. She protected him from the past he found too painful, worried that any mention of it would cause him to shatter.

His silence became hers.

Now she was breaking that silence in the year that would have seen him reach his hundredth birthday. Mary and her children, Henry and Margarita, had travelled the 900 miles from her home in London to visit the country of his birth, the city he had forced to flee all those years ago. It was a trip designed to honour the man who was forever preserved in her memory in the throes of youth, captured behind the glass of a photo frame. A journey that was forcing her to question the *before*: the time previous to their meeting that had shaped him and her own early life that had resulted in the moulding of her.

The decades that followed Jozef's death had seen Henry and Margarita grow into adulthood and, in turn, grow in curiosity. Their constant questions evolved into ones she couldn't answer, holes in their own DNA that her limited knowledge couldn't plug.

But answers to what? She was sure that knowing Jozef's lineage, the name of his hometown, what he had even looked like before they'd met would make no difference to the love she felt for him. Even after all this time.

Or would it?

There was still that brief feeling of apprehension, a rumbling fear that she couldn't quite flatten. What if something in his past unravelled into something ugly, threatening the memory of those brief idyllic years of marriage? A marriage she remembered brimming with contentedness, a partnership full of love. A lie (God forbid) that caused her to question her own judgement in choosing him as a partner, a man who held all her trust.

These were the thoughts running through her head as she stepped off the plane in Warsaw and contemplated the city she had never visited before; the country Jozef had refused to return to after the bombing had stopped.

"What if we were to start a new life in Warsaw?"

She remembered suggesting it to him, over a Polish meal of *pierogi*, as they sat in their flat on Safia Zaghloul Street, Alexandria, contemplating their future. Things had changed in Egypt after the war. Having embraced the help of the British to keep his border secure, King Farouk was less tolerant of them once the war had stopped. The uniformed foreigners were a painful reminder of Egypt's colonial past and Jozef once again felt unwelcome, unwanted. The newly married couple were forced to contemplate their options and the doughy softness of the Polish dumplings popped the idea into Mary's head.

"No!"

The quickness of his answer and the sharpness of his tone made Mary drop her fork with a clatter. The sound reverberated in amongst the beep of horns, the shouts of Arabic that peaked and troughed outside their window.

He looked pained, hurt, angry even. She wanted to take the words back at once, turn back the clock on that moment in a fruitless wish that it had never happened. And then Jozef returned to her, his eyes bulging in their sadness as his hand reached across to hers. He held her palm a moment, caressed her soft skin.

"No," he repeated in a gentle tone and she was immediately loath to expand on his answer, the silence keeping the pain at bay.

Now, Mary's eyes brimmed with tears at the memory of that moment. Strange how the thought of him all these years later could still bring sadness and a simultaneous smile to her face. What would he make of her now that her eyesight was fading, her thick hair dyed a different shade of black, her posture bent with age and her skin still sun-kissed but a little less supple? This was a time in her life that Jozef had never known, his passing coming too soon in their short fifteen years of marriage.

I wish you were with me, now, in this strange place.

"Much has changed in Warsaw since your husband was here." Mary's son had employed a genealogist to help them make the most of their trip to Poland. A local guide (a woman half Mary's age) to navigate the blanks in Jozef's past. She kept repeating the statement again and again to Mary and her children in an almost apologetic tone as they roamed the streets of Poland's capital. It was a statement accompanied by a dismissive wave of her hand as she brought them past another American fast-food outlet, or another modern building fronted entirely in glass.

Warsaw was no longer Jozef's city. The Second World War had made sure of that. Where other cities bore the scars of destruction, Poland's capital had been annihilated and not just its buildings. Records of births, marriages and deaths, censuses, municipal records – all had been destroyed by the bombing, reduced to dust along with thousands of its citizens. Many of those who survived found their past lives erased.

Jozef Beker was one of the latter.

He had emerged from Poland a different man. His previous identity now lost in the ruins of Warsaw, crumpled beneath the feet of an impenetrable war machine. He had even changed his name, reinventing himself as *Jozef* rather than carry on with his birth name of *Szyja Alter*. He feared the connotations the name Szyja Alter brought with it, a dread of the anti-Semitic feeling it might induce.

We all go through a reinvention at some point in our lives.

Hadn't she done the same? On that miserable day in 1948 when she'd turned up alone at Liverpool docks with her dark skin, not knowing a word of English. A foreigner in a foreign land. Adapt and change. They had both done it. The events of their pasts so altering them that it was only with the benefit of age, the slowing down of life, that Mary found herself discovering what had shaped them: the prejudices, the constant need to fit in.

It hadn't mattered where they had found themselves, they had still stood out. In the dull climate of an English winter the colour of Mary's skin set her apart. Despite the numerous languages Jozef spoke fluently, his accent always seemed to arouse suspicion.

"How do you expect your children to thrive in their education if you cannot speak the language yourselves?"

Those bitter words still sat uncomfortably with Mary all these years later. The insults of strangers cutting just as deeply and raising the same level of indignation and determination.

We tried so hard to fit in, Jozef.

On the fourth day of their trip to Poland, Mary and her children's search for information faltered. Details of Jozef's past were proving difficult to come by.

"If he was a teacher, like you say," the Polish genealogist suggested, "he may have attended the university. They have some records left from that period."

It was a small possibility but worth exploring. They followed the expert's thread of hope there, to the university, Mary hardly noticing her children temper their walking pace so that she wasn't left behind. The plane journey, the constant walking, the anxiety over the Pandora's box she was opening were all tiring her, wearing her out and reminding her that she wasn't as young as she used to be. She hated to be reminded of that. Age wasn't a condition she would allow herself to succumb to.

Later that morning Mary found herself sitting stiffly on a plastic chair, dwarfed in a building her husband would not have recognised. The University of Warsaw's immense library had a high-vaulted ceiling crowned with glass, an architectural feature to make the revived city proud: a phoenix rising from the flames of destruction. She was all too aware that, even though it was his footsteps she was following, they were footsteps since concreted over by a new world, a new order.

The glasses that dominated her face caught the dim light of the waning afternoon sun. She sat and stared at the computer screen, flanked by her son and daughter trying to work out what to think.

Szyja Alter Beker results found: 1.

The cursor flashed in time with Mary's heartbeat. A feeling of anticipation coursed through her veins. Neither Mary nor her children said a word as they waited for the university archivist to retrieve the original file. To have something of his past actually uncovered in print was more than they could have hoped for. She'd always believed they would come to Poland and find nothing and the silence she had known would continue. There would be nothing to rock her world, the life they had led together. But here it was: one single folder lying in front of them on the nondescript plastic table. A folder from Jozef's student days, untouched and unimportant for over eighty years.

Mary's hands with their perfectly manicured nails tightened, whitening her dark Mediterranean skin. Still, her outward expression gave no indication of the thoughts running through her head as she came across a picture of what her husband had looked like before they had met, before he had changed his name from *Szyja* to *Jozef*, before the war had torn his world apart and shaped their future.

How strange, she thought as her fingers gently opened the file, *to be unlocking his past and mine after all this time.* All those moments long ago that had made him Jozef, that had made her Mary, bringing them together – a Polish Jew and an Egyptian Copt. The unlikeliest of couples who fell in love against the backdrop of war.

Harlesden, ENGLAND, 1951

It was early when Jozef awoke. He knew that, long before his eyes had found the bedside clock. He started the morning in the same way as always, only this time he managed to wake himself up before the cry could escape his subconscious and wake his sleeping wife. He had stripped to his pants the previous evening before crawling into bed, in expectation of the night-time sweats that visited him so regularly. He'd been right to do so as the cotton sheets were damp and stuck to his clammy skin. Mary stirred next to him and her lips moved silently and briefly. He wondered what she was dreaming about. Her peacefulness was so perfect, her breath so slow and calm that he felt an envy creeping alongside his love for her. If only his nights were as tranquil as hers. In that moment, he became overwhelmed for his need for her and all that she brought him – the peace and comfort, the understanding. But even she couldn't penetrate the darkness that haunted his night, the dreams that plagued him.

It was no use. He would not sleep now. He would get up and take a walk, enjoy the silence of the streets that inhabited the hour when the night owls had retreated to bed and before the early risers emerged. He dressed in the clothes he'd laid out the night before: the grey pleated trousers that had been folded and draped over the chair, the cotton shirt hanging on the wardrobe door with a navy, diagonal-striped tie, the matching woollen blazer hanging behind the shirt, the shoes (brushed and polished) beside the bed with a pair of socks laid out on top. All in easy reach should he need to get dressed in a hurry.

Habit.

The early morning air hit his grateful lungs as he quietly pulled the front door closed behind him. The streets were relatively silent. The sharp, scraping sound of the early morning street sweeper carried easily over the car-less roads. A blackbird paused on the silver birch that rose from the pavement in front of their house. It peered at him curiously, unused to having its early morning song interrupted. Jozef enjoyed this time. *His* time: the quiet, the peace, before the world got up and reminded him that he wasn't alone.

He kept a sound pace along Bramshill Road, turning left onto Acton Lane, his mind mapping out the familiar route which would take him exactly 1.8 miles, 3,693 steps. The very few people out and about ignored him as if it was an unwritten rule that wanderers at this hour were not to be disturbed. Less than half a mile and he double-backed down Manor Park Road heading towards the High Street. The area still bore the traces of war. Every now and then the dim morning light broke through onto the pavement where a house, a business, a shop was missing. A black hole and brick dust left in its place. He could do this route with his eyes shut and sometimes, if he knew he wasn't being watched, he would do just that. His eyelids became barriers to the stark, broken monuments of a time he'd rather forget.

He shut his eyes momentarily to savour the morning calm when he suddenly hesitated, his right foot hovering on stride number 2,383. He sensed something that hadn't been there before. He opened his eyes, searching for the new landmark that had interrupted his military pace. A new shop had appeared on the opposite side of the High Street, in a building which had previously been a furniture store. It wouldn't have interested him if it hadn't been for one word emblazoned in deep blue against a background of white above the gleaming entrance: *Polski*.

His gaze had been so drawn to the sign that he initially missed seeing the man standing underneath it. The man paused in his task of arranging chairs and tables outside his shop, his muscles bulging as he stared at him. Jozef realised his right foot was still hovering inches above the pavement.

"Morning." Mr Morawski's voice carried effortlessly across the deserted road. A deep voice with a sharp Polish accent.

A few minutes later and Jozef's eyes were eagerly drinking in the neatly stacked rows of Polish produce listening to Mr Morawski talk about his family, his Polish roots, his new life in England and his new Polish delicatessen which he had first opened that morning.

"You are my first customer, Mr Beker," he said, offering him a plate of warm assorted breads which had just come out of the oven. "Here's to many more."

Jozef took a small *Żymła* roll and nodded his thanks. His fingers felt the indented starfish pattern on its top and he greedily sank his teeth into its crunchy crust. Sesame seeds peppered his tongue and his teeth sliced through the heavenly chewiness of the warm dough inside. Mr Morawski smiled at the pleasure it seemed to give him.

"It's good, yes?"

He nodded, his mouth full. It was food that awoke memories: his mother busy baking over the hot stove, her hair covered by a scarf as she hummed the quick haunting melody of a Yiddish tango. The sweet smell of fresh bread would send him and his brothers into a frenzy, their small hands reaching for the irresistible yeasty goodness. And then her short temper, a flick of her wrist and her quick tongue cajoling them to get out of her kitchen so she could get on with her day.

"I tell you something," Mr Morawski said, "since you are my first customer. Anything you buy today I give you ten per cent discount. Eh?"

He retraced his steps back home, laden with Polish sausages, bread and sweet treats and his name first down on the order book for a delivery the following Friday. The world was awakening, and he smiled at the thought of his family's happy faces as he came through the door. Sure enough, his daughter's young face lit up with excitement as he emptied the brown paper bags and laid out a feast on the kitchen table.

"*Hein!* And what are we to do with all that?" Mary asked, brushing her thick black curls into a bun as she was prone to do when she meant business. Her hands smoothed down the apron that bulged over the baby bump in her belly.

"We cook it and eat it," he replied, in response to her concern.

"*Pour le petit déjeuner?*"

"*Oui, pour le petit déjeuner,*" he agreed, his smile broadening. "Today we eat like kings. And queens," he corrected himself.

"And how am I supposed to cook all *this* with *that* thing?"

Jozef recognised the look of distaste and suspicion that flashed over his wife's face as she eyed up the range. He knew her opinion on British kitchenware, and it wasn't flattering.

"I will help you. And so will Margarita," he said, ruffling his daughter's hair as she babbled along to her father's enthusiasm.

It was days like this that could make a man feel truly alive: his daughter smiling and laughing around the kitchen table, his wife, with that serious smile of hers, still holding on to the beauty of youth.

Life was for the living. *Wasn't that what it was all about?* Living.

It was only later, when his belly was full and Mary was busy putting their daughter down for a nap, that he unwrapped the issue of *The Jewish Chronicle* as he sat alone on the edge of the marital bed. The door to the bedroom remained shut. The light-green eiderdown that stretched across the mattress gave way to his weight, distorting the geometric pattern at its centre with its diamonds and squares.

It was not that he had anything to hide. Far from it. He knew Mary understood. He knew she fully endorsed his painful search, even helping him on occasions. He just needed the silence to concentrate.

Just in case.

He didn't need to turn many pages before he found what he was looking for. They covered the pages in neat little lists. Always the lists. The Germans had started the list-making before the outbreak of war, singling them out, branding them, sorting them and confining them into an easy-to-manage order. Those early lists had led to the lists of the dead that conveniently turned people into numbers. After all, how else would the Nazis be able to measure their success? And here they were now – six years after the war had ended – arranging themselves into yet more lists in order to bring the strings of chaos back towards some sense of normality.

'Anna Kosinski seeks any information on the whereabouts of her cousin, Erna Golde, last seen in Warsaw in 1942. Believed to have been sent to Auschwitz and then Ravensbruck. No further information known.'

It sat heavy on the heart. Each little plea spoke of a personal tragedy that hadn't diminished with the turning cogs of time. A family ripped apart, leaving questions unanswered of a life cut short in the most brutal of ways.

There was nothing, only emptiness in the space where

their names should have been. But he read each summary of those brief little lives just in case, dissecting each short paragraph in the hope that it might yield a clue as to their fate (no matter how insignificant).

There was none.

Eight years and counting and still no end to the mystery. Despite knowing that they were no longer alive, it was still difficult to accept that fact armed with only the piecemeal information as to *how* they had died.

Mary had not pressed him for information. As each week passed and each copy of *The Jewish Chronicle* was scrutinised, she did not ask him anything. There was no need to. Their little world in this three-bedroom semi on a quiet road in Harlesden was far away from those pre-war days.

Warsaw, POLAND, 2005

"It was so long ago." Mary suddenly realised that her thoughts had escaped out loud.

She watched her son, Henry, disappear in search of refreshments leaving her with the genealogist, this stranger they had invited to share in the most intimate details of their lives. The café they were sitting at in the old town market square was busy with tourists and the waiters were stretched in their task of serving, greeting, carrying. The discovery of Jozef's university file had filled Mary and her children with a sense of urgency, a hope that there was more to discover. They hadn't the time to waste.

"Yes," the genealogist agreed. "Although these buildings are newer than they look." Misunderstanding Mary's statement, the woman suddenly delved into an explanation of this place, this chocolate-box town square, with its soft pastel-coloured buildings. "All rebuilt by the people of the city using old maps and salvaging as much of the debris as possible."

All Mary wanted was coffee.

"That scarf suits you," she offered to the stranger that was helping piece together the parts of Jozef's life. It was a light, opaque thing with flowers that matched the colours of the buildings around them. "You should wear it loose, without the knot. It's for decoration, not warmth."

The woman's cheeks flushed and Mary watched her gaze flit uncomfortably away. Still, she undid the knot and Mary allowed herself a smile. *That's better.* It was a habit of hers to embrace an honest opinion. What was the point in stopping yourself from saying what you think?

"Are you from a Jewish background like your husband?" the genealogist suddenly asked.

That was an interesting question born out of the silence and the inquisitive mind of a historian who dealt only with the past.

"Oh no, no," she replied with a laugh, finding humour in the thought that anyone could think she belonged here. She found herself looking at her hands resting peacefully on her lap, her dark slender fingers slightly crooked but the skin well kept. They belonged in the sun, in a place far from here that, like Warsaw, was now a shadow of its former self, physically gone but tangible in memory. A place she would find as difficult to go back to as this journey of fancy she now found herself on.

Alexandria, EGYPT, 1920

Alexandria was known as the 'Jewel of the Mediterranean' back in those pre-war hazy days of calm. The wide bustling streets with their imposing neo-classical buildings had begun to welcome Western cars that vied for space amongst the donkeys, horses and horse-drawn carts of ancient traders. Palm trees waved in the permanently warm breeze. Smart shop fronts advertised their goods in English, Italian, French and Greek whilst down in the side streets, the Arab street market holders spread out their wares over the dust-trodden earth and gestured in welcome to shoppers as they passed.

"*As-salaam alaykum!*"

"*Wa alaykum as-salaam!*" came the standard reply.

Vibrant rugs, cups and pots were a feast for the eyes

whilst neighbouring stores were full of the fresh smells of earthy potatoes and the abundance of ripe tomatoes and figs. The clatter of languages from a dozen different tongues gave the city a cosmopolitan air. It was a melting pot of cultures and Mary Hawash was born right into the heart of it to parents of the minority Coptic faith. The year of her birth was 1917 or 1916 or 1915. Only her parents knew for sure. Delaying the registration of her birth was the normal thing to do back then. After all, if an Egyptian woman reached her twenties without a ring on her finger, it was unlikely that she was ever going to be proposed to at all. Better give her the leeway of a few years here and there to snag herself a man.

But in 1920, this destiny was a long way off. She was, for now, an only child. Her mother, Zakia, and her father, Hawash (from whom Mary took her last name as tradition dictated), made a handsome couple. He, a smart man with a perfect moustache and his wife, a tall Mediterranean beauty with dark eyes and olive skin. He had chosen her. She had not chosen him. Zakia had shown much promise in life and, at her mother Zatoona's insistence, she had benefitted from a decent education in an American school. But then Zatoona had died suddenly after a long fight with tuberculosis whilst Zakia had barely entered her teens. Zakia's studies were abruptly halted, and she had barely set foot back into the family home before she was found a suitor and thrust into marriage.

Life seemed to stop for Zakia even before she'd reached her thirteenth birthday.

Mary's birth followed soon after; a painful, bloody affair that was thrust upon Zakia without the comfort of a mother to hold her hand. Mary was, of course, ignorant of her mother's struggles. As a toddler she was still wrapped up in the protective bubble of early childhood.

The sun glinted off the heavy gold necklace around Zakia's neck, dazzling Mary as she bobbed sleepily in her mother's arms after a morning at the beach. The jewellery had been a present from Hawash to show the world that business was booming. The sun was at its fullest and the streets were emptying of the babble of tongues as people sought refuge from the heat. Through her sleepy eyes, her father's *galabeya* flapped in the dust-choked breeze like the garb of a pure white angel protecting them from the world. He walked close to them, ahead of them, as an Egyptian man should, leading them through the cosmopolitan streets back to their comfortable house in downtown Alexandria. The light seemed to falter as they entered the narrowing warren of dust-ridden alleyways full of barefooted children and the small-time pedlars selling street snacks and trinkets. The fragrant waft of kofta kebabs caused her nose to twitch and her eyes to open briefly in anticipation. High above them she saw the women draped over balconies, some dressed entirely in black with only their dark, impenetrable eyes showing. The sharp call of their Arabic tongues echoed off the crumbling exterior of the tall buildings as they hung wet washing out to dry. Through her tired eyes they looked like black crows pecking at the scraps carelessly left by the street sellers.

Peck, peck, peck.

The entrance to their house led straight off the pavement. The cool tiled floors and whitewashed walls soothed the heat and Mary's eyelids started to droop once more. She felt the tender caress of her mother's shawl as she felt herself being laid gently down on the tight, starched sheets of her cot bed.

In her childhood slumber she didn't see the difficulty with which her mother put her to bed nor the sharp grimace on her mother's young face. Zakia's belly was visibly swelling now with the rapidly developing baby in her womb. It would be Zakia's third pregnancy and it wouldn't be her last. They weren't to know that then.

For now, Mary slept cocooned in the warmth of two doting parents with no siblings to compete against. Her thick hair covered the pillow, which crinkled slightly from the small depiction of the Virgin Mary on coloured paper that her mother had placed under her head. Four crosses, one on each wall, guarded her cot to ward off any bad dreams. A necessary intervention. It was a habit of her mother's to continue the deep-seated superstitions handed down from Copt to Copt. Life in Alexandria was harder for them than their Muslim brothers. Opportunities were less easy to come by, education and government jobs more restricted because of their faith. In this environment, superstition meant a lot.

Mary awoke the next day to the smell of her father's cologne. The sun was only just beginning to rise and the house was sleepily silent. There was mischief in her father. His spirits were high.

"We are going on an adventure, you and me," he announced.

They left Zakia fitfully sleeping, disturbed by the movement of the unborn baby. This hour belonged to Mary and her father. She giggled at the prospect of having his full attention as Hawash bounced her along on his broad shoulders, humming a tune she didn't recognise. Her childish hands lay gently on the top of his head as she steadied herself against his purposeful sway. He was treading the well-worn route to his shop by the harbour, leaving the comfort of home to focus entirely on business.

Her eyes were open now to the world around her as the city awoke for the day. Sleek Rolls-Royce cars trundled up to the front of the Paradise Inn Le Metropole Hotel whilst porters bustled around them in their immaculately clean suits and bright red jackets, their red felt tarboosh bobbing about like cockerels calling to the morning sun. Past the tall, white villas with their swaying palm trees.

Her father swayed her this way and that, in between a chain of camels plodding towards the market with their overloaded backs, groaning and snorting with the effort. Her fingers reached out to touch the wiry hair that bristled on their backs. To the market now, with its narrow streets where stallholders with caged chickens and fresh legumes heaved and puffed as they set up their wares for the day. Onwards her father took her, navigating the ground with the snake-like tracks that carried the trams into Ramleh Station. Her dark eyes soaked in the smart cafes with their doors still shut and their tables empty whilst the smell of freshly brewed coffee puffed into the air. Her father conducted the scene as if he were leading an orchestra, laughing at his daughter's wonder.

He paused on the pavement outside the entrance to his shop so that Mary could see the large lettering of her father's and her uncle's names above the door. Gold, shiny lettering that popped out of the brickwork in a loud broadcasting statement. She had yet to learn to read but, buoyed by her father's excitement, she giggled and smiled obediently in her eagerness to please him. The metal shutters squeaked open as he unveiled his domain; the place where he resided as king from day to day. There was a coolness in the air inside that had yet to be penetrated by the harsh Mediterranean sun. Her little eyes grew wide at the rows of eggs lined up ready to be boxed for shipment, the sacks of rice that dribbled their contents carelessly onto the floor. That was a happy morning, feeling the shiny, delicate shells as she popped the eggs carefully into their boxes on her father's instructions. Her father chatted and sang whilst they worked, and she felt that they could easily be the only two people on earth at that moment and they would both still be happy.

That was until Goued, Hawash's older brother, breezed into the shop, an unwelcome intrusion onto a cheerful, intimate scene. She didn't like her uncle, but she was yet to understand why. He was taller and broader than her father and had a rasping clip to his voice that spoke volumes of his disapproval at such a young child fiddling with their livelihood.

"You spoil that one."

Hawash aimed a playful punch to his brother's shoulder designed to snap him out of his disagreeable mood. "Ah, Goued, life is for living!" He smiled, his moustache bristling.

"There won't be much living if we don't concentrate on making our business a success," he reminded him. "It's so much harder for us Copts. So many doors closed to us…"

Mary's father grunted. A snort-like sound that reminded her of the hairy-lipped camels of the market.

"Goued, why do you complain so much? Business is good, our pockets are full. We cannot hope for more than that."

"You heard they refused the church's permit to extend the building again? Now if that had been a mosque…"

"*Khallas!*" Hawash snapped, before gathering up his daughter and twirling her in his arms. "What good is all this talk when we have so much to be grateful for? Live for the now, Goued! Don't concern yourself for the future. We cannot plan for something we know nothing about."

Harlesden, ENGLAND, 1951

"What *are* you doing?"

Mary turned to see Jozef standing at the top of the stairs, the corner of his mouth upturned slightly in a half-amused smile. She didn't appreciate his relaxed attitude. It was difficult enough going up and down the stairs with her belly swollen with baby number two, let alone with her arms full of the objects she'd collected from the living room.

"Two days!" She paused on the landing and grabbed a picture off the wall to add to her pile. "Your mother will be here in two days and I have so much to do!"

"Why are you stripping the place of all our possessions? We're not moving again just because my mother's paying us a visit."

Mary would not return his smile.

"Your mother is coming. We cannot have these things around the house!" She waved a picture of Jesus at him that had been given to her by her mother at her confirmation.

"Oh, Mary, it really doesn't matter..."

"*C'est important pour moi!*" She softened at the fleeting look of concern on her husband's face. "Oh, Jozef, I just want her to *like* me," she added quietly.

She did not object as he gently took the photographs, the cross and the framed pictures of Jesus and the Virgin Mary and laid them down on the floor before taking both her hands.

"You are my wife, Mary Beker, *elle t'aimera*." He kissed her. "Besides, what on earth is wrong with this one?" He picked up the photograph of Mary standing outside St Catherine's Church on their wedding day in Alexandria. She was dressed in a white suit that she had made herself, her black hair with its thick curls running down a face that couldn't help but smile.

"It's a church." She shrugged.

"It's a photograph of my beautiful wife on our wedding day."

"It's a church."

"Put it back where it belongs." Jozef had hung it back on the wall before she could protest any further. "You have nothing to worry about. Nothing at all."

Mary had everything to worry about. The house wasn't ready, her mother-in-law's room wasn't ready. She had no idea what to say to this woman whom she had never met. Their little world was being invaded and there was nothing she could do about it.

On the day Tumera Beker arrived in England, the

sun retreated behind a greying sky. Mary thought how appropriate a reflection of her mood as she waited at the docks in Liverpool completely alone, heavily pregnant, waiting for the mother-in-law who remained a mystery to her. Jozef had been taken ill at the last moment, unable to make the journey from London up north to collect the mother he adored. There were no means of contacting the ship before it docked, no prior warning that the pickup plans had changed.

Mary scrutinised the passengers that picked their way down the gangway, hunched in their furs as the shock of embarking into an English autumn from the warmth of a South African spring assaulted their senses. In her hand, Mary clutched the only photograph her husband had of his mother: a touching natural scene of mother and son walking arm in arm down a street in Johannesburg. The photographer had caught Jozef's smile perfectly. His mother, on the other hand, seemed to glare from the picture directly out at her, challenging her to dare encroach on their little scene.

She held the object carefully, anxious not to bend the edges in fear that it would further any resentment she was sure Tumera harboured towards her. A resentment barely concealed in the fangs of the lifeless fox that was currently draped over her mother-in-law's shoulders.

"*Dzień dobry, Matka.*" Mary's voice faltered over the unfamiliar Polish greeting as she addressed the woman walking towards her down the steps of the gangway.

"*Ojej!*" Tumera stopped abruptly and withdrew her foot back from the solid ground of the English dock.

The photograph Mary held was brandished as a peace

offering between them. Clearly, her mother-in-law saw it as anything but that. The displeasure that was sticking like make-up to the older woman's face mirrored that in the photograph and Mary realised that their relationship was doomed from the start. She attempted, in stilted Polish, an explanation of who she was and why Jozef couldn't be there to meet her. The words only appeared to further her mother-in-law's frown and, without another sound, Tumera had forced herself back up the gangway, brushing past the human traffic coming the other way. Mary was left on the dock, her face flushed with embarrassment at the curious stares.

Twenty minutes later and the last of the passengers had left the ship. All except Tumera, and Mary, who had called upon the ship's captain to placate the situation. Perhaps her mother-in-law would be more likely to listen to someone of authority.

"I can assure you, madam, that this lady is your daughter-in-law, and she is here to take you to London to see your son."

Despite Tumera's high heels, Mary was still the taller of the two as they stood on the deck of the ship listening to the Captain's attempts to persuade Tumera to leave. How odd it must look to the crew now depositing her mother-in-law's luggage in a pile beside them. A gentle hint that they were both outstaying their welcome.

At least look at me.

Mary tried to suppress her growing indignation. The baby turned restlessly in her belly reminding her that she had been on her feet too long. The clock was ticking towards the time the train was due to depart to take them back to London.

"*Twój syn czeka*," Mary tried, referencing Jozef in a bid to get her moving. *I'm waiting.*

Would it be such a bad thing for her to return to London alone? Could she justify leaving this woman stranded on a boat halfway between this country and hers?

"*Chodź*," Tumera finally agreed, the flattened face of the fur fox spinning round to land over her shoulder: a watcher at her mother-in-law's back as she abruptly turned and re-trod her footsteps down the gangway.

The greeting that was served up to Jozef was in direct contrast to the one Tumera showed her daughter-in-law at the docks in Liverpool. Mary watched the tender hand of a mother's love gently brush at her son's arm where he lay, delirious with fever in their house in Harlesden. A touch that caused a smile to crack slowly open on Jozef's face.

"*Ima…*"

She smiled at the beauty of it, knowing that Tumera had experienced things with Jozef that she was not a party to. The indignation unravelled like bandages over her bruised pride. For the sake of her husband, she would make this work. From one mother to another, she understood. The love, the hurt, the happiness.

***

A baby boy came in December. Jozef waited anxiously outside the labour ward, hopping from foot to foot whilst Margarita was treated to jelly and ice cream by a kindly nurse with motherly tendencies.

When he was finally allowed in to see his wife, the anxiety was immediately replaced by elation.

"He's beautiful."

"He is."

It was a small statement that seemed to fail miserably at describing the enormity of the feelings coursing through him. He gathered the newborn up into his arms, holding him, protecting him. This child so new, without blemish, lying against his own skin darkened by his constant tending of their vegetable patch. So unaware of the world.

"What should we call him?" his wife asked through the silence.

"Henry," he stated.

There was a slight frown on his face as he said it, and a brief struggle to hold back the tears that threatened his eyes.

"So it is," she replied.

Henry. Just a name. Only a name.

Alexandria, EGYPT, 1920

Mary woke one morning to find that she had a brother. He turned up in their lives one day in December; a tiny little thing that seemed to be unhappy about everything. They were selling salted pretzels outside the window when he arrived. She remembered how the street seller's voice cracked as he shouted louder and louder in an attempt to be heard over the baby's screams. It was hot, the dust wouldn't settle, and the flies were bothering the barefooted children playing with sticks on the street corner. But the screams...

Her parents didn't seem bothered by all the noise. In fact, it was a day when nothing seemed to upset them. Her father was spinning the little creature round and round, his cheeks flushed with delight whilst his *galabeya*, billowing in the breeze, brushed Mary's hair, causing her thick black curls to fall out of place.

"Let me look at you. Ah, *ya amir!*"

"Hawash! You'll hurt the child!" she heard her mother scold, her delicate fingers scooping up the baby to press him back protectively to her chest.

It had been quieter yesterday, Mary recalled. She had spent most of the day playing shop with the gold coins from the large wooden chest in the hall, counting out change for her imaginary customers. Her father was clearly distracted, otherwise he may not have been so accommodating towards his daughter playing games with the family's wealth. Her mother had disappeared for a few days, her belly swollen and her walking slow and laboured. Hawash had not been to his shop by the harbour that morning. Instead, he had entrusted his brother, Goued, with the sole responsibility of opening up and tending to their customers. Even in her young mind, Mary recognised that things had not been as they should. And as that thought niggled at her curious mind, her mother had returned to the house with a baby in her arms.

It was funny how things just happened like that. Little Ghali's entrance had been as sudden as Zaki's departure. If Mary screwed her eyes tight shut, she could just about remember what Zaki, her brother, had looked like. A bubbly, tubby little man who toddled about their house stealing Mary's toys and pulling her hair. And then he had got sick, and it wasn't long before he just wasn't there anymore.

"Say hello to your brother, Mary," her mother demanded, bringing the screaming child with its inconsolable puffy cheeks closer to her.

She froze. Ghali's face looked like a red balloon; watery streaks slashed across his cheeks. She found herself moving an exploratory finger towards him which he grabbed with an angry fist. And then it happened: Ghali stopped screaming. He didn't open his eyes, but his grip tightened and Mary knew then.

"Zaki," she said softly in the sudden silence.

She failed to see the pain wash over her father's face as his flushed cheeks cooled. Nor her mother's body stiffen, her smile left hanging.

"No, Mary," Zakia corrected her, "Ghali."

She looked to her father who nodded.

"Zaki," he conceded. "A good name. A solid name."

Zaki was back in his father's arms and before any further words could be said on the matter, his lungs filled with air and he was back screaming again.

It was settled.

A name is never *just* a name.

Łódź,
POLAND,
1920

The smell of the place hit without warning to any outsider entering the city for the first time. Those who had the fortune or misfortune of being raised in Łódź were used to its stench and could ignore it with the same practice reserved for the incessant hum of the textile mills that ran both day and night. Sewage was a problem alongside other inequalities between the city's inhabitants who were all drawn to Łódź by the opportunities rapid industrialisation had brought with it.

The majority of Jews congregated in the northern Baluty district with its narrow streets and crowded wooden houses, families sometimes sharing one bathroom facility with ten or more others. Pedlars spilled onto the cobbles. Wiry bearded men jostled through the crowds alongside smartly suited individuals. Orthodox Jews and those less so living alongside each other under the backdrop of a growing Zionist movement, all huddled together as if they had some pre-warning of things to come.

Szyja Alter Beker was a bright boy living directly south of these rumblings in a sparsely furnished, tiny apartment in a tall and imposing large-windowed block. A boy born under the shadow of the death of an older sibling. The name Alter (meaning 'old') spoke of the hope of a long and successful life, a way of confusing the Angel of Death into believing that the child was older than he appeared and not a prize worth taking. He was, indeed, a bright boy turning into an exceptionally learned young man. They all were, he and his brothers, Morduch and Aron. All intelligent young men from an impoverished background with a Jewish mother who doted on them all.

Their father had died a few years previously when Szyja was just twelve years old. A victim of the First World War, killed by a German sniper. Their mother was scraping a living at one of the many textile mills that were scattered across the city. It was an industry frequented by Jews and she worked her way up to become an overseer of a small team of women on the factory floor.

Szyja attended a public school near his home in southern Łódź. It had been important for the family to educate their boys in a secular school. Such an education would hopefully open the doors to wider career opportunities when they reached maturity. Even at that young age Szyja was hiding his identity without consciously knowing it. It was an education pitted with Polish pride at the country's recent victory over the

Russians. The Poles' natural aggressor had forcibly entered Poland in 1918, eager to spread the communist way of life throughout Europe, before they were halted in their tracks on the outskirts of Warsaw.

The Poles would not be so lucky next time.

It was a Saturday in June and Mrs Dabrowski was not pleased to see him. He could tell. No matter how many times he apologised for his tardiness, the look of disapproval was still very much evident on her face. The textbook on mathematics Szyja was clutching slipped from his sweaty fingers and into a pile of dust at her feet. Mrs Dabrowski made no move to pick it up. He bent down and as he did so, a waft of freshly baked bread crept its way around her voluptuous figure and into his nostrils. Ah, so he had disturbed breakfast! His stomach growled in anticipation of the invitation to join them. He had not had time to eat before leaving the house that morning.

"Is Tomasz ready for his lesson?" he asked loudly, in an attempt to hide the growls from his stomach.

"We're having breakfast."

A statement, not an invitation.

It was a hot morning, unusually so for this time of year, and his cloth cap was sitting uncomfortably on his head. His wide shirt collar was sticking to his neck, and he resisted the urge to free it in case Mrs Dabrowski thought she had succeeded in making him feel uncomfortable. It had been her husband who had called on his services. Tomasz had fallen behind that year and Szyja had already tutored a number of other boys at the school with success. Times were hard and a schoolboy tutor was a more financially viable option.

The silence continued. Szyja thought of his brothers being dragged to the synagogue whilst he sweated on the Dabrowskis' doorstep. No doubt his mother would blush at the Rabbi's queries as to his whereabouts. *What was a good Jewish boy doing, working on the sacred day of rest?*

Needs must. Things had been financially difficult since his father's death.

Without another word, Mrs Dabrowski turned her back on him and disappeared inside. Szyja took the open door as reluctant consent for him to enter and followed the noise to the kitchen.

Four pairs of eyes looked up at him from the breakfast table. A large effigy of the Christ figure on the cross hung above the family's heads and seemed to glare at the intrusion – Szyja was the odd one out in this homely scene. Jam, butter and a large loaf of brioche sat in the middle of the table, and he couldn't keep his hungry gaze from it. A chair groaned as Mrs Dabrowski took up the last remaining seat. He stood in the doorway, not sure where he should place himself.

"You hungry?" Mr Dabrowski asked. There was a small fleck of jam on his beard that wobbled as he spoke.

He nodded.

Mr Dabrowski inclined his head at his wife and she reluctantly eased her mass from her seat. A stool was pushed towards the corner of the table, and Szyja awkwardly took it. Awkwardly, because its purpose was to help Mrs Dabrowski in the garden to assist her in getting near the tomatoes she was tending. It was far too short for the kitchen table.

He could almost taste the sweetness of the freshly baked

bread in his mouth when his hopes were disappointed. A plate with two small pieces of dry rye bread was placed in front of him. Before he could reach for the jam and butter, Mrs Dabrowski had cleared them away. He ate in silence, washing down each dry mouthful with the water she had provided. The children stared at him. Mr Dabrowski helped himself to more brioche and dunked the sweet bread lavishly into his frothy cup of warm milk so that the white goodness dribbled down his chin. His cheeks bulged and his lips smacked with a pleasing satisfaction. He left the rest of the bread uneaten on his plate.

Szyja swallowed uncomfortably and coughed as the dark bread threatened to stick in his throat. He tried to ignore the curious stares from the younger members of the family.

Nobody likes a Jew.

He was reminded of his father's words as he ate. His father had come home once with a black eye and a fierce temper and when his young son had asked him what had happened, that was all he had said.

Nobody likes a Jew.

Over time he had stopped asking why and slowly the statement had permeated his consciousness as pure fact. That was the way of the world. It was no more agreeable to him, but he had come to accept it all the same.

When war broke out against Russia in 1918 the Jews and non-Jews had all fought side by side. When the soldiers returned, they were greeted as heroes and then it had started again. The remarks, the looks, the beatings that couldn't be pinned on anyone in particular. Yes, that was the order of things. In a way, it was better that his father had perished during the war. He had taken his exit in a timely manner. An undeniable hero.

"Finished?" Mrs Dabrowski had taken his half-empty plate before a reply could be made.

Nobody likes a Jew.

Łódź,
POLAND,
2005

"Did you know Dad had another brother?" Henry asked. "This Aron?"

Mary was pinching the birth certificate the genealogist had produced between tentative fingers. No, she didn't know. Was it strange that he had never mentioned him? Did it even matter that he hadn't?

"We couldn't find any other documents relating to Aron." The genealogist's tone was matter-of-fact, blank. "He may have died before World War Two."

Another mystery. Another life that vanished.

The table was littered with documents that showed this and that. Little snippets of information that were all that was left of those that trod these streets all those years ago.

The archive they found themselves in was dusty and stale. It was old. These documents were old. Official bits of paper that had been written carefully in ink. She didn't like to think of herself as old but these markers in time had been written not long before her birth and some of them not long after. If they were old then, what did that make her?

"His father must have been a soldier then, to have died during the war?" She listened quietly to the questions her children asked about the lives laid before them.

To lose a father by the age of twelve. That must have been hard. Oh, Jozef, I wish I'd known…

Alexandria, EGYPT, 1923

Hawash came home one day complaining of feeling unwell. He had closed the shop as his brother, Goued, was away on business and no cover could be found. Mary had watched horrified from the doorway as her father had clutched at her mother, panting and grimacing like the donkeys pulling their carts of wheat to market.

"Baba…"

He glanced at her with bloodshot eyes, and all Mary wanted to do was shrink back into the doorway.

"Get Azziza to bring me water."

She hurried to his request but stopped short of asking the lady who helped her mother with the chores around the house. It was something about the way her mother glanced at Azziza, the way her voice barked with a harshness when she spoke to her. It was the same voice she'd use to let Mary know she was misbehaving. *If Azziza was so disobedient, why did her father let her stay?* Instead, he issued his reprimands in hushed tones directly into Azziza's ear in the quiet corners of their house when her mother wasn't looking.

Mary plunged the cup she had fetched into the deep jar in the courtyard where the rainwater was stored. The cool, refreshing liquid splashed over her hand, immediately offsetting the morning heat. It landed in small droplets, scattering the dust on the floor as her small hands struggled to complete her task.

"Should I call for the doctor?" Her mother was removing her father's sandals as he settled back onto the freshly clean sheets on their bed.

"Don't fuss!" His hands waved fitfully over his head at the flies drawn by the perspiration on his forehead, or at her mother, it was hard to tell. "This damned heat!"

It was cooler than yesterday. Her mother's temper had been less prone to explode, her walking less laboured from the swollen ankles that matched her swollen belly. Another brother or sister on the way. Mary handed her mother the now half-full cup and shrank back behind the curtain that billowed across the doorway. Her father tugged at his *galabeya*, pulling the white cloth up to expose his knees and the paler skin of his thighs where beads of sweat raced each other across his flesh. She knew it was wrong to continue gazing, but she couldn't help but wonder if all men were supposed to be like that.

"Hush!" Zakia's voice was scolding, impatient. "Now drink."

"Is Baba OK?" She looked up at her mother as she made to leave the room, peering round the bump of her mother's swollen belly in an attempt to see any hint of reassurance on her expressionless face. It was a question said with concern, with fear.

"Baba's just feeling a little unwell," said her mother.

"I could make him feel better."

"Tsshh. Go find your brother and play quietly. Your father needs his rest."

Only this morning, Hawash had scooped Mary into his arms and twirled her as she giggled and played with his moustache. Mary loved him. It was as simple as that. Once, when she had suffered from a sickness that took her energy and sapped her strength, he had sat beside her mopping her brow and told her how she was his little princess. He had asked her what she wanted, what he could get her to make her feel better. He had smiled when she requested the wooden clogs with the blue flowers on them. Smiled but said nothing. And then, when she had woken up later, there they were on the end of her bed with a ribbon wrapped carefully around them.

They were scuffed now, the flowers had faded and there were cracks that looked like veins running over the wood. But she still cherished them.

What she didn't have now was her father.

She had woken up one morning to the shouts of the water-bearer clanging the metal cups of his trade, his sandals making flop-flop noises on the dusty path like wet fish, only to find that her father had gone. He had disappeared from the house in much the same way as her brother and younger sister had vanished from their lives.

Only, her siblings' disappearance had been accompanied by howls from her mother. Men in black cowls and dark faces had scurried around the house with two small boxes that they'd packed away into the back of a veiled cart.

Her mother didn't scream when her father left.

"Your father has gone back to his family to rest," she had stated with a curious dullness in her tone.

Zakia was sitting in her chair, her belly now flat after the birth of another daughter who slept contentedly in another room. Smoke spiralled from the cigarette that dangled from Zakia's fingertips as she emitted a serene state of calm. Her elegant leg with its black patented shoe rose up and flicked her skirts as she crossed her legs. The pose reminded Mary of the posters she'd seen outside the Rex cinema. Hollywood beauties with perfect faces clutched in the arms of clean-shaven men. Except, there was no man holding her mother up. Instead, she sat alone, her flowered dress tumbling softly onto the floor. A flutter of ash narrowly missed the hem of her skirts, but she didn't seem to notice.

"It was his choice." Zakia shrugged and then Mary realised that the heavy gold necklace her father had given her mother on the birth of Alice (Mary's only surviving sister) with its braided coils was missing from its usual place around her neck. The image of that last time she had seen her wearing it sparked in Mary's mind. It had been a cool evening but despite this, Zakia had sat dabbing a cloth to her father's brow as he lay sweating on the bed.

There had been a knock at the door. Her six-year-old frame was just about big enough to reach the latch. Her uncle, Goued, was standing there in his white suit, his moustache twitching like a caterpillar. He said nothing to her. Men were there to be obeyed and she had merely stepped aside to let him pass.

There had been shouting, her mother's pleading voice, but she had not understood any of the words that trickled down the steps and peppered holes through the walls towards her. Goued had returned, flushed, down the stairs a moment later, a handkerchief dabbing at his brow and Mary silently wondered whether her father's disease was catching. If anyone was to get ill, she wouldn't have minded it being her uncle.

The tall man loomed above her and he hesitated, his sweaty hand on the door.

"Be a good girl and look after your mother," he told her.

Mary promised herself that, despite the man who gave the instruction, she would do just that.

Harlesden, ENGLAND, 1952

The thought crossed Mary's mind that her mother-in-law might never leave. Watching her husband's happiness at having her around had been satisfying at first but, as time went on, that satisfaction soon turned into a genuine fear that this subtle invasion on 23 Bramshill Road was turning into trench warfare. It was the little things that made her suspect the worst. She would wake in the morning to find breakfast already made, mother and son talking happily in the kitchen. A vase would find its way to another point in the house because *it was better suited there*. The flowers she'd picked one morning were dwarfed the next day by a bunch Tumera *had just happened to buy at the market*.

She couldn't blame her mother-in-law's resolve to stay. Their semi-detached house in Harlesden was, in itself, a little piece of Poland with the constant comings and goings of the Polish outworkers they employed to assist with their growing belt-making business. A steady stream of men and women displaced from their country of birth were all welcomed into the Beker's hospitable home. All had lost something or someone and were piecing their lives back together, much like the constant pasting and gluing of the belts they collectively made.

On Sunday evenings, they gathered in the Beker's front room, hiding their invisible scars behind evenings filled with bridge and laughter in a bid to keep the trauma at bay.

"Skerczenski, you old dog!"

"How's your head this morning? Eh? Left all your luck at home, I bet."

"Luck! Luck he says. As if luck came into it. Jozef, have you ever met such a sore loser?"

Tumera visibly revelled in the sound of her native tongue as she fussed about their guests with dishes laden with Polish treats. She insisted that her daughter-in-law needn't trouble herself with the preparation of food she assumed would be alien to her palate. Mary tried hard to tame the rising anger that bubbled inside her and assumed the stiff upper lip of her adopted country. It was clear that her husband was happy to have his beloved *Matka* around and she was not going to be the one to upset his happiness.

"I thought I would make *bigos* stew for Jozef," Tumera announced one morning, emptying bags of shopping on the kitchen table.

"Oh. I was going to make *ful medames*." Mary stepped

over an onion that rolled across the floor in front of her as she tried to comfort baby Henry to sleep.

"Oh, you don't want to do that. All that Middle Eastern food can play havoc with the digestion!"

"But I—"

"Go and sit down, dear. Let me be mother for a change."

Mary decided to take a walk before her mother-in-law ended up in the cooking pot along with her onions. It was a dry spring day, and the sun was threatening to make an unlikely appearance. Yes, a walk would do her good. Henry bounced along in his Silver Cross pram and was soon fast asleep. She'd left Margarita with her mother-in-law. It had been a last-minute decision in the hope that having a child to look after would prevent Tumera rearranging the house in her absence. At four years old, Margarita was mindful of what she did and did not like, and spending the morning alone with her grandmother was certainly one of her dislikes. The child had clung onto Mary's knee as she'd tried to navigate out of the front door, and she'd had to peel her off before hastening down the road without glancing back.

She made her way onto the High Street with a selection of belts she kept as samples tucked into the pram's vast undercarriage. Every morning she walked the streets looking for new clients to keep their business afloat. She was more adept at that than Jozef. Years of living in an Arab country had taught her how to haggle and it was as ingrained in her as the language of her birth. Here and there a cap would be tugged in her direction, the shop holders familiar with this tall, well-dressed lady with her dark foreign features walking with a purpose through the morning shoppers.

Something flashed out of the corner of her eye. A man was standing by a stall draped with fabrics of every imaginable size and shape. Yellows and reds and blues. Gold-embroidered stitching along the rim of an emerald-green ream of lightly netted fabric. He was shaking the creases out of a deep-red silk sheet, the sun bouncing off it as it fluttered through the air. She was drawn to him. A potential client. Not only because of what he sold but because of what his face was trying so hard to conceal. He was dark, a foreigner, with guarded features. An unmistakeable Jew. A man with connections.

"Hello," she addressed him. "I am looking for work."

She showed him the belts, pointing out the fine stitching and challenging him to find better quality anywhere in London. He held an amused expression (not unkindly) and listened intently as she showed him each handmade belt.

"What's your name?"

"Mary Beker."

"Well, Mary Beker. Go upstairs and show these to my sister-in-law, Millicent Rothbart. Say I recommended you. She will find you work."

Mary followed his pointing finger to the narrow staircase that led directly off the street behind him. Henry was still fast asleep and there was little hope of bumping the enormous pram up the stairs to the floor above.

"You will have to watch the baby," she decided.

He was taken aback and looked quickly from the pram to the tall woman in front of him with the dark eyes and the stance that mean business.

"But I couldn't possibly – I mean – I don't know you—"

"Your name?"

"Ben, Ben Kaye."

"Good. Now we know each other." She already had her foot on the first step. Then she hesitated and called back over her shoulder. "Don't touch him or you'll wake him up."

Millicent Rothbart was a shrewd businesswoman of average height with wiry hair that spilled into waves over pale, pinched cheeks. She counted the stitching on the samples Mary showed her, putting on her glasses so that she could scrutinise the handiwork and ensure there were twelve stitches to the inch. She placed an order for five dozen and, anxious to acquire a new client, Mary promised a forty-eight-hour turnaround.

Heaven knows what Jozef was going to say...

They usually managed to fulfil orders of up to 300 belts per day, but there were yesterday's orders still to finish and material to source. Her mind went over the figures as she bounced the pram over the uneven pavement on her way back to Bramshill Road. Jozef wouldn't be back until later that afternoon and so it would be tight. But workable. Always workable.

"You promised what?" he asked her later, barely through the door.

Her tongue flicked over the order again as she made coffee, aware of her mother-in-law sitting disapprovingly at the kitchen table. She did everything disapprovingly, as if it was the only natural way to get things done.

"You look tired, Jozef," Tumera said pointedly as she took the offered cup.

He turned to face his mother sitting elegantly at the table, her fingers pinching the coffee cup as if worried she might catch something. Margarita was chasing the chickens in the yard and their irritated clucking pierced through the kitchen window, intermingled with her sudden childish exclamations of joy. There was a clatter as Mary busied herself laying out plates and cutlery for supper whilst Henry slept in the pram by the door. She had her apron on and a few strands of hair escaped the bun she had fashioned on her head whilst she worked. Her feet danced around the kitchen as she moved this pan and that and Jozef was reminded of the dance hall in Ramleh; he with his military suit and she with her A-line dress as he whirled her around to both their delight. Her presence settled the darkness, awakening feelings he had never hoped to experience again.

"Well, then, we'd better get started." He smiled.

Al Asirat,
EGYPT,
1924

It was a stroke that took Hawash in the end. Soon after she received the news, Zakia took her young family to her husband's birthplace in Upper Egypt. A small, insignificant place called Al Asirat, north-west of Luxor.

As they stepped into Hawash's family home with its small, shuttered windows and dry, mud-brick walls, Mary found herself lost in a sea of black and instinctively clutched at Zaki's tiny hand before he could toddle off and leave her. The wailing mourners at her grandmother's house were all a mystery to her. Neither she nor her mother had shed a tear since stepping off the train. Men and women that she had never met before in her life openly lamented her father's loss. Funny, but she had never seen any of them when her father was alive. She felt an odd sense of irritation at the emotion they displayed. They didn't *know* her father. How dare they pretend to love the man she had known all her life?

As the tide of mourners glided past, she saw one face she recognised. Her Uncle Goued had made the journey from Alexandria separately from them, citing that he needed to catch an earlier train to take care of some business. He was talking to her mother or rather he allowed Zakia to talk at him whilst he feigned interest. A small bead of sweat trickled down his nose and hung like a beaded jewel at its pointed tip. He dabbed at his nose but failed to catch it as it clung there. Her mother was agitated, her face strained, her one free hand gesticulating wildly whilst the other clutched Alice to her hip.

"You are young, Zakia, you can work."

A black figure swept past, momentarily blocking out the scene and the next time she looked, Goued was gone, and her mother stood alone, her eyes moist. The mourners had separated. The men were outside in a colourful tent that raged a silent battle with the sombre mood that clouded its occupants. The women scurried like black cockroaches all over the small house that was Hawash's family home.

"Mama?" Mary touched Zakia's arm, suddenly aware of the rough feel of the black laced veil that shrouded her.

Zakia was looking past her at the painting of her late husband that hung on the wall by her grandmother's chair. A large likeness, draped in flowers, which looked out of place in such a small room. Zakia's lips parted softly as she stared, mouthing words too quietly for her daughter to hear.

You stupid, stupid man.

"Mama?" Mary tugged at her sleeve again, her fingers slipping on the grip she maintained on her little brother.

Her mother's eyes slowly swivelled round to look down at her.

"Mama, I'm hungry. Are we going to eat yet?"

Zakia sighed. The black-veiled women were gathering around Mary's grandmother who sat in her chair sobbing uncontrollably as she held empty hands towards the painting of her son. Their backs were soon turned towards them.

"OK, Mary. Let's see what we can find."

She ate bread whilst they sat in the church watching the funeral service. It was a pale, flat saucer of bread that melted on Mary's tongue. She tore off tiny pieces and savoured each one. It was a good meal and she reluctantly shared it with her younger brother and sister who shifted impatiently on the hard wooden seats. Mary had no interest in the bearded men with their white robes and doughnut hats who wailed incoherent incantations over the wooden box her father now called home. The church was smelly and filled with black. Black robes, black shawls, black skirts, black veils. Her mother was shrouded by one and she sat so still that Mary thought she had been replaced by a statue. A large image of a man or woman (she couldn't tell which) seemed to stare down on her from its golden place above the altar where the thurible spouted its puffs of smelly smoke. It seemed to be asking her what she was doing there, and she shivered under its stare.

There was too much sniffing. She wasn't sure if it was the overpowering scent of the sweet, woody incense that caused the congregation's noses to crease or the never-ending grief the adults felt obliged to emit every few minutes. The wailing was getting on her nerves. Her father had never enjoyed noise in the house, so much so that Mary would learn to tiptoe sandal-less across the stone floors on those last few days he had spent withering in his bed.

She wondered what he would think of it all now.

The service dragged and the bread ran out. His hunger now satisfied, Zaki curled up next to her and promptly fell asleep. Alice was playing with the edges of their mother's black veil and Mary wondered if she should stop her before her mother's rage erupted from underneath her shroud. Her mother was prone to rages these days. Once, a few weeks ago, a cup had slipped from Mary's hand as she'd prepared coffee for her mother. The dark eyes flashed, and they had both looked at those scattered shards of porcelain with two very different emotions: Zakia was furious whilst Mary was terrified. The belt was already on the dresser, waiting. Mary hadn't been able to sit down for a week.

She imagined her mother exploding now; the veil flapping wildly, fire in her eyes, her cheeks puffy and red. The strange doughnut men would stop their mumblings and the whole congregation would turn and stare. Would someone have said something? Would they have been able to? Or would they have been sucked up in the tornado of her mother's rage? Let them stare. They were used to it. Adults had done nothing but stare at them since her father had died.

Her mother still didn't move. Mary looked at the women surrounding them in their matching dresses of black that sapped the sun. She knew none of them. Aunts that she had never met before had cooed and pinched their cheeks whilst uncles had ruffled her hair. They looked unfamiliar, they looked unfriendly and smelt dusty, old. She longed to get back to their lives and their future, whatever it might hold.

***

The green train puffed up to the platform with a prolonged squeal that reminded Mary of the death noises of a rat a stray cat had killed outside their house – an awful sound that had stayed with her for weeks. Her mother had packed up their suitcases and marched them back to the railway station a week or so after the funeral. Her grandmother had said goodbye to them in much the same way as she had greeted the sad little procession: with wailing and an abundance of tears that made sticky patches on her cheeks. The patches stayed there no matter how hard she scrubbed at them with the corner of her black dress.

They had been sitting on a bench at the station for what seemed like an eternity. As the train stopped before them, there was a sudden burst of activity. Passengers alighted, new passengers heaved themselves into the carriages, porters ferried luggage up and down and people greeted and waved their loved ones off. Mary looked to her mother, wondering if this was the train they were waiting to catch, but she made no move. Instead, Alice continued to bounce up and down on her knee whilst Zaki propped himself up against Mary, his eyes heavy with sleep.

"Zakia?"

Mary's eyes adjusted to the glare of the sun as she tried to make out the figure standing above them. Her heart sank.

"Goued." Zakia seemed to crumple next to her.

"I was unaware you were taking the train back today."

"Yes. We were just waiting – we were just waiting for it to arrive."

"Would you like help with your luggage?"

He eyed the small suitcase resting by the bench – a tiny thing holding one change of clothes for each of them, all black.

"No. No, we're fine."

Please go away. Mary wanted him to leave, wanted her mother to stand tall.

"You know my offer still stands."

Zakia's lips collapsed into a tense smile.

"Your offer, Goued?" Her mother's voice was dangerous like the lull before the storm. She recognised the tone that preceded the belt or the broom and wondered if she would be treated to the sight of her uncle cowering beneath her mother's rage.

"You would be helping the family and being paid for it at the same time."

How could her uncle not notice?

"A servant in my mother-in-law's house? No," she said firmly. Her moment of rebellion. "*Shukran gazilan.*"

Mary allowed herself to breathe again in the uneventful silence.

"Well, I'd better get to my carriage," her uncle said as he rocked back and forth on his heels. He inhaled loudly – a noisy sound that reminded Mary of the waves on the beach at Al Max, her father chasing her into the sea, the cool water slapping at her calves, her mother laughing...

"Yes," Zakia agreed coldly.

He nodded stiffly like a seagull and clip-clopped his way to the first-class carriage, a porter laden with luggage running to catch up with him.

"Mary." Zakia roused herself from her seat and dropped Alice onto her lap. "Look after your brother and sister. I will be back in a minute."

Mary waited anxiously for her mother to return as Alice fussed incessantly on her lap whilst her brother kept on dozing. The train was filling up, the piles of luggage diminishing on the platform as the last available spaces in the carriages were plugged. They nearly missed their transport back to Alexandria. Their mother returned to them in a hurry, her dark form emerging through the steam clutching a single railway ticket in her hand. Through the chaos of the departing train, Zakia threw Mary up into the carriage before following her inside with the rest of the children and their luggage. A man was selling cigarettes, pushing his head through the narrow windows as he strained to reach his customers. There were frantic Arabic exchanges before a guard bundled him away.

"Mary, you must hide under the seat and not make a sound."

She looked at where her mother was pointing. It was dusty and dirty.

"But why?"

"Because I have no ticket for you. Unless you want to stay with your grandmother in Al Asirat?"

The old woman scared her. All she had done was brush

her cheeks with her gnarled fingers declaring again and again how much she looked like her father.

"No. No, Mama," she said hastily, scrambling into the narrow space and drawing her knees up to her chin. Her cheek pressed onto the dirty floor of the carriage; she could hear the click-clack of the track as the train puffed out of the station. Her mother's skirt caressed her skin and she closed her eyes to the smell of her familiar perfume. Her dreams were pitted with the indiscriminate faces of the mourners at the funeral. Aunts and uncles, cousins, friends of the family all reaching out sympathetic fingers towards her, grabbing her, crying with a grief that would never match her own. As she drifted off to sleep, her father's face was there, smiling at her.

Funny, but she couldn't remember her mother ever smiling like that.

Skierniewice, POLAND, 1923

Szyja's head lolled where he sat on the eight o'clock evening train service from Warsaw to Skierniewice. The day had started early, just as the sun was rising. He had been careful not to wake the family he lodged with as he prepared a meagre breakfast from the last remaining egg in his cupboard and a stale piece of bread left over from yesterday. His stomach barely full, he had spread out his lesson plans on the bed and worked solidly until it was time to walk the half a mile to *School Number 5* to begin his day. The morning had dragged as he coaxed and cajoled a classroom full of small boys through algebra and arithmetic. They yawned and fidgeted as they took turns to recite answers to the questions he had thrown at them. It was with disappointment that he rarely saw the spark of any passion for education that had fuelled his own learning a few years previously. A disappointment that, nevertheless, rarely led to the use of the instrument of correction his own teachers had been so ready to use. He didn't believe in scaring his charges into submission.

The afternoon had passed off in the same way as the morning and he counted down the minutes to half past three. The fidgeting in his classroom had intensified as the lazy afternoon sun lapped in through the school's high windows. And then the afternoon bell had been joyfully rung and the boys scurried like spiders out of the school gates to fill their stomachs on their mothers' carefully prepared lunch, their *obiad*, before playing mock battles in the parks nearby. He envied their abandonment. For himself, he had no time to eat as his day was far from over. It was a dash to get to the station to catch the train to Warsaw to arrive in time for his afternoon lectures in the study of philology – the analysis of language in texts and oral history. The teacher became the student.

The evening train carrying Szyja back home gently rocked him so that he almost forgot the empty pit at the bottom of his stomach. It hadn't been full since breakfast, save for the half cups of strong black *kawa* that kept his mind functioning throughout the long day. As he dragged weary legs through the emptying cathedral-like expanse of Skierniewice's train station he treated himself to a *bułka z pieczarkami* by the entrance, dimly lit in the waning light. The toasted bread and mushrooms tasted of years long ago: his father showing him the abundance of wild fungi underneath the pine trees in Las Ruda-Popioły. A bountiful harvest which his mother would then fry with butter for him and his elder brothers as they impatiently danced around her worn-out feet.

His stomach now finally full, he would almost sprint the 800 metres back to his lodgings in a modest house opposite Park Miejski and collapse into bed to rest both an exhausted body and a tired mind. These split days were taking their toll, but Szyja never complained. He was not one to dwell on the harshness of life. You were dealt from an unknown pack of cards and it was up to the individual as to how and when to play them.

The teaching was a means to an end and enabled him to continue the further education he had so desired. He would have perhaps earned a higher wage in the textile mills of his birth town but that wasn't for him. The hours of a teacher fitted better, and he enjoyed the challenge the job presented him. That was all that counted. As his pay cheques came in, the money he accrued quickly haemorrhaged on rent and university fees leaving only enough to fund a meagre lifestyle and a non-extravagant diet.

But it had not been the funding of his course that had been the initial issue in his plan but getting accepted onto the course in the first place. Certain professions were less open to him because of his background and a university degree for a Polish Jew was almost unheard of. He had been accepted due to the fact that he didn't *look* Jewish and he didn't volunteer that information. Life in Poland depended a lot on what you looked like.

As soon as he was old enough to work, he had eagerly left his home in Łódź for this new endeavour in Skierniewice. His family had remained in Łódź, his eldest brother now married with children and settled on a career as a painter and decorator that would eventually take him further east to Grodno. Szyja couldn't wait to be rid of the place. His new home was quieter, less industrialised and within a half an hour walk he could be amongst the soft rolling fields of the Polish lowlands with the smell of the pine forests heavy in the air. In the summer months, the Rawka River would provide respite from the heat. This rural life was far more palatable.

His lodgings were small – a tiny room in the attic of a family home. A small window provided a view of the trees in the park that shone red, yellow and vibrant gold in the autumn months and luscious green in the summer, the smell of blossom lying heavily in the air. His possessions were limited to a writing table and a bed with a crate by its side and a fraying lamp, all of which were strewn with open textbooks of the works of Wolf, Scaliger and a number of exercise books with childish scrawls and neat, red corrections.

His life followed a similar pattern of teaching, studying and long walks in the open air. When money would allow, he would visit the theatre, the cafes and the occasional dance. He visited the synagogue less and less as the distance from his mother meant her influence slowly waned. Instead, he chose to live his life as a secular Jew but a Jew nonetheless. When he found more than he expected in his pockets, he would play cards with his friends, and they would while away the evenings setting the world to rights over a glass or two of Krupnik in the homely warmth of one of their living rooms.

Then he met Rozia.

Rozia Frajdenreich was a well-educated woman with three sisters and a dominant mother who was well known in the town. Unlike her sisters, she stood out with a hint of red in her otherwise deep-black hair. Softly spoken, she brought a sense of calm into the class where she began teaching; a class in the same school as Szyja. They met over *kawa* in the staff room and spent their breaktime talking of politics, their mutual love of language and aspirations of a distant future. The chats continued after work in Kafka Café, which spilled out onto the wide marketplace of Skierniewice's city centre. Then, it was dinner and then soon the letters from Szyja's mother were filled with questions that focused on Rozia's lineage and her family's prospects. He was able to placate her with reassurances that the Frajdenreichs were Jewish, with Rozia's own stepfather rising up through the ranks of local politics. There were rumours that he was even tipped to take over as mayor one day.

The next two letters from his mother remained unopened on his bed. They had arrived in frantic quick succession and Szyja was able to guess their content. There was plenty enough time for marriage, plenty of time before the thought of settling down would enter his mind.

Skierniewice,
POLAND,
2005

There was no photograph of Rozia. The only windows into Jozef's former life were photographs his mother had kept safe from the war in her villa in South Africa and none of those preserved her likeness.

I wonder what she was like?

It was a question Mary had probably asked herself in the past but only fleetingly.

"Did he ever talk about her?"

"No."

The question was shot dead with the plain truthfulness of her answer. He hadn't. He had laid down the facts of her once and that was that.

Mary recalled how Jozef used to spend weekday evenings in their workroom with a man who helped him punch eyelets into the half-finished belts. The two of them would sit with only the methodical sound of the machine they used breaking the silence between them. Now, with the passage of time, the man's name escaped her, but she still remembered his head shining in the dim electric light where his hair should have been. As well as his hair, the Nazis had also taken his mind. When you had lost so much, no amount of words would bring it back. That was why the man with the shiny head and Jozef with the gaps in his past left the words to the silence and got on with the business of living.

Alexandria, EGYPT, 1924

Life was different. Even at the age of seven, Mary noticed that. Azziza had been the first to go from their comfortable house in downtown Alexandria, and then slowly, but with a quickening pace, the gold coins that Mary enjoyed playing with in the family chest started to diminish. Then, it was the chest itself and then various bits of furniture so that it wasn't long before Mary and her sister were sharing a bed. Neither minded. It was comforting to have a warm placid body to snuggle up to after the fits of rage that accompanied their mother's daily despair.

Then it wasn't long before even the house disappeared.

A cart piled high with the remains of their belongings waited for them outside on the street and their mother closed the door to their previous life with a sigh that carried longingly on the breeze. Zakia didn't say where they were going and none of the children thought to ask. Mary's feet scuffed the pavement as she watched the sweat drip off the street porter as he heaved and dragged the cart behind him. A distant memory of the camels she had seen struggling under the weight of sacks of grain in the early morning drive to market entered her mind, their backsides sore from the whips of their guardians hollering and whistling at them. Her father had pointed them out. Her father. She had only mentioned her father once after the funeral. She had not dared to mention him again.

"Your father should have looked after his family," her mother had raged. "He knew what was to happen after he was gone but he did nothing about it. Now look at us! Don't speak to me about your father."

Mary's eyes followed her feet and she kept a tighter hold of her brother's hand in case he ran off amongst the cartwheels that kicked up dust from the road. Her mother, with her black veil of widowhood, shielded much of her face to the world as if she was ashamed of this lumbering caravan.

They turned down a much narrower side street that seemed to squeeze out the sun. There were children running barefoot on the uneven road that bore no pavement. Little urchins were scurrying back and forth through narrow open doors where Muslim women eyed their progress suspiciously. Mary squeezed her brother's hand tighter. She was in as much need of his loving, reassuring touch as he of hers.

Their new home was small. That was all Zakia could say about it. The porter left them at the door and, in the absence of the crooked figure of a *boab* guarding the entrance, the family wondered how they were going to drag their belongings up the two flights of steps to the top floor.

With another sigh, Zakia pushed open the wooden door with its worn handles and entered the small lobby area. It was cooler in here with its windowless walls and worn stone steps. Mary could make out the small blue handprints that clung to the peeling plaster following the route of the stairs; an effort to protect the occupants of the flats from the evil eye. *Was there a need for protection here?* She watched her mother pause and then cross herself before leading the children up the steps. There was a momentary struggle with the door lock and then they were in. Empty doorways led off into a small kitchenette, two small bedrooms and an adequately sized living area which led onto a substantial balcony. Mary pushed the shutters open, eager to escape the oppressive air stagnating in the rest of the flat. The shutters creaked to her touch, their small, slatted panels breaking up the light like bars on a jail cell. She reached a hesitant foot onto the balcony area, suspicious of the many holes that speckled the wooden floor. They created a broken view of the street far below where pedestrians scurried by with only their heads and the occasional foot visible. There were dark black bars surrounding the balcony giving her enough of a sense of safety to allow her feet to explore further. Her feet pitter-pattered carefully to a corner by the peeling plaster where two large clay jars with crumbling rims stored rainwater for drinking. She scooped a mouthful into her hands and drank, the water dribbling down her dusty chin. Her thirst satisfied, her eyes scanned her surroundings. The opposite building felt so close she could touch it and she reached out a finger to try just that.

"Mary! See to your sister and brother whilst I get us settled."

Their meal that night was meagre in comparison to their usual fare. They sat cross-legged on a rug on the floor as they usually did but there was only one large sharing platter and still that only afforded a couple of handfuls of macaroni each and a few green vegetables mopped up with flat bread. Zakia explained almost apologetically that she hadn't had time to prepare much due to the move and that she had done her best with what they had. This same excuse would be used tomorrow and the day after and the day after that until it became such a part of their routine that no further excuse was required anymore. Cushions had been spread out onto the floor in the children's room until new mattresses and beds could be sourced. Their mother was nothing if not resourceful.

A new normal was reached the next day. Mary was left in charge of her siblings and a list of chores too big for small hands, whilst her mother trundled off down the road with their empty cart. Zakia's jewellery (the only remaining link to that time of plenty when Hawash was still alive) was used at the pawn shop to free up cash and now she was off to the wholesalers. Deep-yellow rich s*emneh*, pulses and reams of fabric would be loaded onto that cart and sold on for profit. But for now, Mary watched her mother dressed in black disappear off into the distance much like a beetle scurrying from the midday heat.

The trundling sound returned later that morning and

Mary, expecting it to be her mother, rushed to the balcony to see. On the street far below, a cart of a different kind was working its way down the street. A cart loaded with sweets. The seller's headscarf bobbed as he heaved his load, calling out (as he did so) the items he had for sale with a jovial air. Other faces appeared in the vacant doorways and windows to watch his progress; eager young faces escaping from busy mothers.

Mary's mouth salivated and she licked dry lips. Her brother had come to see what the fuss was about, and he looked hungrily from the seller to his sister (his surrogate parent for the day) his eyes wide in a silent plea.

Zakia had left a few piastres before she'd left that morning. Mary was under strict instructions to use them to get a bit of bread from the bakers to go with the white, milky soft *domiati* their mother had left for the children's lunch. She had yet to go to the shop with its grilled front and racks of fresh loaves. The coins glinted tantalisingly from where her mother had left them on the shelf out of reach of the youngest ones. Just a few jellies wouldn't hurt, she told herself. Her tongue could taste their sweetness as she reasoned that she would still be able to purchase what else she needed with the change.

The three of them sat on the floor in the hallway, their backs resting against the door to their mother's bedroom, which Mary had guiltily shut behind them. Juice ran down Alice's chin as the three of them sucked and slobbered over the handful of jellies Mary had purchased a few minutes beforehand. The deed was done and, whilst she tasted the sweet softness of a cherry-flavoured delight, she felt no guilt. It was only when her mother returned later that day that the enormity of what she had done finally hit her. Literally.

"Where is the change, Mary?"

She could tell her mother was tired. Her sandals had rubbed raw red marks onto her feet from the constant trudging from client to client with a heavy load.

She knew she had to come clean. The punishment would be worse if she didn't.

There was anger in her mother's face as she listened intently to the story her daughter now told. Anger, exhaustion, disbelief all rolled into one.

When she had finished the punishment, Zakia replaced the belt onto the hook by the door and left her lying on the bed. Mary, her eyes smarting from the onslaught and a backside that was throbbing from the reprimand, watched as the belt swung gently from side to side. Just a belt. No longer a disciplinary tool.

She smiled. The taste of cherry was a ghost still evident on her tongue. A sprinkling of sugar could still be sought at the corner of her still-to-be-cleaned mouth. She licked every crevice carefully clean, holding on to that brief feeling of satisfaction that her disobedience had brought.

Despite the pain and the guilt, it had still been worth it.

Skierniewice, POLAND, 1923

"I'd like you to meet my mother."

Szyja had been lounging on the Frajdenreich's sofa whilst Rozia's fingers skipped lightly over the keys of the Irmler piano in her mother's parlour. His mind had been wandering as he listened to the melodic tunes of Chopin and Bach, helped on by the two glasses of Zubrowka and the homemade pickles and cheeses he had been plied with. The thought had suddenly popped into his head and the mood compelled him to say it.

"Oh?"

Rozia's fingers had paused on the piano keys, her head tilted to one side so her long dark hair fell softly over one shoulder.

"She asks about you," he continued, his mind still thoughtful. "A lot."

"I'd like that," she conceded before her fingers returned to the melody that had caught in both their ears.

***

"She's a fine Jewish girl!" It was the second time Tumera had declared the excited statement, her hands cupping Rozia's cheeks as her beaming smile continued not to falter. "I couldn't have picked a better girl if I'd have gone and employed a *shadkhan* myself."

Szyja felt the embarrassment warm his cheeks and tighten his collar. In his mother's eyes the wedding had already been set.

"*Ima*," he warned quietly. "Perhaps I can help you with refreshments?"

"Oh, the cake! I completely forgot. Rozia, my dear, please sit. You must be tired after the journey."

Szyja ushered her into the kitchen and closed the door. "*Ima…*"

"A mother has every right to be happy for her son!" she teased him. "See, I made an apple cake. Your favourite. It's been so long since you visited your mother."

Her playful tone couldn't quite hide the subtle hurt at their enforced separation. Between work and study, there had been little time left to visit his hometown and the mother whose children had all left the nest.

"I'm sorry I haven't come sooner." His hand brushed her arm where the sleeves from her purple and white dress puffed in a fashion he hadn't seen for a while.

Tumera's hand clasped his. In the two years since he had last seen her, she seemed frail, smaller than he remembered. Behind her joy was a sudden sadness in her eyes.

"Your father would be very happy," Tumera tenderly fixed the non-existent crookedness in his tie and stroked a finger down his freshly shaved cheek.

"I hope so," he agreed. The face of his father was fading now, lost in the eyes of a child but forever in his mother's memory.

"You have worked hard to get where you are. You have a good job and now a good woman behind you."

"*Ima…*"

"Tshk! Let me say my piece. You, Aron and Morduch are all that I have now and if I have to lose you all to your own lives, at least allow a mother to be proud."

He smiled and kissed her on each cheek.

"Of course. Now, what about this cake?"

Alexandria, EGYPT, 1924

The sweet seller would pass their door again on other days, but Mary had learnt by then not to squander the piastres left for their lunch. This rule had not been written on her backside from the belt that day but rather in her awareness that life was more precarious than she remembered it to be when her father had been around. Her mother returned home in a daily state of exhaustion from the miles she had walked around the city. She would sit in silence in her chair, her sandals kicked off to relieve swollen feet, until she had rallied herself for her children. This short period, Mary had learnt, was the most critical time, for her mother was quick to anger when she was tired and was best left well alone until rallied by the coffee Mary had prepared.

At the start of the week, Zakia was refreshed and adorned in the jewellery Hawash had given her when he was alive. And then, after spending a moment in silent prayer with her fingertips lightly touching the feet of Jesus on the cross by the front door, she would disappear for the day, returning with a bare neck and a heaving cart. The cart would then slowly empty so that by the end of the week, the goods would be replaced by money and by Sunday they would be able to supplement their diet with a little meat and the necklace returned to her neck just in time for church.

Mary liked Sundays. For that one brief day of the week, her mother would return to her. The day would start with Mass and not the trundling of her mother's cart. Zakia would get up early and spend a while in front of the mirror, touching up her make-up so that no one else would see the true nature of her daily toil. She would return to the mother Mary remembered from her younger years: tall, beautiful and darkly serene. And then the children would be dressed in their best clothes, their hair smoothed and their faces washed, and they would sit stiffly on the ornate wooden pew in the church that Zakia herself had financially contributed to when times had been less hard. The four of them sat like any other family surrounded by the golden hue and exquisitely painted walls of God's house and dutifully thanked Him for a life not quite yet fulfilled but a life nonetheless.

After worship, Zakia would spend the afternoon squatting over the Primus stove cooking the chicken she had killed and plucked the night before, the smell licking around the children's noses as they played amongst the remaining poultry on the balcony. Sometimes, if they were lucky, it would be a little beef. And then they would all collapse with exhausted stomachs, smiling and occasionally laughing as Zakia told them stories in the glare of the afternoon sun.

It was a day of peace and calm and family normality.

That peace was shattered one day in early January.

Her mother was out and Mary answered the door in her absence. A delivery boy was standing there, his arms loaded with boxes of all different sizes. Unsure what to do, Mary had allowed him to squeeze them into the short hallway by the front door. They stayed there all morning, stacked so high Mary could not quite see over them. She chewed on her nails and tried to think. Her mother had mentioned nothing of a delivery and she had double-checked with the boy that they hadn't been sent to the wrong flat. They remained there tantalising her as she walked back and forth from the hallway to the living room and balcony and back again. Her behaviour puzzled her brother and sister. Alice's little fingers tried to touch the wooden slats and Mary quickly scolded her as her mind wrestled with what she should do. It was a few hours before she summed up the courage to take a peek in one of those boxes. Her careful, eager fingers prised open the crinkly paper that covered the contents of the top box. Her nose twitched. She covered the contents again quickly with wonder and amazement creeping over her face. She dared herself another peek. Her nose had not deceived her. Shadows from her hair partly covered the sweet-smelling *baklava* and melon fruit. She covered it hastily and scrambled for the second box. It was larger and twice as tempting.

Meats. Some cured, some raw. The third box held legumes and bread: sweet-smelling, fresh crusty rolls and flatbreads all eagerly waiting for her to devour them.

She couldn't sit still for the rest of the afternoon. At every sound from the street below, she would rush to the window in the longing hope that it was her mother returning. Alice, with her baby eyes and chubby cheeks, watched her sister dart this way and that. A sprint to the window and then a shrug of disappointment before she returned to the boxes and the excitement would return once more.

She met Zakia at the bottom of the stairs when she finally arrived home, hot and exhausted, her cart nearly bare. Unswayed by her daughter's urgency, she loaded Mary with the remaining wares and the two of them went upstairs – Mary hopping from foot to foot, words tumbling out of her excited mouth, and Zakia wearily trudging behind.

Her mother stared into the boxes for quite some time, never uttering a word. Mary's babble finally came to a halt, her mouth dry, her eyes staring at her mother expectantly.

Zakia took an age before she finally nodded and took the boxes to her Primus stove.

All the children watched her cook those meats and fry those vegetables. As each tasty morsel left the large cooking pot, three pairs of eyes watched it being laid carefully back on the plate. The smell in the flat was excruciating. Time passed slowly.

When she was done, the frying pan was cleaned, the stove carefully wiped down. She left the room for a moment and it was all Mary could do to stop herself from falling on that pile of food in her absence.

It took a while for Mary to forgive her mother for what she did next. Her ears were blocked to the explanation she provided as her stomach dominated all the thoughts running through her head. The food, the sweets, the fruits, the meats, the bread all disappeared back inside the boxes. Without another word Zakia and the feast left the flat with the salivating children huddled inside it.

All of it was sent back to the person who'd sent them: Goued, her uncle. Her father's business partner. The man her mother cursed for enjoying the wealth they had once had; the wealth taken from her as a widow, as a woman. A victim of her sex.

"When you are older," Zakia told a distraught Mary later that night, "you will understand."

Skierniewice, POLAND, 2005

Mary clipped on her watch and studied her make-up in the hotel mirror. It had been an exhausting day spent mainly on her feet going from one location in the city to another. Each journey had ended in much the same way with a gap in the line of buildings where a place known to Jozef should have been. They had gazed up at polished modern buildings that had replaced the houses of the previous century holding bits of paper with their meaningful typed addresses, trying to picture his world.

It was still alien to her.

You don't need to wear all that make-up, you're beautiful as you are. The mirror caught her smile as she remembered his words. She'd been waiting for him at the train station in Ramleh one evening and had been furious as he'd alighted the carriage and then walked straight past her.

"Jozef, why are you ignoring me?" she had shouted after him.

"You don't need all this!" He had gesticulated wildly at her rouged cheeks and bright red lipstick. "You don't need to do that for me."

Her hand hovered to her lips, her fingers lightly gripping the lipstick with its deep shade of red. The reflection looking back at her was older now than that young, unblemished youth waiting at the train station. What would he now think of her thick-rimmed glasses that corrected her fading eyesight? The loose skin that caused her mouth to fall in permanent seriousness? The hair that was a different shade of black to the one he would have known?

She replaced the lipstick onto the dressing table unused and smiled at the memory of the man who could no longer see her.

OK, Jozef, you win.

She may be altered like the buildings he'd have known in his youth, but he would still have recognised her, still have loved her. Some things were destined never to change.

Luxor, EGYPT, 1924

Luxor was not like Alexandria. The streets were littered with trinkets catering for the many tourists that filed dutifully to the Valley of the Kings and back again, fuelled by the discovery of a little-known boy king in the desert not two years before. There were bawdy golds and vibrant blues leaping out of withered hands eager to cash in on Egypt's newfound popularity. It was hot, dusty and crowded and Mary didn't like it. She did not know why they had come, but Zakia walked with such purpose off the train with her children in tow that she imagined a mission of great importance. Mary knew better than to dare question the reason why. When Zakia's mind was made up, it was made up and that was that.

Iskandar was a wealthy man. He owned a jewellery business just short of the city centre. He was also Zakia's brother and in the absence of her father who had died long ago, he was also head of the family. As far as Zakia saw it, he was also her only hope.

The door to the family home opened and the children huddled together against the onslaught of cousins that tumbled out onto the street and excitedly danced around them. Copteya, Iskandar's wife, greeted her sister-in-law with open arms and it was all Zakia could do to hold back the tears that threatened to bubble over.

When Iskandar returned, he was patient and sympathetic to her plight.

"What is it you want from me?" he asked once the silence had fluttered like a veil over the choking onslaught of Zakia's story.

It was clear from the coolness of his tone that his sympathy might not yet stretch to practical help.

"I want you to help recover what's due to me, what's due to my children. Hawash owned half of that business; without him, Goued would have nothing. I want to get it back."

"You are a woman, Zakia." Her brother sighed, his fingers busily stroking his neat beard. "But to leave you with no provision… that was certainly a lack of foresight." To emphasise the point, Iskandar's hand flicked in illustration at the roof above their head as they sat in his study. Zakia was aware of the trinkets lined up on the dresser in the corner; the paintings hanging neatly on the walls; a large image of their parents on their wedding day seemed to loom over them as they talked. Their parents' faces beamed with excitement as if promising a future that their daughter could never dream of having. Zakia felt suddenly cowed in her widow's veils and sank further back into the cushions on the patterned chair.

"Stay with us a while." Iskandar's hand sneaked over her tightly curled fist and squeezed, his moustache and goatee breaking into a smile as his eyes retreated back under his furrowed brow. "Rest and regain your strength."

And so, the family swapped the oppressive emptiness of their life in Alexandria for the family home in Luxor. The children adapted swiftly to the sudden abundance of playmates and, with the help and comfort of her family, Zakia did forget the hardships from which she had flown.

For a while.

It was not long before Zakia was forced to find some sort of income to keep her and her young family afloat. Her brother's generosity could only stretch so far and his patience with three extra children in the house could only last so long. A childhood friend who worked at a nearby school told her of an Arabic teaching post that had become available. She jumped at the chance, not least because the school were also willing to take on Mary as a pupil despite her being two years younger than the usual school age.

Mary did not relish the opportunity.

The school was big and oppressive. The adults were overbearing. She sat dwarfed in between children who had two years further growth on her. The letters on the blackboard made no sense. The words in the books laid out before her danced and flew from her understanding. Nobody would play with her in the playground. She was too babyish, too little for their games. She longed for the comfort of her brother, sister and cousins and the inclusiveness they provided. She hated the school. She hated the teachers and the children and most of all, she hated her mother for sending her there.

"How was your morning?" Zakia asked her as they strolled back home in the heat of the day for lunch and a nap.

There was no answer from a sullen Mary as she trudged along the pavement like a condemned prisoner, destined to spend a lifetime in the confines of a place that oppressed her.

As they neared the family home, the children were playing with sticks in the street outside her uncle's house laughing and screaming as they made up mock battles, challenging an unseen army. They fell about her and begged her to join in, hunger and the heat not diminishing their enthusiasm.

The bread with the remnants of a fava bean stew stuck heavily in her throat as she lingered over her lunch, her knees scraped and dusty from the game she had joined. She was 'warrior Mary', battling the injustices and fighting for the freedom of her playmates. A hero amongst her fellow children.

"Hurry, Mary," her mother reminded her, clearing the rest of the dishes away. "We will have to leave soon or we'll be late."

She'd forgotten about school. The afternoon session had yet to be tackled.

"I don't need to go back today." The words were out of her mouth before she could stop them, spoken with an authority that convinced even herself.

Her mother hesitated with the platter she held. Slowly

and methodically, she was gathering what leftovers there were into a bowl.

"Oh?" she asked, not turning her back. "And why is that, Mary?"

Her mother was giving her a choice and the rest of the day would go one of two ways. She could either take the offered path of correction or plough on with the deceit. The latter may result in a beating, but it was also sugared with the temptation of more playtime with the people who loved her and that was far more preferable than another afternoon at school.

"It's a school holiday this afternoon." Mary sat up in her seat as the lie continued to buoy her spirits. "The teacher said that we didn't need to go back because it's a saint's day."

"Oh?" The plate had been returned to its rightful place. "Which saint?"

"Peter," she said with such conviction that she even convinced herself.

"Really? That is strange."

"Why?" She had failed to see the warning signs.

"Because I haven't been told such a thing. Do you not think as a teacher at the school they might have thought to tell me too?"

She shrugged, still convinced she was winning the conversation. She just needed to keep believing.

"Perhaps they forgot." It seemed a credible excuse and she was pleased with herself. "Yes, perhaps they thought that it would be up to me to tell you."

"That does sound exactly the kind of thing the school would do." Zakia's tone shifted dangerously. "Forget to tell me of all people whether I should be working or not this afternoon."

She had turned to face her daughter with a look that dared her to retract the lie before it snaked its way further across the situation. Mary faltered a little.

"That's what they said," her voice trailed off.

"Mary?"

"It's a school holiday," her lip had started to tremble.

"Mary."

Zakia took her to their bedroom and locked the door behind her.

The belt was not used on her backside that day. Instead, Mary looked on in horror as her mother reached for the *falaka* – that instrument of torture used to keep her feet still whilst the full force of the broom came down swiftly onto the soles of her feet.

She could hardly walk for a week.

But at least she was able to have the afternoon off from school.

Harlesden, ENGLAND, 1952

Mary realised that something wasn't quite right just as soon as she stepped into the hallway of Bramshill Road. The kettle was screaming and not singing. It sat neglected on the stove announcing to the world that it had been left on too long. Margarita's teddy – a pitiful bunny with worn-out ears and a nose that had been chewed off during previous months of teething – lay discarded at the bottom of the stairs.

She took the kettle off the heat and tutted.

"Margarita? Tumera?"

More toys were dotted about the lounge floor.

"Margarita?"

Her daughter was sitting outside the toilet door on the landing, her back against the white-painted wood. There was a sullen look about her, her lip curled in childish anger as she hugged her knees to her chest.

"Are you all right, Margarita? Whatever's the matter?"

The question was answered when the door Margarita was resting against rattled violently on its hinges. Mary noticed the bathroom key, which looked enormous in her daughter's hands.

"Margarita Beker! You let me out this instant!"

Mary suppressed the urge to laugh.

"Margarita, why have you locked *Babcia* in the bathroom?"

She thought about it for a long while.

"I just don't like her."

Oh, my angel, I don't like her either, she silently agreed. It turned out that Margarita had a reason that day for not liking her grandmother. Tumera had taken her on a trip to the shops in Shepherd's Bush and in Woolworths they had both spent a while staring longingly at the sweet section. Jars of pear drops, liquorice and rhubarb and custards had taunted Margarita as her eyes bulged and her lips salivated. A tub of broken chocolate had been requested and it had sat on the counter directly in front of her eyes as her grandmother reached into her pocket. A few pence had been exchanged and the two of them had left the shop with a small white paper bag. Tumera had marched them to the park to sit on a bench opposite the duck pond. That bag had sat on Tumera's lap and Margarita couldn't take her eyes off it. She had then watched her grandmother pop every last piece of that broken chocolate into her wrinkled mouth. The hairs on her top lip bristled like porcupine quills with every salivating suck. Not once had she offered the bag to her granddaughter.

"She is your *Babcia*, Margarita." Mary sighed. "You cannot lock her in the bathroom." She leaned close to her and whispered with a wink, "No matter what she has done."

"Mary? Mary! Is that you?" the door called. "I demand that you open this door immediately!"

Would Jozef be all that upset if they just left her in there? She brushed the thought out of her mind before it could take a firm root over her senses. She scooped up her daughter and unlocked the door. Tumera, her face puffy and red with anger, tumbled out onto the landing.

"That child is a menace! She has no manners, she is rude—"

"Are you all right, Tumera? Good. No harm done, then."

Margarita was shaking in her grasp but not through fear. And there it was. A memory sparked in some corner of her mind that had lain undisturbed for nearly thirty years. It occurred to Mary how alike she and her daughter were as they held each other. The child was shaking with rage. She knew that feeling. She could see her own mother – degraded, broken. She could feel that same rage sprung from a child's unconditional love. She felt that same urge to protect her family at all costs.

Alexandria, EGYPT, 1924

Once again, Zakia, Mary, Zaki and the young Alice were on the move. They left behind Iskandar's house, the cousins with their infinite energy, the school that provided Zakia a job and Mary a constant source of frustration. They returned to Alexandria. Despite the hardships awaiting her there, Zakia was light in spirit with the thought of being free. Men, she had learnt over the last nine months, were all the same, expecting the women to wait on them hand and foot. Even family.

It hadn't been long into their stay in Luxor before Zakia had learnt that, as a woman, she could expect no help from anyone. Iskandar had waved off her constant questions. He had made little effort in his pleas to Hawash's family to release the money she was owed. Her dead husband's share of the business was left firmly in the hands of Goued. The money she made from her small and insignificant teaching job started to disappear into her brother's lap. Money for rent. Money for food and clothes. The fact that the house was a family home and that her father had tried to share it out amongst his children seemed to be long forgotten. When she wasn't working, she was cooking and cleaning, her knees red raw from scrubbing the floors her brother trod.

It was not the life she wanted. It would be better to be on her knees scratching around for a living than to be on her knees for another man.

Their landlady was waiting for them in the lobby to their flat in the dusty street of Harah Mussa. It was late in the day and they were all exhausted.

"You're late with the rent." Their landlady stood, hands on hips like a bulbous teapot, her wide girth bulging in anger. She looked like she had been standing there a while.

Mary had always regarded her mother as tall but against Rashida, she seemed small and vulnerable. The dark circles around her mother's eyes seemed to make her cheeks shrink so that the bones that held her together were sharp and raised.

"Can this wait, Rashida? We've just this minute arrived back and the children are tired..."

"I have a dozen other tenants who would be happy with such a flat. I'm running a business here. This is not the first time I have had to remind you about payment."

"Mary, take your brother and sister inside. I will be there shortly." Mary hesitated on the foot of the stairs, her arms full with Alice's heavy weight. She was suddenly aware of how vulnerable her mother seemed, overshadowed by Rashida's towering strength. Her head was bowed, her shoulders shrugged, her fingers barely gripping the small, tattered suitcase she had dragged back from the train station. "Go, Mary. Take the children inside."

Mary's feet lingered on the stone staircase. She didn't want to leave her. The harsh tone of Rashida's voice carried like the pitter patter of tiny bullets up the stairwell. She could hear her mother start to sob. It was a quiet, mournful sound.

"Do you realise how lucky you are to have such a landlord? Anyone else would have chucked you out onto the street, children or no children."

"*Min fadlika*, my husband…"

"I don't want to hear it, Zakia. Every other family has a story like yours and still they pay up on time."

Mary opened the door to their flat and pushed her brother and sister inside. She gritted her teeth, closed her eyes, and took a deep breath. She could feel the rage bubbling up inside her, little angry bubbles that popped in her skull. She was her mother's cooking pot: a hot, boiling cauldron that danced and spat onto the living room floor.

"Please, I will pay you, just give me time—"

"Time? Do you think I have the time to come down here chasing tenants that drain my generosity by—"

Rashida got no further. Mary had reappeared, red-faced and breathless. She leant over the banister brandishing one of the wooden clogs her father had bought her in her right hand. Zakia saw her first. Her mouth opened like a fish catching air but no sound came out. Rashida turned to follow her gaze. Her eyes hooked on the clog as it spun slowly towards her before catching her right on the nose. She toppled backwards, her arms drawing large circles in the air as she tried to steady herself. She lost her balance and landed with a bump on her ample bottom, the clog landing on her lap.

"*Khallas!* Don't you dare talk to my mother like that!" Mary screamed.

Zakia looked from the landlady at her feet to her daughter and back again. She had stopped crying, her face contorted in abject horror. Mary's brain allowed her mouth the briefest of smiles as she watched Rashida's nose swell and redden before the enormity of what she had done caught up with her. Her hand flew up to her mouth and a cold shiver encompassed her petite form. She hesitated long enough to see her mother's lips part and stiffen before the fear kicked in. She flew down the rest of the stairs, hobbling with one foot bare, leapt past her mother and the stricken landlady and crashed out into the small courtyard. The toilet door was half open and she jumped inside, losing her other shoe in the process before bolting the wooden door behind her and curling herself up into the corner. She sat there shivering despite the heat, her chin burrowed into her knees.

Tap, tap, tap. Her mother's fingernails knocked on the toilet door. Mary could see her toes in their familiar sandals poking underneath. She drew her knees tighter to her chest, her teeth clenched.

"Mary?"

Tap, tap, tap.

"Mary?"

"I'm not coming out!"

"Rashida has gone."

"I don't care. I'm not coming out!"

"Why ever not?"

"Because you'll beat me."

"And why do you think I'll beat you?" Her mother's voice was strangely calm with no hint of the rage that normally accompanied a thrashing for bad behaviour.

"Because – because I hit Rashida on the nose!" There was a pause. The toes under the door stirred slightly, rippling restlessly like the waves on Stanley Beach. "She shouldn't have talked to you like that. She shouldn't have made you cry."

There was a sigh from the other side of the door as long as life itself.

"She shouldn't have made you cry," Mary repeated, aware of the small droplets of salty tears cascading down her face. "I didn't like that."

Another sigh and the door sagged as her weary mother leant up against it. The toes disappeared and the soft black cotton of her mother's dress settled gently into the gap under the door, draping the ground in its sadness.

"It's not the first time I have cried, Mary, and it won't be the last," Zakia addressed the air between them. "But you just cannot treat adults like that. It's just not done." Another sigh to signal the reprimand had finished as gently as it had begun. "I promise not to beat you, just open the door."

The door opened silently, and to her surprise, Mary found herself caught in her mother's arms, the powerful hug crushing her with love. They stood like that for a while, neither wanting the moment to end.

Harlesden,
ENGLAND,
1952

A ghost turned up on their doorstep. It was early in the
year, when the smog sat heavy on the streets, gasping
and choking the Londoners as they scuttled this way
and that. Daytime was turned to a permanent dusk,
all yellow and sickly and for once, children didn't play
outside but gawped out of their windows into the haze as
they dreamt of the far-off summer. The ghost had tightly
curled hair and a scarf stretched from cheek to cheek as
a barrier to the world around her. Her dull brown shoes
and brown woollen suit spoke of a war now gone. Mary
had answered the door and she squinted at the figure on
the porch as the smog struck a match in her eyes and the
moisture blurred her vision. She had asked for Jozef. No,
she had asked for *Szyja Alter Beker*. That was what the

ghost had said: three words in a thick Polish accent. A ghost asking for a ghost.

Mary hesitated and wondered whether it was *her*. Had the advertisements she had helped her husband write actually worked? Had the woman Jozef – no, not just Jozef – *they* had always assumed had perished, just been waiting in the fog to make her entrance into their settled lives? She had to invite her in. The smog was snaking around the woman's legs and dragging itself over the doormat. She didn't want it reaching her sleeping children. The woman's eyes thanked her in place of the anonymous mouth that remained shielded behind her makeshift mask. Mary left her hovering on the mat with her back against the front door as she fetched her husband. Tomorrow they were due to make a large delivery of orders and he had spent most of the evening checking each belt for quality in their makeshift workroom. There were glasses perched on the end of his nose.

She followed him back into the hallway and was unable to see his reaction to the ghost. The woman's eyes brightened over Jozef's shoulder and she removed the scarf to reveal electric red lips which contrasted sharply to her modestly rouged cheeks. The face didn't match the severity of her clothes.

"Zusana?"

"Mr Beker!"

And almost at once, Mary relaxed in the knowledge that this wasn't *her*. A sudden change in Jozef as the excitement danced in his eyes as he rushed to explain to his wife who this woman was: a fellow teacher from the school in Warsaw where Jozef had been employed as assistant headteacher before being promoted to head. Here, on their doorstep, miles from Poland, was a remnant of his previous life.

"It was difficult to track you down," Zusana conceded, as she dabbed the cream from her lips from the offered cup of coffee in the Bekers' living room. She sat, perched on the edge of the sofa, like a bird ready to take flight. She looked uncomfortable.

"It's difficult to find anybody these days," Jozef conceded. "How are your family, Zusana?"

The lips pursed.

"One brother killed. The rest are living." There was no emotion in her voice as if she had tested that statement numerous times over the years. Perhaps the sadness had been wrenched out of her. "And yours?" Her eyes darted up to meet Mary's in an almost apologetic way. "I heard that…?"

"Yes, well…" He shrugged.

Mary felt compelled to plant a hand firmly on Jozef's shoulder and the touch immediately made him visibly relax. The silence held.

"You were good at your job, Szyja. Those boys learnt a lot from you." Zusana drained the last of her coffee and returned her cup with a clatter that meant business. "The school has started back up and we are looking to fill the gaps."

A smile escaped his lips, a wry, bitter smile. "The gaps in the staff or the building?" he eventually asked. "I heard there was nothing left of Warsaw after the Germans and the Russians were finished."

"People are rebuilding, Szyja," she ignored the direction his tone had taken. "It is rising from the ashes, and we need good people to help make it what it was. Come home."

"This is my home." He caught Mary's hand. "We are settled here. I'm not going back."

Zusana reverted to their native tongue.

"Warszawa was your home. The buildings, the people you once knew may be gone but it's still Warszawa. You and Rozia were happy there—"

"Please do not say her name," Jozef replied in English. "She is no longer here."

Zusana nodded, almost apologetically. Mary watched the woman's eyes flit across their English living room with its paisley sofas draped with lace headrests and the pink and white teacups stamped with flowers. She'd forgotten to remove a large box of belts which held tomorrow's orders from the corner of the room, and she saw Zusana's eyes rest on it a while.

"So, you are happy being a tailor now? A man with a university degree—"

"I am happy," Jozef interrupted her. "My belly is full; my family is safe. I have a roof over my head. I no longer fear who knocks on my front door. The years have taught me what's important in life."

The woman sat in silence until her head began to nod in understanding. It was a look that Mary had seen before amongst the faces of their Polish friends as they shuffled the cards ready for bridge. That brief glimpse of a moment of unity only those that had shared in similar hardships could hope to understand.

"If you change your mind," Zusana said, rising to her feet, "the offer will always stand. The school will welcome you and your family with open arms. Think about it."

Mary drew the curtains against the smog, the night

and the woman with the electric red lips. She had been enveloped in the mist as soon as she had stepped back outside after taking her leave of them. Mary knew she couldn't ask her husband what he was thinking. He had replaced the glasses onto the end of his nose after the woman had left and put Chopin onto the record player, his hands running over the belts looking for any discrepancy that would lead to a reduction in price.

"I meant what I said," he suddenly told her without turning around, knowing she was still there, standing behind him, silhouetted in the doorway. Waiting. "Why on earth would I want to go back there?" There was a bitterness to his voice that she hadn't heard before. "I've only just learnt to sleep at night."

Skierniewice,
POLAND,
2005

The place where Szyja Beker and Rozia Frajdenreich were married in the late autumn of 1924 was now an electrical repair shop on the corner of an unassuming road not far from the city centre. It was quiet; the birds were singing. Their song filled the silence where the congregation had once been. The low building had been painted a vibrant orange that spoke cheerfully against its bright red roof.

Mary didn't want to go in. There wasn't any point. The toasters and microwaves that cluttered the beautifully arched windows were not going to give her any of the information she was looking for. Instead, she listened carefully to the genealogist's considered estimations on the aspects of that wedding from the dull resurfaced car park. The two were probably married as was the Jewish custom underneath a *chuppah*. There would have been a large celebration afterwards due to the Frajdenreichs' respectability in the community – Rozia's stepfather was a member of the municipal council. Mary imagined them dancing and drinking into the night. But where?

Did they both know then? Did they have the slightest inkling of what was to come?

The information was flat and sparse. A few official lines in the synagogue's archives scratched out in copperplate writing. That wasn't exactly what she'd wanted to know. What had she worn? This dark-haired woman. This woman who had captured Jozef's heart in this previous life of his that he had kept so hidden.

The leaves in Park Miejski would have been glowing like fire. The warmth of the waning summer had yet to be extinguished. She imagined Rozia, her face covered modestly in a thick white veil, taking Szyja's hand as they broke the glass with a satisfying stamp of their feet. A ring of flowers would have been placed on Rozia's mother's head and the sisters would have all danced around her as they celebrated the marriage of the last of the Frajdenreich women.

And when the dancing and singing were finished, when the cries of *Mazel tov* had fallen silent, did they suspect then? Or did they truly believe that Poland was changing, that the new prime minister, Józef Piłsudski, was ringing in change with his policy of assimilation of all ethnic minorities?

All this, Mary contemplated on the bare tarmac in amongst the Toyotas and Skodas. She knew none of this could be answered by a few lines of text scrawled by an official over eighty years ago.

Skierniewice, POLAND, 1924

"My little brother, all grown up." Morduch had his arm around his brother's neck, his speech slurred from the wine that had flowed freely. The two were surprisingly similar in looks: both had thick black hair that puffed up on the tops of their heads. Morduch's eyes were more guarded than his younger brother's but with the same tense look with lips thin in constant thought.

"It's about time, you were about to say?" Szyja remarked.

"Let's just say *Mazel tov* and leave it at that." He winked. "She's a good Jewish girl," he continued. "*Matka* is pleased."

Tumera had given up trying to hold back the tears just as soon as she'd rearranged Szyja's *kittel* on his shoulders before escorting him down the aisle.

"The last of my sons," she had told him, flattening the creases in the white linen again and again whilst her mouth showed dissatisfaction that her touch couldn't achieve the perfection she wanted. Those same dexterous hands that were used to manipulate the looms in the factory where she worked had lit the *yahrtzeit* candle in memory of Aron just a few weeks before. It had been just over a year since the death of Szyja's brother, the glue between Morduch (the eldest) and himself, the youngest. Over a year and the tragic accident had written lines on his mother's face that matched the ones left by his father's death.

Sometimes happiness and sorrow become interchangeable.

"So, is it children next?" Morduch continued his teasing, his fist planting a playful punch to his brother's shoulder.

"One thing at a time," Szyja reminded him.

"Rozia will need something to do once she gives up teaching."

How quickly my life has turned! A teacher and a student, now a husband and they are already lining me up in preparation for fatherhood!

The newly married couple moved into a traditional wooden house with a tall roof and dark wooden walls in Czysta, just west of the city centre. It was near enough to retain links with family and friends in the established Jewish community directly south of their little home, but far enough away that their heritage was not immediately obvious to their neighbours.

Friends and family brought them furniture and crockery and all the other trinkets a couple would need as they started out in life.

They may not have had much but they did feel blessed.

The flowers blossomed and vegetables started to grow in their little patch of Poland, carefully tended to by Szyja as a break from the constant teaching and the studying he undertook in Warsaw. Rozia would frequently walk the half mile or so to the train station in the evening to meet him. As life edged its way into the summer months, the trees bloomed with cherry blossom and the two took advantage of the lighter evenings to take a detour through Park Miejski on their way home. Rozia took his arm and laughed as she recalled a day spent tending to their home and chatting with friends. Szyja forgot the tiredness that ached his bones and smiled at her happiness. The willows dipped their branches into the lake, rippling the water in the gentle evening breeze. He liked this time of day as the world crept towards a peaceful calm after the toils of work and study.

"Poland is so beautiful this time of year," Rozia remarked as she leant over the painted wooden railings of the stark white bridge in the park where the willows trailed and wept.

Her hair fell in cascades over her shoulders, reaching for the cooling water far below. He noticed how her slender fingers, which had once skipped lightly over the piano at her mother's house, were dry and cracked from the manual work she had undertaken that day. She had gratefully accepted their new life, but he could tell she still craved a spark of interest to work her mind. Many an evening would be spent with her quizzing him on the studies he had undertaken that day in Warsaw as if it was the juiciest apple on a tree that she just couldn't reach. Her mind craved excitement and he suddenly felt a pang of guilt that he was pursuing a dream at her expense.

Then she was off, running across the narrow bridge to reach a clump of corn poppies that lay undisturbed in a bed left wild by the gardeners. Their nodding heads waved in the breeze and she picked a bunch of them.

"These will go well on our dining table."

He smiled. Their 'dining table' was an upturned crate Rozia had rescued from the market. She had covered its original purpose with a makeshift tablecloth that was fashioned from the lace from her wedding dress. Rozia was good at that. Making something out of nothing. It helped when the bills became harder to ignore and the cupboards became a little lighter of food.

Tumera had always taught him that life was hard and he was gradually finding out how hard it could be.

Skierniewice, POLAND, 2005

Mary imagined the wooden house on a leafy road and couldn't help but think how different this life with Rozia was compared to the hustle and bustle of their life on Bramshill Road. The constant toing and froing of friends and outworkers. The piles of belts that were deposited in and out of their living room. The trundle of the traffic outside their door. The only aspect of this place and theirs that bore even the remotest resemblance was the vegetable patch in the garden. Jozef always liked gardening. Whatever the weather, however tired he was after a hard day, he was always in amongst the vegetables, his muscles bulging as the earth yielded to the constant digging and turning. Was he the same with Rozia, here, in this quiet piece of Poland?

It was at this house, in this leafy, sleepy street, that the anti-Semitism they had tried so hard to avoid came knocking at their door. The genealogist had found it. In amongst the gentle news stories of a typical town. The death of Israel Spichler.

It was a name Mary was entirely unfamiliar with but a name that her husband would have known well. The stepfather of his then wife. The man who had risen to a job on the municipal council and the unlikely Jew tipped to be mayor one day.

He stood out and a Jew should never stand out.

Skierniewice,
POLAND,
1925

The bad news turned up one morning as spring was trying to move the cold depths of winter from the town. Szyja had been getting ready for work, cramming children's exercise books into a heaving satchel, when there had been a knock at the door. He had found Rozia's brother-in-law standing there, hopping from foot to foot as he'd tried to find the right words.

Szyja knew it was bad news from the simple lack of a tie. Shmuel always wore a tie. If he had not been in such a rush to cover the mile or so from the family home, maybe he would have put one on and then Szyja would have been less prepared for the words he was about to utter.

Don't say it. Don't break the peace.

Shmuel delivered the news quickly, and almost

apologetically, as if the offence lay in ruining their day rather than the actual crime itself: Israel had been walking home late the night before after meeting friends from the synagogue when he had been set upon. Somehow, he had managed to stagger home but died soon after, leaving Rozia's mother distraught.

There was a gasp. Rozia tore her shirt. It was an action he had seen his mother do years before, an official letter from the darkness of the previous war resting limply on her lap. Anguish and despair visibly laid out for the world to see.

He realised his brother-in-law was still standing on the porch; a neglect on their part as they had failed to invite him in. He stood on the steps in the quiet street, his breath fogging up the air between them. There was perspiration on his forehead despite the cold.

"Come in, Shmuel," Szyja offered, his face pale whilst his wife clung to him.

"I have to get back to Zenia and her mother. I'm sorry for..." he fought for the words. "I'm just sorry."

Szyja didn't go to work that day. Instead, he forfeited the loss in earnings in order to prop up his wife and help in any way he could. The family stood quietly in the Frajdenreichs' living room. No tears were shed, no angry words spoken. They knew that there would be no investigation into his death, no effort to corner the culprits. The deed would go unpunished, and a large memorial stone would be placed in the Jewish cemetery to commemorate the memory of a Jew who had dared to excel in local politics.

Rozia's mother, Faiga, hung a portrait of her second husband over her bed as a constant reminder of his missing presence. She shut the shop she owned selling liquors for a week to gather her strength whilst a steady procession of mourners held her hand in the silence and told her how sorry they were and what an excellent man Israel had been. It was a well-practised outpouring of grief that was an all-too-familiar sight in the towns and cities up and down the country. It was not the first tragedy to strike a Jewish family in Poland and it certainly wouldn't be the last.

Harlesden,
ENGLAND,
1952

The Rainfords came for tea. There was always a visitor to the Bekers' house on Bramshill Road. Whether they were Polish, English or any other nationality, they were all welcomed into the sitting room and fed *Pieczarki marynowane* and rye bread all washed down with a glass of Krupnik.

Today, the Rainfords were visiting.

They sat around the kitchen table and passed the time laughing over small talk as Mary fussed around them. Mr Rainford had a new job at a tailor's in the West End. Mrs Rainford had started training as a nurse – a profession Mary knew much about – and she offered happy memories in support of her guest's chosen career.

"Ah! *Ima*, come join us." Jozef pushed a chair out for

his mother, Tumera, who had come into the kitchen on hearing voices. He beckoned her to sit.

There was an awkward moment that Mr and Mrs Rainford were all too used to. A look of horror passed over Tumera's face as a glance turned into a stare; a smile in greeting turned into anger without a cross word being spoken. The Rainfords' eyes looked towards the table in the hope of retaining some sort of human dignity; not their own, but hers.

"Oh!" was all Tumera could muster.

The chair remained empty in the space between them as an open invitation. Tumera seemed to look from the chair to the Rainfords, wondering what to do. The Bekers' guests went back to sipping their coffee, refusing to rise to any sense of indignation. This was the way of the world. After arriving from Jamaica in the spring of 1949, they were used to the stares and the whispers. Jozef was not so understanding.

"*Ima*, please sit." There was anger in his voice that made Mary turn, a plate of *racuchy* dangling precariously from her hands threatening to spill sweet pancakes over the kitchen floor.

"No, Jozef." Tumera's face had hardened to stone as she gathered herself together. "I shall take my coffee back to the living room."

He confronted her later, after their friends had left in order to save them more embarrassment.

"That was unacceptable," he told his mother through lack of any other words to say.

"How can you allow people like *that* to sit with you?"

"People like that?!" His voice rose loudly and Tumera

flinched in surprise that her son had forgotten her matriarchal status.

"Jozef!"

"Whilst you are living in my house, under my roof, you will treat my friends, my family, with the respect they deserve."

"Ah!" A wry smile as if she suddenly realised what this was really about. "*Your* family. I see now. Jozef, you know my opinion on the matter."

"Yes, *Matka*, I know your opinion on the matter but that is not to say that I agree with it."

"I just want to know why, with all those good Jewish women out there, you settle for…"

"*Matka!*" He cut her off before the words could be released into the air like a ten-foot wall between them.

"You deserve a better life, Jozef. Rozia, the children… You are an educated man. A man with a degree from the University of Warsaw of all places! Yet here you are making belts like a common tailor with a woman from…"

Jozef left the room. He left the house and if his legs would have taken him, he would have left the city, the country, the continent, and the general world around him.

Tumera packed her bags the next morning and a peace ensued as she boarded the ship at Southampton docks. A ship that brought her back to her life in South Africa with her clothes factory and the racism she had embraced as her own after fleeing the hatred and the anti-Semitic violence of her homeland.

Skierniewice, POLAND, 2005

Mary was contemplating the mother-in-law that disliked her. The woman with the stony face who clutched her youngest son's arm in that photograph from Johannesburg.

They couldn't find the gravestone of the brother that died so young. They couldn't find the monument that was supposedly erected in honour of Rozia's stepfather. Any memorials to those tragedies had been wiped away with the hatred that had later gripped Europe.

Hate is a powerful tool.

Did Tumera hate her because of the colour of her skin? Did she hate her because she wasn't Jewish?

"She had a hard life," Mary had to admit. "She'd lost everything – her husband, two sons, the grandchildren." Not an excuse for her behaviour as Mary would never allow her that, but an explanation for it at least.

"She must have moved to South Africa to be with family," the genealogist offered. "She had a sister that moved there in the twenties. Maybe it was because of that."

And Jozef and Morduch and the family she left behind? How did she feel about that?

Jozef had once confessed that, in the height of the war, during their depth of desperation, he had written to his mother to ask for her help in getting them out. For some reason, she had said no. That was something Mary could never understand: how a mother could abandon her child.

Alexandria, EGYPT, 1925

Mary lay in bed with clean cotton sheets pulled tightly up to her small chin. Her chest felt heavy with the pneumonia that had plagued her body since Tuesday. Her temperature soared and then plummeted and was dabbed away by the kindly woman sitting by her bedside.

In her delirium, the woman was a hazy blur of black with a pale face framed in white that reminded her of an angel the priests had talked about in their never-ending sermons. This woman might be an angel, but she was definitely not her mother. In her feverish state she tried to picture her mother standing over her. She could remember her black veil but whenever she tried to pull it back to touch her mother's face, the image twisted and turned away from her fingers and the veil came down again.

Her hands scrunched the bedsheets in panic and Sister Philippine gently clasped her little fist until the moment passed.

"*Chut petite, ça va aller.*"

The calm words soothed her, although she had no idea what they meant. Her fingers relaxed.

"You are not well, Mary," Sister Philippine continued with a kindly smile.

Ah yes. She remembered where she was. The tall dark halls of L'Orphelinat de la Miséricorde came back to haunt her: the French school for orphans on Al Saba Banat Street in Alexandria. It was a large building (enormous in relation to her small size) with faded brown cement walls and tiny windows with grills that spoke of inmates desperate to get out. She had wanted to leave. In the first few weeks of her mother leaving her in the nuns' clutches they had had to physically restrain her. She was convinced her mother was still waiting outside, clutching Alice to her chest with Zaki clinging to her skirts. Her mother could not have simply *meant* to leave her there. She had done something terribly wrong. That was it. Her mother was so upset with her that no amount of beating would correct her indiscretion. She had had to leave her in the presence of God to cleanse her of her wickedness.

"Can you remember where you are?"

"Am I in hell, sister?"

Philippine frowned and checked her temperature with her soft silky hand.

"Tsk! *Non, petite fille. Non!*" She paused and muttered under her breath. "Don't let Maman Ancette hear you talk like that."

The fever subsided again for the fifth time that day and the woman beside her came into focus with her black habit and pure white wimple. She smiled and the warmth radiated off her.

"Are you hungry? Some *chocolat*, perhaps? *Du pain?*"

She ate hungrily despite the tightness in her chest and, for a while, she forgot about her mother with her blurred face and distant smile.

They say angels visit us in our moment of need. Philippine was there consistently in the years she spent at that school. And it was years. The hope that her mother would return to collect her vanished just as soon as the harshness of school life became her reality. Hope was replaced by stubborn strength and a resolve greater than her age. She had stopped crying on the day when one minor mistake had seen her dressed in nothing but a hessian sack and forced to stand like a statue at the school's entrance all the way through lunch. Her mistake had been to refuse to answer to the name Mary *Goued*. She was Mary *Hawash*. Always had been. But the nuns shunned the custom of using the father's first name as the child's last in favour of the Western tradition. Her last name must be the same as that of her father's. She kept forgetting and that was her punishment.

It was hot and itchy under the sack and people stopped and stared. A little boy passed by with his sombrely dressed mother. His little finger lifted to point, and a hand stifled a snigger that escaped his smiling lips. He could have been Zaki. He was small enough, but little of the memory of his face remained in her tired mind for her to piece him back together. To her surprise, the thought of her brother and mother no longer invoked a sense of sadness inside her. Instead, she felt the rage twirling inside her stomach. Tighter and tighter it whirled until it became a ball that bounced and rocketed in a desperate bid to escape her body and the school that imprisoned her.

She would cry no more.

She would not give them the satisfaction.

Skierniewice, POLAND, 2005

The coffee in the hotel room was rich and satisfying. Perhaps it had only been the English who had been obsessed with Camp coffee in those early years after the war. That sweet, nutty syrup; such a poor substitute for the real thing! Thankfully she had tried none of it since.

Her feet were taking a break from the long walks into the past that occupied their visit to Poland. Laid out on the dressing table in front of her were the various papers and documents she had been encouraged to bring from London in order to aid their search.

Such beautiful children!

In amongst the official papers, the hastily written scraps to assist an aging memory, Mary had brought along the photographs her husband had possessed. Most of these had come to London via his mother. He, himself, had left Poland with nothing. She remembered how the small parcel from South Africa had landed on their doorstep, how Jozef had sat down in contemplative silence as he'd sifted through the images of the people who now only existed in his memory. Then they had been put away in a cabinet and not looked at since.

Was it just too painful?

Some (the pictures of Tumera's sons as young men and the faded photographs of her grandchildren with smooth, chubby cheeks), showed signs of gradual fading by sunlight. It was as if they had been put on a mantelpiece on proud display so that the faces of those captured in time could enjoy the sun once more. Mary knew that hadn't been at their house.

Tumera must have done that.

In the warmth of a South African climate, thousands of miles from her original home, Tumera would have openly kept reminders of all that she had lost in plain sight. It was a thought that hadn't occurred to Mary before; this dour woman with her open dislike, clutching hold of the years and the people she had lost in Poland. Her son with another woman, with children she didn't recognise, showing signs that he had moved on when Tumera herself could not. Unlike her son, she was too old to start anew, too bitter to begin again.

In amongst those photos that had been loved so dearly, Mary found herself reaching an understanding, a compromise with the mother-in-law who made it quite clear that her son could do better.

The past had such a habit of shaping the present.

Alexandria,
EGYPT,
1926

The small rooms of the family's flat on Harah Mussa had been replaced in Mary's young mind by the vast expansive halls and corridors at L'Orphelinat de la Miséricorde. The uniform with its straight lines of blues and greys had eroded her previous life and even the clogs her father had bought her had become too small and worn for her growing feet. The Arabic she had spoken everyday was becoming hazy with its replacement by the soft French tones of the nuns who glided down the corridors and instilled their lives of virtue and perfection on the young girls under their care.

Mary found new friends in place of her brother and sister. Young girls of her own age and from all backgrounds who giggled and played with her hair. She was also struck (as she came to know these new playmates) by how different her life had been to others in the city. The relative comfort she had enjoyed when her father had been alive and well enough to provide for them was just a distant memory and those harsh times of wanting were the only childhood she knew. Her newfound friends spoke of cafés and a life in Alexandria she had never seen or known. Laurens, a particular good friend of hers, told her about the film she had seen at the Rex cinema with her mother immaculately dressed in a suit of lilacs and mauves. Mary's mouth salivated at the image Laurens painted of the pure white vanilla ice cream melting on her tongue as the Hollywood cowboys rushed across the screen and into her imagination. Laurens' mother had taken her to a café afterwards and she had spooned the cream from her mother's coffee into a mouth that had been numbed by other delights not two minutes before.

That was when she realised what 'poor' actually meant. It was the ants she had tapped out of the stale bread her mother had kept in the loft to dry. It was the dull pain in her tummy from a diet that was left wanting. It was the swollen feet of a mother who walked the streets with a heavy cart for a few piastres a day.

She was ashamed and angry.

It was a warm day in November when Laurens showed Mary what she had really been missing. The hot heat of summer was calming in time for the cooler Mediterranean winter and the girls had a rare moment before afternoon prayers and the lessons that followed. Laurens took Mary's hand and she allowed herself to be led with some trepidation through the empty halls towards the refectory. Her friend was giggling and exchanged excited looks with

Therese who jogged along in her pinafore dress in a bid to keep up.

"*Dépêchez-vous*, Mary!" The hand that was tugging hers was warm and slippery to the touch. "Come on!"

They demanded she close her eyes at the heavy wooden door whilst Therese navigated the iron latch. Girlish hands clamped on her face to make sure she didn't peep. They pulled and pushed her, being careful that she didn't trip.

"*Voila!*" Laurens exclaimed in finality, removing her hands from over Mary's eyes with a flourish.

She blinked as her gaze adjusted to the harsh light that cascaded in from the full windows behind the serving area of the large hall. Her friends could hardly contain their excitement as they waited for her to see their carefully laid out surprise.

"There, Mary, there!" Fingers pointed and faces beamed.

On the serving table before her, dotted on a cool, marble board, were sugary delights that Mary could never have imagined in her wildest dreams: silky eclairs, shiny baklava sprinkled with nuts and sugars, dainty biscuits and rich, velvety cakes. The girls squeaked and clapped their hands with delight.

"Happy name day, Mary!" they called in perfect unison, their voices bouncing off the empty refectory walls. A birthday was rarely celebrated, but the saint's day of the saint with whom you shared your name was a cause for celebration.

"Oh!" was the only word she allowed to escape her mouth. She was acutely aware that there was moisture on her eyelids and a solitary tear escaped from the corner of her eye.

"Oh!" Laurens subconsciously copied her friend's cry and flung warm arms around her. "Have we done something wrong?"

"*Non, non!*" Mary caught her arm and squeezed, her face lighting up into a smile. "This is wonderful! *C'est merveilleux!*"

They filled their stomachs with the treats, not allowing a single crumb to remain undevoured. Their faces sticky and their fingers thoroughly licked, they slumped onto the floor with their backs against the wall and giggled.

"When Maman fetches me this weekend," Laurens decided with some finality, "you will come with us. Oh, say you will, Mary!"

She nodded with a smile, her stomach too full to utter a spoken reply.

The three of them sat in silence waiting for the courtyard clock to strike an end to their fun; three girls in three grey pinafores with bright white cotton socks pulled tightly to the knee; three girls that all now looked the same but with a former childhood that was miles apart.

Laurens and her mother spirited Mary away from L'Orphelinat de la Miséricorde that Friday. The girls were sleepy from Mother Ancette's dull tones during afternoon prayers and they both slumped wearily on the expansive leather seats of Laurens' family car. Mary was too tired to even notice that this was the first time she had ever sat in an automobile.

They took her to a café by Stanley Beach and had ice cream on the sand. Mary had been there before when her father had been alive but none of it seemed to be familiar. Beautiful women clad in swimsuits stood on the sand in the centre of the circular bay as if they were famous actresses in a theatre. Light bounced off the circular row of beach huts behind them and bathed them in light as if a hundred spotlights were upon them. Vibrant reds, yellows and blues dazzled her eyes in asymmetric patterns and floral displays. She sank her teeth into the pure white ice cream and smiled as the delicious mixture smothered her chin and touched her nose. At the age of nine, her eyes were being opened to life outside the sheltered living her mother had provided.

Laurens insisted on taking her to the Rex cinema and Mary was happy to recreate the scene her friend had painted for her back at school. She sat mesmerised by the handsome actors with their pencil-thin moustaches and crisp clean suits and the women with their dark lips, petite noses and perfectly curled hair. The two friends left the plush seats to run into the open air and daydreamed about Antonio Moreno. Laurens adopted the sultry look of Greta Garbo and the two laughed and smiled.

The weekend ended as quickly as it had begun and the two were back in their grey pinafores listening to Mother Ancette's morning assembly with her tightly wound coif and stern, pointed face.

"You must come out with me and Maman again," Laurens whispered with a finality that didn't allow for any objection.

There started a pattern once a month where Mary was welcomed into her friend's family and, for that weekend, she had a surrogate mother and sister who loved her as their own. This pattern turned into habit and was a welcome retreat from the stuffiness that haunted her time at school.

And then her mother returned.

Maman Ancette called her into her study during embroidery one spring morning in 1927. The nun was sitting stiffly behind a vast heavy wooden table. There were glasses pinching her bony straight nose and a cane lay ominously between them. Mary's stomach contracted as she desperately tried to remember what misdemeanour she had committed to have the privilege of being punished in private. Her gaze was so intent on that instrument of torture that she did not see the other lady sitting on the edge of a chair, in the shadows, in the corner of the room. A woman dressed in a black dress that halted just below the knee with dull black shoes and a dark veil that draped over shoulders that were hunched in fatigue. A face that was proud with a hint of propriety and a determination that challenged anyone that looked at her.

"You don't recognise your own mother, Mary?"

Mary recoiled at that statement and the tears began to flow freely and readily down shocked cheeks. She stood still, staring at the woman in the corner as if she had seen a ghost. Her feet refused to move. She seemed older than she remembered. Older and thinner.

"Mary?"

A voice that was so silky soft that she wanted to wrap herself up in it and immerse herself in its silkiness. There was a sudden spark of a feeling inside her that she hadn't felt for years. She crumpled inwards, invisibly, and the two years she had spent in the French school independently growing in confidence seemed to melt away. She was seven again, crying on the threshold of an alien world, surrounded by nuns as her family walked away.

"You've got so tall!" There was an emotion in her mother's voice that she couldn't place as she didn't remember hearing it before: a feeling of sadness, of pride and love. Zakia walked towards her and placed a hand on her cheek. Mary realised with a start that the top of her head was nearly parallel with her mother's chin. She shrank back from the hand that was no longer soft as she remembered it in her dreams, but hard and wrinkly from physical work.

There was pain in her mother's eyes that she immediately tried to hide. Zakia cleared her throat and addressed the Mother Superior, who remained unmoved by the scene.

"Mary will be coming home for the weekend," she stated with some finality.

Home? And where exactly was home? This place was all she remembered. This was the space where she belonged.

It turned out that home was still the two-bedroomed flat on Hara Mussah. It smelt musty and unkempt, devoid of a family for too long. She gazed shocked at her brother and sister, unable to believe that the little girl who walked confidently around her was little Alice whom she remembered as barely fitting into her arms. Zaki was losing his boyish chubbiness and held himself like he wanted to be treated – the man of the house.

And there, squatting by the Primus stove, the familiar smells of her mother's cooking brought her back to the family she believed had abandoned her a couple of years ago. As she ate, crossed-legged on the carpet, scooping up the greeny goodness of the *molokhia* stew with a piece of flat bread, she mulled over the question that she knew she could never ask and if she had had the courage to ask it, would never have been answered anyway: *Where on earth have you been?*

Skierniewice, POLAND, 2005

That question had never been entirely answered. Mary had asked her mother about it once, when she was older, when an adult mind could look at the past with more of an understanding.

"Why did you leave me in that school?" she had asked, her lips pursed and her body tense in anticipation for an answer she suspected she wouldn't like. "So young and alone for so long?"

A shrug and a slight pause in her sweeping. She was cleaning the living room in readiness for the guests Zakia had invited over for cigarettes and a game of bridge.

"I couldn't cope," she'd offered with her back to her. "I had things to do and Alice and Zaki were too young to leave."

So, her crime had been her age?

Her mouth had opened to continue the questioning, but her mother's back had acted like a barrier to the past. The silence told her that it wasn't the right time. It was still too early in their lives to smooth the wrinkles of the past. Still too raw for them both.

Mary had never returned to that question in the years that passed. It had always been something she intended to raise but life got in the way and she was left with the regret of unanswered questions. Just like those questions she had failed to ask Jozef which she now found herself trying to answer in the silence where he should have been.

Was it right to feel angry at that?

"Why is it you always seem to have a tear in your eye when you talk about your mother?" Henry's question had popped up in this trip to Poland and it had startled her in its directness. Funny that she found herself talking about her mother in this European country that bore little resemblance to her country of birth, to Zakia's home.

The truth was her mother was always on her mind. Always had been. A part of her that she felt needed protecting.

When she was eleven, she had asked for her sister to join her at the school for the firm reasoning that one less child at home would lighten the load of her mother's cart, ease the pressure on her weary feet and allow more time for her to rest. Perhaps the answer Zakia had given her later in life – the statement that she couldn't cope – had been something she had known at the back of her mind even at the cusp of her teenage years. An answer that had led to an overwhelming desire to help.

Poor Alice! To be going to school so young! She had asked the nuns to push a small cot next to her own bed and had thrown herself into the role of surrogate mother and protector.

Her old grey pinafore had dwarfed her younger sister's fragile frame. The tall ceilings and large hall had scared her, just like it had scared Mary all those years ago. How alike they were with their short, tightly curled hair and sharp facial features, although Alice was obedient and polite and anxious to please, having none of her elder sister's forceful determination.

"Why can't you be more like your sister?" Sister Julienne had exclaimed in exasperation as Mary yet again refused to follow the strict rules guiding every minute of their young lives. "She is seven years younger than you, yet even she knows not to answer back. How you two are from the same mother, I will never know!"

Mary had needed Alice as much as Alice had needed her. Her sister's calmness soothed her. She never had a bad word to say about anyone – a natural beacon of light and laughter. A quality like that needed protecting. She hadn't wanted her own childhood experiences to take that from her. She hadn't wanted her sister to become aware of how their mother was getting thinner, quicker to anger every time she came to collect them from school for a weekend of chores and labour.

And Zaki?

She hadn't resented *him* but more his unfortunate status as the only male in the house. The best of everything came Zaki's way. It was the way of life in Egypt. All hopes placed on him just because he was a man and destined for better things.

Mary remembered once how, one Friday, her mother and brother had come to fetch them from school, and she had noticed, with horror, her father's tarboosh resting casually and haphazardly on Zaki's thick black head. She hadn't been able to help herself. The hat was snatched from her brother as their mother looked on horrified.

"Did no one ever tell you? You must take off your hat in a place of worship!"

The hat was fiercely clutched in her hands as if the tarboosh still held the smell of the father she missed, the life she grieved for whilst her mother hissed at the children to stop making such a scene.

"I have never been so embarrassed in all my life!" Zakia had declared, mortified, as she'd bundled them into the street and away from the staring nuns.

The hat had been promptly returned to Zaki's head and Mary had wanted to cry at the unfairness of it all. Perhaps that was why, all these years later, she couldn't bring herself to talk about her mother without those tears in her eyes. It was as much the grief and longing of losing her as it was about the grief of a childhood cut short and the questions that found themselves unanswered.

Harlesden,
ENGLAND,
1956

The nightmares had started again. It had been a year since a mild heart attack had taken them both by surprise – Jozef always seemed so strong, so young. His now fragile health had worsened the night sweats and left Mary in a constant state of worry. He screamed in the night, loud pitiful whimpers that erupted from his sleeping lips as his eyes darted behind their wrinkled veils.

"Jozef?" The whisper was delivered directly into his ear as she gently held him, willing him back to the present.

He never directly spoke of the *horrors*, but Mary couldn't help but imagine the images that haunted his dreams and made him scream in the night; the cattle trucks, the death, the despair, and the inhumanity of it all. His eyes darted open. Bright white eyes in the blackened room searching in fear for the next onslaught on his senses.

"Jozef."

Mary used her voice, her calmness, to bring him back to reality. Her hands stroked his fists that clutched the bed sheets and he slumped back onto the pillow that was drenched in his own sweat.

"I'm sorry I woke you."

She said nothing as she turned on the bedside lamp knowing that her husband would want to read for a while to shake from his mind the images that haunted him.

She was worried that the screams would wake the children, so she padded across the landing to check on them. They lay undisturbed, Margarita clutching her withered fluffy bunny and Henry lying on his stomach, the covers pushed off his small frame as his chest rose and fell rhythmically; both in an innocent slumber that only the young can enjoy. There was nothing to haunt their dreams. Mary and Jozef tried hard to keep it that way. Their life in Britain was miles away from the uncertainties Egypt had to offer or the horrors Jozef had seen. It was not a perfect life in any way, but it was safe from the rumblings that threatened violence and war.

The day clawed out of the night. Margarita was making breakfast when Mary came downstairs. She had woken later than usual due to her sleep being disturbed. Jozef had not been there when she'd opened her eyes and the cotton sheets were devoid of any crumples from his sleeping frame. The book he'd been reading was flattened face down on the bedside table so that the spine was creased. His reading glasses lay carelessly open on top and the lamp was still glowing as it fought the rays of sunshine from the gaps in the curtains.

There he was, sitting at the kitchen table, his arms folded, staring into nothingness. He wore his flannel trousers and a creased shirt but there was no tie around his neck, no socks or slippers on his feet. His face was unshaven, the small hairs adding to his tired look. Bacon and eggs sizzled in the pan where Margarita tended them, the noise perfectly accentuating the tension in the room. She turned when her mother entered, her gaze full of anxiety.

"Some coffee perhaps?" Mary's soft hand touched her husband's shoulder and he flinched. She withdrew her hand and gave her daughter a reassuring smile that forced itself out of her uncontrollable worry.

"Yes." His voice was metallic and thick.

The breakfast and the coffee seemed to rally him at last. The nightmares had always existed at night, but this was the first time they had penetrated the light of day. Mary insisted he delay his trip to the West End to deliver the order they had completed yesterday. It was not due until the afternoon and he would be wise to rest in order to shake the fatigue of the previous night. For once, he did not disagree with her suggestion and that was why he was there when the postman delivered the unwelcome news.

It was a telegram from South Africa. No one liked to receive a telegram. It invariably meant bad news. He took the small piece of paper with its anonymous, typewritten script and brought it into the sitting room, closing the door behind him. Mary was left watching that closed door as the kitchen clock ticked on through the silence.

Tick tock. Tick tock.

He left the house when her back was turned, without his jacket despite the coolness of the autumn air. Mary noticed it hanging in the hallway as she heard the front door click shut. Her face full of worry, she dashed to the front step and just about glimpsed his form disappearing around the overgrown laurel hedge on the corner of their street. The children were at home, otherwise she would not have hesitated to run after him. The clue to his disappearance lay abandoned on the worn green and red carpet beside his usual chair; a one-page, typewritten script with the crown of the post office mark at the top. The factual message was taped in brilliant white to the tea-coloured form and seemed to shout at her in capitals with an urgency that transcended the few thousand miles from its source.

TUMERA BEKER DIED YESTERDAY.
FUNERAL MOST LIKELY NEXT WEEK.

So, Jozef's mother was dead. The how didn't seem to concern the sender nor Mary for that matter. The point was that Tumera, Jozef's last link to his previous life, was gone.

His nightmares became even more vivid that night and the next. It became harder for Mary to wake him as if, with each night, the terrors were gaining more of a grip on him, pinning him down into a darkness that was unrelenting in its onslaught of fear. There was nothing that could be done. There was no magic cure to take the demons away.

The dreams, the physical work, the long hours wrote a strain in lines across Jozef's face. Long, deep ridges that made him seem even more serious. He was tired. Mentally and physically. He was short-tempered and words were said in frustration.

"Are you calling me a liar?"

Henry had come home from school to say that he had had no lunch money in his bag to pay for his school dinner that day. Mary was adamant that she had given it to him that morning. Jozef had quipped that she must have been mistaken as children did not lie. She baulked at that. She did not like the implication that it was *she* who lied.

"The boy is adamant that he had no change for his lunch. You must have been mistaken," he persisted.

"I am not a liar!" she hissed.

The children stared. Margarita's bottom lip trembled. The kitchen seemed to bubble and boil with the angry mess of their parents' anger. No further words were said, the looks on their faces were words enough. Mary did the only thing she could, which was to grab her handbag and leave the house. She powered down the steps and down the road. *And then what?* There was a sudden realisation that the one person she wanted right at that moment was thousands of miles away. She closed her eyes at the end of the street and took a deep breath as she thought of Zakia and the longing she stirred inside her. Right at this moment, England didn't feel like her home with its grey weather and its dull, predictable population. She wanted the bright, clean streets of Alexandria. She wanted the cosmopolitan air, the culture, the colour. She wanted Zakia and Alice and the friends she had left behind.

Her feet took her to the only place she felt she could go, Our Lady of Willesden Catholic Church on Nicoll Road. Its tall, imposing red-brick façade welcomed her in and she slumped exhausted onto one of the hard wooden pews in the centre of the church. The building absorbed the angry, echoing tread of her patent-leather shoes and she was suddenly lost in the hollow silence. With her eyes closed she could almost hear the haunting chants of the nuns from her infant school back in her homeland. Oddly peaceful and strangely ethereal. They had scared the life out of her during her childhood but now, the memory of those voices was sweeter. That time was gone. Lost.

This was not her place – this England.

Perhaps you will visit us when we are settled? She remembered those final words to her mother as they had parted at the docks in Port Said, off to a new life in Europe as the situation in Egypt became untenable to any possible future. Zakia had nodded in blind agreement to that promise, as people tend to do when they know the more truthful answer is too painful to bear. There were tears bubbling at the corner of her eyes and the typical black attire she was prone to wear spoke of a new mourning that superseded the events all those years ago. The loss of a daughter as well as a husband.

"Hello, Mrs Beker."

The voice startled her and Mary's hand flew up to stop a gasp from escaping shocked lips. She had not heard Father Keegan slip into the pew behind her. She immediately dabbed at the corner of her eyes with a handkerchief to hide the shame of her emotions.

"It is unusual to see you here at this time," he remarked, as his large frame caused the wood to heave and creak.

The statement did not require an answer but she provided one all the same. The incident with the lunch money was recalled with careful censorship and her predicament laid bare as she succumbed to her vulnerability.

"I have nowhere to go, Father," she admitted. "I am not sure what to do."

"Your home is where you should go, Mrs Beker." The priest laid a calming hand on her fingertips. "And by that I don't mean the bricks and mortar that gives you shelter. Your home is in your heart, and I believe your heart lies firmly with your family."

Liverpool,
ENGLAND,
1948

It was early September. The *Empire Halladale* eased into the Liverpool docks on a day when light rain covered the view of the city stretching out for miles in front of it. The white troopship, which had increasingly greyed throughout the long journey, was dwarfed by the tankers around it. Mary had staggered out onto the deck to watch the welcome sight of solid land rushing up to greet them. There were soldiers spilling out around her calling out to loved ones far below them on the shoreline. A lady called Lilly, whom Mary had not known prior to the journey, had a tight hold of Margarita who was sleeping fitfully in her arms.

The three-week journey had not been kind. Mary had discovered soon enough into the trip that she did not possess the sea legs of the eight other ladies who shared her cabin. The room swayed and turned in ways unimaginable and soon she was doubled over with a sickness that stayed with her both day and night. The sting of vomit at the back of her throat and the smell of the sea and the oiled workings of the ship was an assault on her senses that she neither welcomed nor relished. Through her helplessness, the other women in her cabin (young mothers, all of them) had taken pity on her. They were all wives of English officers with soap-white skin who busied themselves cleaning the cabin, bringing her water and a tasteless soup that they encouraged her to sip with exaggerated nods and anxious looks. Their babble went completely over Mary's head, and they resorted to communicating with each other through gestures and pointing, accompanied by smiling faces and noises of concern and compassion. Margarita had become ill and as the fever gripped her, the ladies doubled their efforts to help her stricken mother and nurse the child back to health.

Mary was just over thirty years of age and this was the first time she had ever left Egypt. The first time she had travelled anywhere outside her country of birth. The pain of separation from her mother was all too much to bear during that three-week voyage beset with vomit. This was a different world, a drab world, and she longed to hear the sound of people speaking Arabic – some small connection to the home she had left behind.

She leant over the railings and tried to pick out Jozef from the crowds of people along the front. She was aware that she was now in a place that she didn't know, had never visited before and whose language largely escaped her.

The decision to leave Egypt in 1948 was a difficult but necessary one. Mary had always thought Alexandria would be her forever home, but then anti-British feelings after the war had changed all that. Jozef was advised not to wear his uniform whilst on leave. His adoptive country started to echo the intolerance of his country of birth. Shops were targeted with stones and fists. There was a feeling of tension in the air that Mary had never known before, a constant threat hanging over them.

"We go to England, with the Polish Resettlement Corps," Jozef told her. "I'll be demobbed and then we start our lives over, away from all this…"

England was a gateway into a new world. And what a new world it was with its smoke-filled chimneys and busy docks of faded red, black and grey. The war seemed to have sapped the colour out of this island as well as its strength.

She thanked the women who had kept her going through the past three weeks with smiles and nods of grateful abandon and they parted at the bottom of the gangway.

Now what?

She placed her suitcase down and hoisted Margarita onto her hip. She was jostled by soldiers spilling off the ship returning home. She envied their excitement. It was getting late into the afternoon and the sun must have been fading wherever it was amongst the clouds that enveloped this drab country. She glanced at the troopship that had become her last connection with home and decided to walk further up the dock to see if she could spot her husband in the thinning crowd. It smelt of sweat, oil and dust. Large cranes loomed high above her. Lorries snarled and sputtered precariously through the gaps between the warehouses and the water's edge. Everything seemed dirtier and more unkempt.

Where was he?

She was struggling with the weight of her limp daughter who had fallen asleep again and the meagre contents of her small suitcase. She needed a coffee to lift her spirits.

"Mary! Mary!"

The khaki military suit he was wearing blended in with the rest of the soldiers milling about around her. It had been a few months since they had seen each other and she noticed his thick dark hair was shorter and there were a few extra pounds hanging loosely around his belly. She wondered if he had been eating healthily or if the army rations and lack of formal exercise were starting to take their toll.

"Jozef!" Her laden hands didn't allow her to wave back so she stood exhausted as he powered his way through the crowds.

Mary, Margarita and their small brown suitcase were all picked up and crushed in a bear hug.

"How was the journey?"

She frowned at the unknown language that came out of her husband's mouth. He repeated the question pronouncing each unknown syllable slowly and carefully.

"*Pourquoi parles-tu comme ça?*" she scolded him.

"It's the language of this country, Mary." He laughed, mirroring her French. "You'll have to start learning. I'll teach you. Come!"

As they walked the streets of this strange new city,

Jozef eagerly acted as her tour guide. The yellow-tinged brickwork of the Royal Liver Building loomed above them and she couldn't help compare the scenery to the clean lines, intricacy and majesty of the Montaza Palace or the ornate Italianate styles of the Little Venice buildings of her home city. The only similarity she could see was the busyness with which the city's people seemed to go about their day. It was late on in the afternoon and still traders were shouting their wares on street corners whilst men and women carried goods here and there.

"Jozef, I could really do with a coffee." She was struggling to keep pace, her weak sea legs only just getting used to the normality of solid earth beneath her feet.

They ate fish and chips out of newspaper sitting on a park bench washed down with a strongly brewed cup of tea. No coffee. Jozef warned her that the coffee here wasn't the same strong silky brew she was used to. Tea was a better bet. She was surprised at how well it revived her. As she ate, she couldn't help but stare, wide-eyed, at her surroundings, trying to take in this new city. There were piles of bricks haphazardly plugging gaps where buildings once stood. How vast a war it was that had touched her own country and this one, stretching its twisted bomb-ridden fingers across the world. The potatoes were soggy and salty and sat heavily on an empty stomach that had now eased from the choppy voyage. It was a strange stodgy dish which lacked the intricacies of the delicate spices of home but it was welcome all the same. Her eyes tried to decipher the mysterious words on the paper that encompassed her meal and she tested some of them out on Jozef, who laughed at her pronunciation.

This was going to take a lot of getting used to.

By the time the sun had almost set on the wet, smoky horizon of Liverpool's industrial heartland, Jozef and Mary had still not secured a room for the night. Jozef had digs in the military camp on the outskirts of the city but there was no space there for Mary and the baby, so the two of them, with a sleepy Margarita in tow, trawled the B&Bs in the city centre in the hope of a room for the night.

"Why are you laughing?" Jozef asked. They were walking back down the steps of a large Victorian villa. Behind them, the proprietor was flipping a sign announcing 'No vacancies' in the window after filling his last room.

"Oh, Jozef! Can you not see the irony? Mary, Jozef and a baby looking for a room for the night and all the rooms are taken?"

They found a double room in a small establishment on Mount Pleasant Street. Once Jozef had translated the name of the road, Mary raised her eyebrows in wonder at the absurdity of a place announcing its pleasantness when it was clearly anything but. Peeling wallpaper greeted them as they stepped inside from the busy road with its dust-choking lorries and cars with squeaky brakes. The owner insisted on payment up front, her eyes looking at Mary curiously as Jozef talked. The room overlooked a small courtyard that stank of urine. It was sparsely furnished with one double bed and a sink with a dripping tap in the corner. A quilted eiderdown, which was clearly the host's pride and joy, was placed squarely on a bed that sagged and groaned from its many previous occupants.

"What did she say?" Mary asked curiously when the door had shut and they were alone at last.

"She said hot water comes on for half an hour at 4pm and there's no leaving the guest house between 11pm and 6am."

"Jozef," Mary scolded as she wrestled with the dripping tap. "What did she say?"

"She wondered where you had come from. I told her you were a princess from the Middle East and the rest of your entourage would arrive tomorrow morning."

She laughed and slapped him playfully on the shoulder.

"Oh, please say you didn't say that!"

They refreshed themselves as much as they were able to at the tiny sink and Margarita was put to sleep on a makeshift bed of cushions and blankets, stacked up with the puffy eiderdown.

"So, this is England?" Mary was lying on the bed, staring at the dark stain around the single light bulb dangling above her head. There were muffled voices from the room next door. She had yet to take off her shoes since, looking at the carpet, its congealed tufts were likely to stick to her stockinged feet.

"Yes, this is it," Jozef agreed, lying down beside her. "Do you like it?"

"It's…" she chose her words carefully, "hard to tell…"

"Yes," he agreed. "It's different. But," he rolled onto his stomach and looked her directly in the eye, "they do a good beer."

She laughed and then for a moment she realised she had forgotten the sad wrench in her stomach from leaving her mother behind. Guilt seemed to suddenly overcome her.

"Hey." He observed her feelings. "It's not forever. Just until my paperwork's sorted and I become a free man. Then we will move on to France and invite your mother over. And then you and I and Zakia will enjoy wine and cheese in a French chateau with Margarita and our many other children running riot amongst the grapevines far below our little terrace."

She closed her eyes at that thought and smiled. The plan had always been that England was a stopping point; a means to an end so that Jozef could be demobbed from the army and they could start a new life anywhere they pleased. France was the natural selection with its common language for the both of them. Far enough away from the trouble brewing in the Middle East but with friends already established there (including old school friends of Mary's).

This drab, wet, alien country would not be their forever home.

Harlesden, ENGLAND, 1956

Mary returned to their house on Bramshill Road with some trepidation. Her pink leather handbag was clutched in her hands as she followed the noises to the garden where she heard the children playing.

"Mummy!"

The relief on Margarita's face to see her mother return was plain to see. She threw her arms around her waist and clutched Mary to her, handbag and all. Henry was sheepish and hung back, looking from his father to his mother and back again in case any action he took caused another scene between them.

Jozef was dressed in his old military uniform with its faded knees and torn sleeves from the rose bushes in the corner. He had been gardening, as he was prone to do when his soul desired peace. He looked at her, his face severe but anxious, his two hands resting on the hoe he had been using on the soil in his vegetable patch.

"We were worried." It was a statement that more likely described his own feelings rather than the feelings of the rest of the family.

"I went to the church."

"Whatever for?"

"Because I had nowhere else to go."

"Of course you didn't," Jozef said matter-of-factly, his face grim. "This is your home. Where else could you have possibly gone?"

For some reason, his practicality made her smile and then, she put her handbag down and went over and kissed him on the cheek.

"I'll take that as an apology," she decided with some finality.

Skierniewice,
POLAND,
2005

Home.

This had been Jozef's home once. His street. The shops he'd once known. But a place was never the same without the people you knew in it. As much as Mary's home had been with her family, her Jozef, her children, wherever they had led her, where had Jozef's home been? Had it been with Rozia? It wasn't a question to ask when Jozef had been alive, but it haunted her now in this strange town when time had taken the one person that she could have asked away from her.

Were you happy here?

She was acutely aware that their happiness had been intricately intertwined with the nightmares of his past. A past that he just couldn't shift. A cross word would be said in exhaustion, escaping from a mind so busy trying to keep the horrors at bay. As she stood in the place that was all of him but none of him at the same time, she couldn't help but feel a slight resentment. Not towards Rozia – the woman that had first captured Jozef's heart was not a reason for jealousy – but a resentment that her own short time with him was so shrouded in the horrors that were yet to reach the young Szyja and Rozia here, in this nondescript town in Poland.

Her own early years of marriage had been one of upheaval, crossing continents and starting anew. What had things been like for Rozia and Szyja? What obstacles had they had to overcome?

Skierniewice, POLAND, 1925

It wasn't long before Szyja started to fall behind with his university fees. He didn't want to tell Rozia at first. She had enough to contend with due to the meagre living his salary provided and the increasing adaptations she'd had to make with the household accounts. But soon, he had little choice. As he arrived at his daily lectures, he was soon filled with apprehension in case a financial clerk was waiting, the red lettering of an outstanding bill waving in his hand for the whole world to see. He worried that soon there would be a knock at the door and the debt collectors would be there with their suits and hats and a demand for final payment.

"What's wrong?" she'd asked as he'd sat pensively one evening, his university text books untouched on his lap and a piano concerto playing on the gramophone.

"Nothing for you to worry about." She had caught him off guard, and the dismissive wave of his hand and the half-conjured smile did little to alleviate her worries.

"Szyja?"

There was no use hiding anymore.

"I'm behind with my course fees. We simply don't have the money." The textbooks were pushed from his lap and landed, flapping like birds, onto the floor.

"We'll manage," she decided after a few pensive moments. "You'll not give up after coming this far."

The gramophone was sold the next day. Szyja arrived home to find the corner stand empty and a clock missing from the shelf in their bedroom. He was angry at first, but when the bills were paid and the risk of being called out in the middle of one of his lectures diminished, he agreed that it had been the right thing to do.

And then Rozia announced that she was pregnant.

It was a cold evening in March. Szyja had been eating the *bigos* stew she had prepared the night before. It was a hearty meal that she had fashioned from the rabbit a neighbour had shot in the woods near their home, a small portion of Polish sausage that her sister had brought as a gift earlier that day and bulked out with vegetables from their little plot of land. It gratefully filled a spot in his stomach that had been empty since morning. He had been so hungry he had failed to notice the lilacs propped up in a broken cup on the centre of the table or the flowered dress she was wearing that was always reserved for special occasions.

"I need something to occupy my time," she had begun as she watched him eat. She had yet to pick up her knife and fork.

"Perhaps it's time we found you some tutoring to do? Piano lessons perhaps? If it's a household with an instrument lying idle, I'm sure they could…"

"I'm pregnant, Szyja."

The knife and fork clattered back onto his plate. Shock gradually turned to excitement, mirroring the hesitant joy that was etched on his wife's face. He scooped her up into his joyful arms and spun her around, upsetting the flowers on the table, which spilled into his *bigos* stew.

"Oh, that is wonderful news!"

"But how will we manage?" Rozia's anxiety spilled over. "Things have been difficult…"

"We'll manage just fine. Everything will work out. It all has so far." His practical, matter-of-fact attitude cut through their anxieties, the worry that had lain below the surface of their careful existence. "Just you see."

Alexandria, EGYPT, 1929

It happened during assembly one unusually hot day at the end of April. The girls were all clustered on the uneven wooden floor chanting the prayers they'd been taught that started and ended every one of their days at L'Orphelinat de la Miséricorde. There was sweat already on the back of their knees and under their armpits, generated by the warm bodies of over 200 girls and young ladies crouched closely together in their itchy grey pinafores.

Maman Ancette was reminding them not to run in the corridors and that there had been too much talking over lunch the previous day. It was the same speech as yesterday. Her bony finger wagged over their heads and Mary wondered how their headmistress was immune to the sweats that plagued the rest of the school on these hot days. Her forehead below her tight coif was dry and barren and there were no damp marks on her long black dress like the other nuns. It was days like this that the pupils could be forgiven for wondering if she was human at all.

The piano started up and the girls all rose in awkward unison to sing their praises to God. Their mouths moved in obedient, exaggerated movements under the watchful eye of the nuns who gazed down at them from their position on the stage. The piano reached a crescendo, the teacher at the keys swaying this way and that as her head nodded the beat. Mary gazed into the distance as her mind started to wander. Her lips had sung the tune so many times.

And then it happened.

As the music stopped and the girls automatically turned towards the doors that led to their lessons for the day, Maman Ancette's hand rose in silent command to stop. They all halted, turning their faces to her as an orchestra turning for instructions from a conductor. She indicated for them to sit, her face settling into a more severe frown than usual. There were hushed whispers from the girls as they imagined the cause for this break in their usual routine.

"Could the girls Mary and Alice Goued stand up?"

Her beady eyes searched the mass of youth spanning before her. Alice visibly crumpled into herself; Mary felt the fear tighten in her stomach as the colour drained from her skin. The girls around her were leaning away from her in case whatever misdemeanour their friend had dared to undertake was catching.

"I said," Maman Ancette repeated slowly, "Mary and Alice Goued stand up. We are all waiting."

Mary rose shakily to her feet and looked around for her sister. She was nearer the platform with the younger children of the school, her eyes popping out of their sockets in fear as she searched for reassurance from her older sister. Mary tried a smile, desperate to hold her hand but unable to with all these children sitting between them.

"It is a shame that I have had to interrupt my day as well as waste the time of my fellow teachers and that of all these young girls before me just for the sake of the two of you."

Mary could see Alice start to cry, silent little tears cascading down her small chubby cheeks.

"I think you should start by apologising to everyone."

Mary couldn't utter a word if she tried, her legs turning to terrified jelly.

"Well?" Maman Ancette demanded, her hands stretching open in exasperation. "We are all waiting."

"*Pardon.*"

The word tumbled automatically out of her mouth, and she silently willed her sister to do the same. She obliged in a small voice which made Mary want to cry.

"It has come to my attention that whilst we are all endeavouring to further your education by supplying excellent teaching, you have failed to pay Alice's school fees for the past two terms."

The final explanation for the carefully staged humiliation came as an unexpected blow to both of them. There was a snigger somewhere in the audience until Ancette's fierce glare silenced them all again.

"Well?" she persisted, her hands clasped in self-belief. "What do you have to say for yourselves?"

The question seemed ridiculous posed to an almost five-year-old. Alice automatically turned in silent appeal towards her older sister. Mary swallowed and thought of anything she could say.

"*Pardon*, Maman Ancette," she tried. "I'm sure there has been some mistake."

"I can assure you, Mary Goued, that there has not been any mistake and at the risk of wasting any more of our precious time I shall conclude that you will settle the necessary debt by the end of this week otherwise I shall have no choice but to expel your sister from this school with immediate effect."

Alice's shoulders hunched in panic, unable to stop the sobs that reverberated off the stark walls of the school hall. Mary wanted to scoop her up and run out of there, leaving the embarrassment and fear they both felt far behind, but the mother superior dismissed the girls and Alice was immediately swept up with her class as they trotted off to their lessons. Mary had no time to help her.

Laurens could see her friend was fuming.

"She shouldn't have done that," she said limply in an effort to placate her visible anger. "I'm sure there has been some mistake. Will you contact your mother?"

"No. I will deal with it," she said stiffly, forcefully. "I will not allow my sister to be expelled."

The idea came to her during her sewing lesson that morning. Sister Julienne was hunched over the fine stitching on a piece of white lace, her head bobbing with every stroke as she completed a masterpiece good enough for any market. That was it. She could make something to sell. But what did she have to sell? And who could she sell it to? As she was trying to answer these questions, Sister Julienne handed out two handkerchiefs for the girls to practise their stitching. That was it. The next hour was spent practising her hand on one of them whilst the other she kept folded neatly in the pocket of her pinafore. She excelled that day in her work, careful to please her teacher so that she would not be forced to redo her work on the smuggled contraband she held carefully in the folds of her dress.

It stayed with her during lunchtime. That small piece of cloth, the means to her sister's future. She was willing the day to end so that the next part of her plan could be put into action.

"You seem deep in thought, Mary?"

Mary looked up ashamed from her plate of *macaroni bechamel* feeling as if she had been caught out. The lady behind the counter with a ladle in her hand was a kindly woman in her forties known to her as Madame Khouri – a Syrian who had always had a soft spot for her since the day she'd started. She was smiling, her hand hovering over her lunchtime task as the stream of young girls filtered past. The kindness was too much to bear, and the story of the school fees came flooding out of her. It was received with the necessary sympathy and concern, but with the steady file of girls behind her, Madame Khouri could say little else.

Mary ate in silence, barely touching her plate, and when she had finished all her stomach could bear, Madame Khouri was waiting for her by the pile of unwashed dishes in the corner of the canteen. Mary told her the plan she had made and secretly revealed the hiding place of the handkerchief that was to become her sister's saviour.

"Let me help you, Mary," the kindly woman implored, a caring hand on her arm that wanted to take all her troubles away. "I will find you the money. Your sister will not be expelled, I promise."

"Thank you for your concern but we will not accept charity. I cannot take money from you." The words gave her a level of dignity that was way beyond her years, which Madame Khouri could not help but admire. There was a young woman standing before her where a frightened child had once been.

"In which case," Madame Khouri smiled proudly, "once you have finished the handkerchief, let me sell it for you. I know a buyer who would be willing to pay for a piece that is well stitched."

"You do?"

"Of course. How much was it you needed?"

"Two pounds by the end of this week."

Madame Khouri nodded her assent and assured her that she would see what she could do. With the prospect of her plan paying off, Mary gained a new confidence and sense of purpose. That night she waited anxiously in her bed with the cotton sheets pulled up to her chin, as one by one, the other girls in the dormitory gently fell asleep. She waited until she heard the deep breath of the last girl succumbing to slumber before she quietly crept out to the toilet block with her mission in mind. Crouched on the wooden toilet seat and with her feet pressed against the door, she worked for hours stitching a pattern she had taught herself into the white corners of the handkerchief by the light of a candle. She had not dared to turn on the lights in case the brightness stirred the nuns. She couldn't afford to fail as time was of the essence.

Satisfied, she hastened back to bed; the finished article was safely stowed under her pillow. She barely slept, the peaceful sounds of her classmates sleeping next to her did nothing to alleviate the sense of urgency of completing the task in hand.

Madame Khouri was clearly pleased.

"What excellent stitching," she commented, her fingers stroking the fine lines of the red and blue pattern at each corner of the white cloth. The work was accompanied by dark circles under Mary's eyes and a general fatigue that haunted the girl's small frame. "I shall be able to get a fair price for this. Well done, Mary."

She needed an adult's approval. The actions of Maman Ancette had shocked her. She hadn't realised that the world could be so cruel and she was crying out for someone to restore her faith in human kindness.

The Syrian was true to her word. As lunchtime came around once more, she was able to take Mary to one side and slip the precious notes into the palm of her sweaty hand.

"Two pounds!" Mary cried in quiet exclamation.

"Shh!" Madame Khouri demanded, looking around her hastily. "The purchaser was so astounded at the quality of the work, she insisted on paying the full price."

The explanation was delivered with a wink and a nod and both of them chose to ignore the niggling thought that the handkerchief was not worth anywhere near that amount. She could have hugged her but was careful not to arouse suspicion of the illicit exchange.

Mary greeted that Friday with a spring in her step and her chin held high in the certainty that she was now able to right the wrong delivered on her family. She waited outside Maman Ancette's study with Alice quivering beside her on the high-backed chairs. The sounds of footsteps echoed up and down the unfriendly corridors and Mary held her sister's hand in a bid to stop her shaking. She had told her sister not to worry, that she had found the money necessary to keep her from the shame of being expelled, but she still fretted, her hands wringing her panic as the moments passed. Mary was sure the nun was deliberately keeping them waiting. There was no one else inside that room and no sounds of her barking on the shiny black and gold telephone that was the only concession to modernity that she would allow.

Mary remained unmoved. She was ready.

The nun called them both in, her tone indicating that she had given herself enough time to summon the rage that such an occasion warranted.

"Well?"

Alice visibly shrank next to her sister whilst Mary looked the nun straight in the eye.

"We have the fees," she said slowly, deliberately. "My mother dropped them off this morning. She asked me to pass on her apologies for any delay."

The nun's bottom lip twitched as she listened, clearly caught out by the reply. Her hands, which had been clasped together in solemnity, unravelled themselves and bony fingers reached out expectantly towards them.

"Let me see."

Mary reached for the notes which she had carried

around close to her chest over the past few days. They were warm and tactile. She placed them, one at a time, into the woman's outstretched hands. They unfurled quickly amongst the cold wrinkles of the older woman's flesh. Mary felt the Mother Superior flinch at the feel of them as if she had placed a spider on her skin instead of the money she had asked for.

"It's all there." She felt the need to clarify her position in order to alleviate the woman's doubts.

The nun took a while inspecting the notes, fingering the paper from one bony hand to the other, clearly unable to believe what she saw.

"You stole these?"

Mary frowned at the question. *Could Maman Ancette really think that?*

"*Pardon*, Maman?"

"I said you must have stolen these!" The question became a statement as the woman tasted the concept that satisfied her own misgivings. "Wicked, wicked, child!"

Alice edged closer to her sister, staring at the wooden floor in terror.

"Stole them?" Mary was surprised that she didn't mirror her sister's fear. She was meant to cower at the older woman's words, admit that she was right even though she knew it not to be true, but instead she felt the first seeds of utter indignation. *How dare you?* "I can assure you, Maman, that I didn't steal them." Her voice came loudly from a place from within and she marvelled at her own bravery.

"Then where did you get them?" the nun spat, tossing the notes onto the floor between them as if they burned her. One of them fluttered down to rest by Mary's foot. She didn't waiver.

"I told you that my mother gave me the money this morning and asked me to give it to you—"

"Lies!" she shrieked, a sound mirroring the crows that called for their supper in the streets outside the school's walls, pecking the non-existent morsels of food from the dust on the floor.

"They are not lies," Mary persisted, her voice rising in anger.

"Knowing how your mother lives, I find it incomprehensible that she could have just turned up this morning and given you these notes to pay off her debt."

"How my mother lives?" She found herself repeating those words incredulously but against her better judgement.

"Do not propose to answer me back, child!" the woman responded, spittle flying from her angry lips. "I know of your situation and I cannot simply believe you came about these notes how you have said. You have stolen them, and I shall find out from where. I shall sniff out the truth, just you see!"

"My mother gave them to me this morning. I did not steal them…" She repeated the statement with incredulity.

Maman Ancette seemed to bubble and boil like lava and Mary wondered if her veil would explode off her head in a shower of sparks. The nun was lost for words. She opened her mouth and closed it, popping like a fish from the market. Then, to the girls' surprise, the Mother Superior dismissed the two of them with no further threats of expulsion or accusations of thievery, the notes lying discarded where she had thrown them on the floor.

When she closed the door to the study behind her, a tortured sigh expelled its way from Mary's lips. Her body trembled under the tumultuous emotions that rippled and fizzed below the surface. She took Alice's hand and leant down to look at her so that their faces were nearly touching. Her breath was hot and heavy on her sister's face, her expression mirroring the anger of Maman Ancette, powerful and terrifying.

"Alice, listen to me," Mary's voice was low and quiet but compelling in its earnestness. "From now on we will not allow anyone to talk to us like that. We rely on no one but ourselves. We are not lower than them and they are not higher than us. We are equal. Do you understand me?"

There was a change in Mary that day. A forcefulness below the surface that rejected the injustices of the world. A girl on the verge of womanhood where a frightened child had once been.

Crewe,
ENGLAND,
1948

On arriving in England, Jozef was based in a Polish
resettlement camp called Calveley Camp near Nantwich
with the Polish II Corps. It was a bleak place in the North
of England that was at odds with the warm Mediterranean
heat of Alexandria. Although some families were living
on the site, many chose private accommodation outside
the military walls as the camp reminded them too much
of a war that urgently needed to be relegated to the past.
The young Beker family put up with the run-down hotel
in Liverpool for a few days before Jozef found them
accommodation in nearby Crewe. It was an Edwardian
semi on a quiet road with green open spaces and trees
opposite leading down to a small river that cut through
the symmetrical houses that crowded the area. Jozef

had borrowed a jeep from the base that day to drive his family to their new accommodation. They pulled up outside number 21 and were immediately accosted by a swarm of children drawn to the khaki metalwork and shiny leather seats of a vehicle that was alien to the area. They fired questions at the couple as Jozef helped his wife and daughter down onto the pavement and Mary was at a loss as to what they were saying. The first few days in this strange country had been a minefield of gestures and friendly nods that replaced an understanding of language. With the lack of words, she was finding it difficult to express herself fully.

How dirty these children are!

She had always believed England to be a wealthy country, an idea fuelled by the elegant English ladies who rode on open-topped charabancs between the Alexandrian hotels with their parasols twirling in the sun, the men sitting stiffly in high-necked suits despite the heat ordering the workers around them this way and that. These children with their unfathomable accents and unkempt hair ran the roads without shoes and with clothes hanging ragged from overuse; the littlest ones were even devoid of trousers. This was not the England born of imagination. She smiled and waved at the children, Margarita clutched close to her chest. Some of the braver few reached out grimy hands to touch her, and Mary bore their welcome with patience. Jozef was frowning. He said some words in English that made no sense to her, but she could tell by his face they were angry instructions to leave her alone. He ushered her inside the open door of their new home leaving the children to scamper over the seats of the military jeep.

Mrs Mason was a homely woman with hair swept back under a headscarf adorned with flowers and an apron splashed with remnants of a thousand meals tied tightly around her waist. Her puffy hands, which were surprisingly soft considering the endless chores she undertook each day, were curled into balls pressed firmly into her ample hips. She greeted them both with a smile and a cup of tea decanted from the teapot reserved for special occasions, which had been dusted down from the mantelpiece. Mr Mason was a slight man who worked all hours on the production line at the newly opened Rolls-Royce factory nearby. They rarely saw him. When he wasn't working, he was either down the local pub with his fellow workers or on the stands at the football stadium in Liverpool. When in the house, he adopted a pose on his favourite chair by the fire and would fall asleep with a newspaper lying unread across his lap. The Masons had a baby that was only a few months older than Margarita and Mary felt a relief that this presented a means of commonality between the two mothers. Their lives were otherwise so very different. Mary smiled and fussed over the child and Mrs Mason soon returned the favour on a wide-eyed and nonplussed Margarita. They finished their tea, Jozef conducting all the talking for them both before they were shown their room on the first floor at the back of the house. It was smaller than the hotel room but a lot cleaner and more welcoming, with polished wooden floors and a large window that looked out onto the many backyards of the back-to-back houses. There was no sink but an old-fashioned jug and bowl with faded patterns standing proudly on a washstand in the corner. The rest of the room was bare.

Mary looked out onto the brick yard. There was an outside toilet and the remains of a coal shed propped up against it. Children were playing along the alleyway that acted like a barrier between the backs of the two rows of houses. There were children in the small yards, children running across the streets and down to the stream, there were children everywhere. She wondered how they could all fit into the small dwellings that stacked up alongside each other like a precarious house of cards.

They made themselves a home, all the while knowing that it was on a temporary basis, just until Jozef's paperwork came through and his military past was behind him. France was still a tangible dream. He brought two camp beds from the military base, which gave them a place to sleep, whilst Margarita slept in her pram, a monstrous thing that Mary had to bump up and down the stairs a few times each day. Cooking was done on a small Primus stove that had survived the journey from Egypt and whenever they needed to wash, they would commandeer the Masons' kitchen and follow their example of boiling water on the stove for the battered tin bath that had been passed down through generations.

Mary got used to the stares. For the first time in her life, she was made to notice the darker pigment of her skin and the interest it would generate. Jozef had explained that the neighbours thought she was exotic, but the tone of some of the words they spat at her when she was walking Margarita on her own sounded far from complimentary, even if their actual meaning escaped her.

She hated relying on Jozef. She had spent a lifetime

learning not to rely on anyone, but in this strange land she felt powerless and helpless.

He tried hard to keep her spirits up and she busied herself with the tasks she was able to do on a daily basis: washing, cleaning, making meals for them to eat in the Polish way. But everything was different. So different that it was as if she was a child again, learning to demystify the adult world around her.

How the English loved to queue!

They queued for everything; for the baker's, the butcher's, the grocer's. Sometimes she wondered whether the women in their scarfed heads and wicker baskets joined the end of a queue just for the sake of it. It was a polite and ordered experience that was completely at odds with the chaotic haggling of the Egyptian markets she was used to.

The morning would follow a similar routine of joining these queues with Margarita bouncing along in her pram. Rationing was still a cloud hanging over the country, a by-product of war. The ration books became another force to be reckoned with alongside the strange foreign currency. Jozef got into a habit of splitting out their money for the day between different envelopes with scribbled notes in French and English on each, listing the ingredients the money should be used to buy.

"No," she said sharply one day in Jenning's, the butcher's shop, pulling back two large pennies from the 7d she had deposited on the counter. The beef she had ordered with pointing and gestures lay half unwrapped in greaseproof paper between herself and the butcher. He stared at her and then at the coins, wiping his hands on his striped red and white apron.

"Mrs Beker, it's 7d for half a pound of meat."

There were tuts and sighs from the waiting women behind her. She had no idea what he had said but that didn't matter; bartering was an Egyptian habit she was loath to break.

"This," she said sternly, indicating the 5d.

"Mrs Beker." He sighed. "Seven pence, not five."

"Five."

The scarfed heads of the queuing housewives were leaning round each other to voice their silent thoughts on this regular customer with her irregular ways.

The butcher gently reached over and took her ration book and the disputed two pence difference.

"Let me put your shopping in your bag for you," he said with purpose, leaning over the counter with its damp, meaty smell.

She frowned, disappointed, until he placed her stamped ration book back into the palm of her hand along with one of the disputed brown coins. She smiled pleasantly back at him and left the butcher's with the housewives' heads following her.

The strange words in the shops became more familiar as the weeks passed and soon she was trying to sound out the names of different fruits and vegetables in English to the smiling shopkeepers who erupted with delight as her pronunciation became stronger. Buoyant with success, Mary would return home and try and recreate the Polish delicacies she had been used to making back in Alexandria when the couple had built their first home together.

And then their landlady changed.

It was a sudden transformation that Mary could not

understand or pinpoint why. She had been filling the tin bath with hot water from the kettle that whistled buoyantly on the range. Margarita was tottering about the kitchen, cruising from chair to chair as she practised using her feet. The Masons' young child was playing with the pots and pans Mrs Mason had spread out before him. They were shiny and loud and all at once Margarita made a sudden grab for them. Her small hand had barely touched the handle when Mrs Mason screamed and snatched it back, reducing the poor child to tears as she fell and bounced onto her bottom. Mary looked up, the empty kettle in her hand, and tried to ask in broken English whatever was wrong. The other lady seemed hot and furious, brandishing the offending item high above her head. It was under the tap in an instant, covered with soap suds and harshly scrubbed. The Mason boy stared at his mother, dribble cascading down his chubby cheeks. Mrs Mason screamed at Mary. She could only make out a few words of what she was saying due to the ferociousness with which she spat them at her but their tone was clear. Mary baulked at the word 'filthy', which she understood all too well. She abandoned the kettle, the tin bath and the kitchen and rushed upstairs with an inconsolable Margarita, closing the door on the continued shouts and screams as they spiralled up the narrow staircase.

They avoided each other after that. The family were kept clean using the washstand in their room and, rather than use the kitchen to wash their clothes, Mary would take them down to the river to scrub. Neighbours would point and stare but, as she told Jozef, she would rather the pointing and incomprehensible comments than the screaming onslaught of the Mason woman.

"When will your paperwork be complete so that we can leave this blessed country?" Mary was folding clothes on the camp bed. Margarita was playing with a doll on the floor whilst Jozef leant against the window trying to stay out of the way.

"It won't be long now," he assured her. "I had some news today of a teaching job in Avignon. Stanislav has relatives there and he thinks I stand a good chance of getting it."

"*Pas assez tôt!*" she muttered, scrunching a pair of Margarita's tights between exasperated fingers. "When can we leave?"

The smile that escaped his lips as he acknowledged her enthusiasm was not timed correctly and Mary scowled at him over the pile of washing.

"Let me at least write my application!" He laughed.

The application was written along with a letter of recommendation from his commanding officer. It was not long before Jozef was able to rush up the stairs to their little room brandishing a letter of acceptance and, for a while, Mary was satisfied with the knowledge that France was becoming one step closer. The prospect of setting down some roots at last, lifted her spirits. The stability would enable her to invite Zakia into their lives again. With that thought, the daily drudgery of cooking, cleaning, dragging the pram up and down the stairs didn't seem so difficult to bear. Her spirits were so improved that she even managed to find time to start sewing again. Jozef brought home two silk parachutes from the camp that were no longer needed, and she set herself the task of hand-stitching shirts and little dresses to increase their wardrobe. It was a happy task that busied her fingers and passed the time whilst she waited for Avignon to save her. A task that reminded her of Alexandria and the life she had left behind.

Alexandria, EGYPT, 1929

Mary had found a new ability, a new skill for her busy fingers that would help her mother earn a few extra piastres to supplement the household income.

Sewing.

Encouraged by her success with the handkerchief and the positive feedback from Madame Khouri, she set about using the scraps of material her mother had left over from all her bulk buying to teach herself to sew. She had a doll that acted as a model for the tiny little dresses she fashioned out of scraps – a small toy with a cushioned belly and wisps of stringy black hair popping out of a heavily painted head. She was satisfied with the results, and it wasn't long before Zakia allowed her to use bigger cuts of material – bright blues and oranges, along with flowery patterns and asymmetrical shapes. Alice became her model, pleased with the excuse to wear more brightly coloured items than the dull straight dresses Zakia salvaged from the market.

"Stand still!" Mary had her sister standing to attention by the balcony window one afternoon as she tucked and pinned her new creation to just below the knee.

Alice giggled and obeyed, her eyes shining. Even Zakia smiled, collapsed in her favourite chair after a satisfying lunch, a cigarette dangling from her fingertips. Zaki was outside playing with his friends from the opposite building, his shouts creeping up to their flat now and then.

"Now that is pretty," Zakia conceded in an unusual state of calm contemplation.

"I've been working on it for a while," Mary said proudly, through a mouthful of pins.

"You look like a proper seamstress attending to a blushing bride before her wedding day."

Alice giggled again at the thought of marriage, a prospect that was far beyond her years.

"A woman doesn't just have to look pretty for her wedding day," Mary replied abruptly. "Hold still!"

"No, but it helps."

"What was yours like?" Alice asked their mother and Mary tensed. Perhaps they were getting too carried away by their mother's seemingly wistful mood.

"Mine? My what?" Zakia asked, the smoke spiralling in curls above her dark clothes of mourning.

"Your wedding."

Her sister ignored the sharp tugs on the dress she was pinning, unaware that she was trying to warn her.

"Oh, it was a fabulous day!" The dreamy look in her

mother's eyes surprised her. "Lots of food, dancing, the tent was packed! Our families knew a lot of people. It was hard to greet them all."

"I wonder what mine will be like?" Alice thought out loud.

"We have to get your sister married first," Zakia pointed out. It was the way in Egypt: marry the siblings off in age order – the eldest first, the youngest last. Mary spat out a pin.

"I will not get married."

It was said with a finality that laid down a challenge to her mother and the social constraints of the age.

"Ah, Mary." Zakia smiled. "You say that now but…"

"I mean it. Men do not interest me."

"They're not meant to," she said dismissively. "But how else will you live if you do not get married?"

"You've managed, Maman." She was treading on dangerous ground but gambled on her mother's relaxed demeanour to be able to say what she felt. "Besides, who will look after you if I get married?"

A smile escaped Zakia's lips.

"You're good to me, Mary. Always so good to your mother. But there will come a time…" A wave of the hand and she had thrown her head back in her chair exposing her slender neck and sharp features. The conversation was over. She wished for silence.

The dress was completed and packed carefully for Zakia to sell to a waiting client that Monday when she returned to her cart and the girls returned to school. It made a few piastres, which were immediately and unquestioningly spent on Zaki without Mary's knowledge.

It became a pattern, a weekend ritual outside the confines of the nuns and the strict schooling that was the girls' introduction to the world. A weekend of pins and needles, turning fabric into dresses, blouses, gloves and head coverings so that by Sunday night Mary's fingers were pinched and aching, but her mother was proud and pleased.

"Oh!" Mary stopped short on the stairs to their flat one Saturday morning as their landlady's daughter skipped towards her, seemingly oblivious to her presence and in danger of knocking her over. "*Mazeratn!*"

The girl, who was younger than Mary, flushed red and dodged quickly around her, her sky-blue dress brushing against her knee. Mary was troubled. She watched the girl darting down the stairs and disappear out of the front door as fast as her legs could carry her. She knew guilt when she saw it. She also recognised the sharp blue material of the dress she had been wearing.

"Maman, have you seen the sky-blue fabric you gave me last week?" She was knee-deep in material inside her box chest containing all her sewing equipment she had been hoarding for her latest creations.

"No, I haven't taken anything from that box."

She sighed, her cheeks flushing with rage as she remembered the guilty look of the girl in the sky-blue dress with her furtive eyes and almost apologetic smile.

"I'm telling you, she's stolen it from us!" Mary cried, her anger uncontrollable as she tried to make her mother understand.

"I am sure you are mistaken," Zakia was the calmer one of the two, folding laundry on her bed as she tried to placate her daughter.

"Rashida has broken into our flat and stolen my material!" Mary persisted. "I have just seen her daughter dancing prettily down the stairs in it!"

"What would you have me do? Confront our landlady over some unhappy circumstance with a complete lack of evidence? Use something else for your dress. I gave you some offcuts of a pale orange cotton last week. Just use that."

Mary boiled, her fists pumping in tight, angry balls by her sides. *The unfairness of it all!* If she had been the one skipping about in someone else's sky-blue cotton, her backside and the soles of her feet would have been red raw for weeks. The world was unjust, unfair and prejudiced. No one could persuade her otherwise.

Skierniewice, POLAND, 1925

For Rozia and Szyja, a boy arrived later that year. A thin, quiet little boy who was doted on as the first grandchild in Rozia's family. As was the custom, no trinkets had adorned the house leading up to the birth in case these symbols of happy expectancy would bring bad luck on the family. Once mother and son were settled after a protracted home labour, a steady stream of well-wishers descended on the Beker family home, filling it with gifts adorned in blue: a small carved wooden soldier from Szyja's brother, Morduch, a porcelain cup and bowl from Rozia's mother, Faiga, and some knitted baby clothes from Szyja's mother, Tumera. Vodka was exchanged and, after much debate, the couple agreed to hold a *brit milah* for the child on the insistence of both grandmothers on the traditional eighth day after his birth. Arjusz Beker (or Arja as he was affectionately known to his family) was welcomed into the world into a country that was still struggling with its relationship with the Jewish people but was seemingly more relaxed of late. There was a peace into which the new parents settled – a hazy world of joy and sleepless nights. The journey to and from Warsaw became a chance for Szyja to reflect and to catch up on some much-needed sleep. He was now a father as well as a husband, teacher and scholar. The responsibilities of life had crept up on him, slowly at first and then at greater speed over the last few years. He excelled at teaching, encouraging his young charges to excel themselves in their learning so that they could make the most out of their lives in a progressive Poland.

Arja had his father's eyes, large dark eyes with thick black eyebrows which looked adorable in one so young but promised a severe-looking man that would emerge later with age. As the year passed, he trotted after his father in the vegetable garden, his chubby hands pulling up the weeds, copying his father's example. They gathered the apples together from the trees Szyja had planted in the first year they had called 2 Czysta home. Rozia gazed on, noticing the smile that escaped easily from a proud father's lips. With Arja, he was gentle and caring without any of the financial worries that dominated her own conversations with him.

"We shall feast this Shabbat!" Rozia laughed with mock surprise as the two presented her with a basket full of fruit and potatoes the size of a button.

"That we shall." Szyja smiled, planting a kiss on her cheek.

They lit candles that evening as the dusk welcomed in the night, honouring the traditions of their ancestors as they feasted on *challah* and the produce from their garden. The morning would herald Saturday and the traditional day of rest. Life was comfortable and peaceful as it is in the stillness before the storm. Beautiful, light, carefree. But that peace never lasts. It soon washes away like a faded memory.

Hatred, bitterness, death and destruction. It was all descending on them.

The war was coming.

PART TWO

Harlesden,
ENGLAND,
1957

"Who do you hate more, *Tatuś*?" Henry's curiosity over a late Saturday breakfast made Mary nearly spill her tea. He cocked his head as he contemplated the thought that had sprung into his young mind before he delivered it to his father like a brick through the glass of a shattered window, upsetting the order of things. "The Russians or the Germans?"

It was that time of year when the poppy sellers with their medals and worn faces were out on street corners shaking their boxes and teaching the young the significance of the little red flower and all the hurt it portrayed. The scars of the war no one talked about were still evident on some streets; a missing church here, a dismembered building there as everyone waited patiently for the rebuilding efforts to catch up. So much destruction. So much gone. It was only going to be a matter of time before the war would be talked about by the young and the curious, the ones who had had the luck of the draw by not living through it.

There was a stillness in the kitchen caused by stiffening parents. The radio was on and had just begun broadcasting the shipping forecast. Familiar yet unknown names peeled between the static which hissed and cracked. *Forth… Tyne…* Mary adjusted the tea cosy, looking at her son but not daring to catch her husband's eye. She was curious. It had not been a subject she had dared to broach. *Dogger… Fisher… German Bight…* Jozef put his knife and fork down. There was an egg left wobbling on his plate, the yolk slowly oozing over a slice of bread toasted on one side but not the other. Mary watched its path across his plate as the family waited out the rising tension.

"Neither," he said, dabbing his mouth clean with a napkin. His tone was dull, devoid of emotion. "The Poles," he continued. "I hate the Poles more than the Russians or the Germans."

"Why's that?" An innocent question from an innocent mind.

"Because they did nothing," he said simply. His brow furrowed as he sought the right words of explanation. "Because the Russians and the Germans invaded Poland and did all manner of despicable things and the rest of my countrymen stood by and did nothing. And that, in my opinion, is far, far worse. Now, shall we finish our breakfast?"

Skierniewice/Warsaw, POLAND, 1935

Pilsudski, Poland's progressive and liberal leader, died in 1935. By the mid-1930s, Jews were escaping Germany in their thousands, driven out by increasing anti-Semitism. The new German Chancellor who had risen to power just two years before was spreading a message of hate that was lapped up like cream by the German population. Germany wasn't safe anymore. Amongst the struggles of the German people, reason was misplaced and revenge was sought. Many thousands of those Jews ended up in neighbouring Poland, swelling the numbers of the greatest concentration of Jews in Europe. They sought a peaceful life free from jackboots. Some simply sought life. But with the death of Pilsudski in 1935, the gradual assimilation of the Jewish population was all but halted. The Jews in

Poland and the refugees that sought solace within her borders were only on a temporary reprieve.

There was no panic at first in the synagogues, no alarm in the communities built on traditions that rolled back centuries. Why would there be? In 1935 there was no indication of what was to come. Adolf Hitler was a German problem, not a Polish one. And Russia? That age-old enemy that loomed over her neighbour with might and fear? No one imagined Stalin sitting in Moscow greedily wringing his hands over maps of Polish lands. If there was suspicion amongst the more astute of the Jewish community, it was ignored. It would all blow over. It always did.

For Rozia and Szyja in their sleepy street in Skierniewice, there were the sounds of another baby echoing off the wooden walls. This time it was a girl. Marysia Beker had arrived in March 1934. She had dark hair with specks of red like her mother. Her long locks caught the sun and sparkled. She doted on her father and annoyed her brother who had spent nine years having his parents to himself.

Two years previously, Rozia had suffered a miscarriage. The child had been mid-term and was delivered suddenly and without warning at home. Rozia had been by herself, and the ordeal was far too quick and sudden for her to seek help. Arja was eight – too young and too terrified to understand. He had watched in horrified silence as his mother writhed on the bedroom floor before the strange-looking bundle all covered in red had appeared. Rozia had cleaned herself up, sobbing as she wrapped the not yet fully formed foetus in blankets and waited for Szyja to return on the evening train.

"*Oy gevalt!* Why did you not get help?" he had asked in panic as he'd surveyed the scene.

She couldn't answer him through the tears. Grief had her by the throat. They cleaned up the mess and mourned the tragedy alone. It was easy enough for her to blame herself because the previous week she had asked Szyja to recover Arja's old cot from the loft. She had wanted to see if it still fitted in that empty space at the foot of their bed. She should never have started to decorate the house. It is hard to argue with a mother who needed an explanation, any explanation, for the tragedy of losing a baby. Szyja gave up trying.

They gave their dead son the gift of a name – *Henryk*.

The next pregnancy had them both in a continual state of trepidation. Rozia took extra care to lighten her chores and rest as much as her young son and the house would allow. Family and friends were instructed to pop by whilst Szyja was out and through everyone's scrutiny, Marysia was born without any complications.

The house of three was now a house of four. Arja had started school at the same place where Szyja was working and the two enjoyed the fatherly bonding time in the early morning and late afternoon. Rozia was happy with this arrangement. She had heard stories of Jewish boys being attacked on the streets. A friend's boy had had tar thrown at him on his way home a few months before. The warm sticky substance had caught him on the back of the head and they had had to shave his hair to get it off. Stories like that kept her awake at night.

And then Szyja heard of a job opportunity in Warsaw. The role came from a friend from the university who had whispered the idea into Szyja's head. It was right in the centre of the city with lodgings big enough for his family above. An Assistant Director of a large public school; a step up from his position in Skierniewice. It would mean physically moving away from family connections and the friends they had made, but they would be financially better off. He took it without hesitation.

His mother-in-law pulled in a few favours and a family friend provided a horse and cart to ferry them to their new life on Nowolipki Street in Warsaw. The city was vibrant and stylish, and Rozia fell in love with it instantly. Their new home was a large apartment reached via a wide-open staircase with three large bedrooms and high ceilings supporting plain chandeliers. Large windows looked out onto the city's vast skyline with its elegant and regimented rooftops whilst below them were the sights and sounds of a busy road. A constant stream of trams trundled past, scraping along the tracks as the bells ting-tinged to the steps of passengers as they hopped on and off. Old men were ferried around in rickshaws pedalled by the young and the fit whilst horses and carts vied for space on the cobbles. The shops were full and markets regularly competed for space on the pavements outside, selling all manner of goods at knock-down prices. There was a large, vibrant Jewish quarter that wasn't so far from where they lived, although the school where Szyja worked was secular and they were both happy for Arja to attend there. The Jews seemed to meld in better in Warsaw and for a while Rozia felt safe and happy and pleased with the move.

For now.

Alexandria, EGYPT, 1935

Mary was no longer a child. She was now in her late teens and old enough to leave the school she had attended since she was seven. Except, she did not. Her efforts at home and at school had proved her an accomplished seamstress and Maman Ancette offered her a job teaching embroidery to the girls.

"You are accomplished in your needlework," she had told Mary in that same office which had seen so many of her 'corrections' as a child. Except now, the nun seemed frail and fragile with no sense of that awe that had instilled fear and anger in previous years. "The girls will learn a lot from you."

It was not difficult to accept. The job came with lodgings and thirty piastres a month, which would go some way in helping her mother with the finances. It also meant she could keep an eye on Alice who was still a pupil there.

The scholar became the tutor, and her transition was immediately accepted by the nuns and her other fellow teachers who embraced her as their own. It was a happy place that cossetted a young Mary from the outside world – there were no men in the school, no reason to start to question her changing body. Her hips had grown wider and there was a bosom where it had previously been flat. Her face was dark and strong with a long nose and dark Mediterranean skin. She wore her hair down to her shoulders and it bounced softly in thick waves. She was too old now for her mother to beat her and, as the eldest in the family, Zakia increasingly leant on her daughter as someone would a person older than her daughter's years.

Mary still returned to the flat on Harah Mussa at weekends to help her mother with the chores. Whilst the women of the house cleaned and scrubbed, Zaki met up with his friends and carried on his studies unhindered by the never-ending tasks at home. It was hoped that he would attend university, as he was a bright boy who continued to be the apple of his mother's eye.

The piastres that were duty-bound for Zakia's hand were taken from Mary and placed in a box with ibis birds adorning its sides. The birds kept a watchful eye on the growing fund that was destined never to ease the family's meagre meals. If Mary had seen what the birds were trying to hide, would she have questioned what it was destined for? Had she assumed her brother had paid for his own university education?

That Christmas, Zakia saved enough to buy her daughter a Singer sewing machine. It was a beautiful piece of machinery that was received with delight. Its elegant black frame bulged and arched in a tactile way. There were faded flowers spiralling across its sides. Faded because it was, of course, second-hand. Zakia found a suitable table for it to live on in the corner of the living room. It seemed to be displayed with pride, much like an old family heirloom that had been passed down through generations. It was a thoughtful present, but it was also a family investment as it meant she could produce more garments for her mother to sell. She volunteered a mending service for the girls at L'Orphelinat de la Miséricorde and there was always a weekly pile of pinafores and blouses that needed mending and re-threading to be returned to the school on the following Monday.

The gentle whir of the needle and the click, click, click of the foot pedal as Mary worked was a constant sound in the Hawash household. Zakia found it soothing as she worked her magic on the Primus stove, producing a meal out of seemingly nothing to satisfy her daughters' hunger on their return from an intense week at the school.

It was on one of these weekends that Mary made up her mind. She was repairing a grey pinafore, a bright polka-dotted fabric of navy and white lying next to her waiting for her skilful hands to turn it into a skirt that her mother could sell on. The thought had originally occurred to her during one of her lessons that week. It had been during a lesson on stitching for a group of eight- and nine-year-olds when the idea had popped into her head. The girls had sat intently on the floor in front of her desk as she demonstrated the various stitches to their innocent eyes. Fifteen young girls who had not yet seen much in life except for the walls of L'Orphelinat de la Miséricorde and the nuns that inhabited it. It occurred to her that the nuns were her role models and that, apart from her mother, these women were her only clue to the outside world and the adults that inhabited it. Her view of the world was as distorted now as it had been when she had sat on that same carpet looking up at her teacher with those same innocent eyes. She had a sudden urge to see more of the world; to start exploring in a way a woman should.

Maman Ancette, with her frail and withered hands, displayed a rare moment of understanding when she approached her. The older lady permitted herself a smile as Mary set out her plan.

"*Es-tu sûr?*"

"I need to see the world," she decided with some finality. "I think it is time for me to move on."

The elderly nun nodded, disturbing the smoothed-out lines of her crisp white wimple.

"We wish you well, Mary Goued. You have been a good addition to our school."

Mary found a job making dresses in a textile atelier, a workshop that she had to reach by tram. Her first day was approached with trepidation and excitement. The tram navigated her alone from her mother's apartment to her new place of work above a parade of shops in the north of the city. Out of the confines of the school, with its drab walls and introspective view of the world, she looked at the streets of Alexandria in a new light. It was brighter and more vibrant than she had previously cared to notice.

People of all shades and nationalities rubbed shoulders next to each other as the trams trundled, the occasional car sleeked past, and the donkeys and camels vied for position on the busy streets. There were stalls spilling out from the side alleys bursting with large dishes of colourful vegetables, dried fish and food carts with large pans of fried *Kebda Eskandarani*. The smell of the roasting meat carried deliciously to her nostrils.

The atelier was hot and sweaty. Tables were laid out next to each other along a long and narrow room with large windows overlooking the rooftops. The women there were mostly Arabic with long, flowing black dresses, some with their faces covered, others not. Their fingers flicked effortlessly across the materials they wielded across their workstations whilst threads of discarded cotton lay strewn across the floor. There was the hum of the machines and then laughter and then the quick flick of Arabic tongues. She felt at odds, dressed in her white polka-dotted shift and free-flowing hair. As the owner of the atelier (a short woman with a widow's veil much like her mother's) showed her to her workstation, she was uncomfortably aware how at odds she was with this place. She touched the bulge of the small cross her mother had given her at her confirmation where it lay hidden against her chest, trying to glean what comfort she could from it.

She arrived back home in tears.

It was not what she had expected. Had Maman Ancette known as much but failed to warn her? Once the overseer had shown her what to do and left her to it, she had found herself in the middle of conversations both alien in their nature and vulgar in their tone. She had a lot to learn about men, she realised. She was now twenty years old and the same age, if not younger, than some of the other women there but, from hearing their conversations, she was well behind in life. They talked about parts of a man that she never knew existed and she blushed at the thought of the nuns she had known hearing the same words that were entering her ears. *And the language!*

It was not a job which she could see lasting, and she confided this fact to her sister. Alice blushed for her when Mary skirted around some of the topics she had been privy to. She would not tell her mother. She would have been hauled down to the church quicker than her legs could carry her and forced on her knees in prayer.

She needed another job.

Her mother had other ideas.

"Who are they?"

Zakia had pushed her eldest daughter out of the living room and into the kitchenette in haste as Mary returned home from work one day. There were two people sitting on chairs by the open balcony doors. She recognised neither of them. One was a young man with a wispy beard that sprouted indiscriminately from a chin that was not yet fully formed into the chiselled look of manhood. A tarboosh sat firmly on his head and his long legs supported gangly knees that shifted uncomfortably under his *galabeya*. The woman sitting next to him was half his size and twice his width. She wore a pretty floral dress that clutched at her hips as if its life depended on it. Her face was set in a smile that didn't move and she nodded vigorously at her surroundings, keen to show her enthusiasm at everything that caught her eye.

"Who are they?" Mary muttered fiercely to her mother

as Zakia tried to shield their private conversation from their guests with the curtain that hung from the doorway.

"Oh Mary, I'm afraid to tell you…"

There was anxiety in her mother's tone, and she knew at once why they were here. Displeasure erupted all over her face; her lips pursed in disapproval and her eyes flashed in anger.

"*Maman!* How could you!"

Zakia's hands clutched and fidgeted as she tried to placate her daughter without arousing the suspicion of the guests in the living room.

"They came for you," she tried to explain. "I had to invite them in. It would not have been polite to leave them standing outside."

"I don't care about being polite!"

"Mary, tsh!"

The man had seen her boarding the tin tram for work and had followed her home before speaking to his aunt about approaching the family. That wasn't unusual. Most marriages in Egypt began with a chance meeting in the street. But Mary baulked at the thought of this man, barely out of his teens, following her around as if she was an item to be bartered for like the fruits and vegetables on a market stall. Enquiries had been made and now the family were in discussions about marriage, and this was the first she had known about it.

Marriage.

To a complete stranger!

"I am not going to get married!"

"Mary! Keep your voice down and make our guests some coffee."

"Did you just hear what I said?"

"He's a nice young man. Just make him a coffee and listen to what he has to say. There is no harm in that."

"I am not getting married!"

"Please, Mary. For me. For your Maman. Just hear him out. Please." Zakia pleaded and cajoled and when the tears started to bubble in her eyes, Mary relented. Her mother beamed, a smile immediately broadening across her cheeks. *How quickly the tears vanished!* "And make sure you make the coffee properly with a good foam on the top. Just like I've taught you," she called sweetly over her shoulder.

Mary had nothing in common with the man. He failed to look at her. Whether it was through shyness or because he felt that it was beneath him, she wasn't sure. His coffee remained untouched although his companion sipped and slurped before asking for another, which Mary obediently obliged.

There was no froth bubbling perfectly on top this second time. Zakia frowned and Mary smiled surlily back at her. There was much talking but neither of the younger people there were involved as their opinion was of the least concern in the matter. The man was called Abasi and the woman was his aunt. She simultaneously fished for compliments on his countenance whilst brandishing his achievements with exaggerated abandon. There was none in the whole city of Alexandria with more business acumen nor prospects for a brighter future than Abasi. He was the owner of a fishing boat who was doing so well for himself that he recently had to branch out and hire two men. Mary now realised where the smell was coming from. She stared directly out of the window as the woman went on to praise Zakia on her daughter's good looks and strong demeanour with the same slippery tongue. There was no need for Zakia to ask Mary what she thought when the couple finally left with a flourish. It was written all over her daughter's face as their female guest continuously bowed and shook their hands again and again as if that would cement the deal she had come to make.

"I am not getting married to someone like that. I am certainly not marrying an Egyptian. In fact, I am just not getting married," she told her with some finality as soon as the door had closed.

"He's perhaps not quite the right fit," she conceded, subconsciously wiping the invisible smell of fish from the palms of her hands, "but think about it, Mary. For the sake of your sister and your brother, you must consider marriage at some point. They cannot marry until you find someone."

"And what's to stop them?"

"You know the eldest must marry before the youngest finds a partner. It's the way."

"It doesn't have to be." Mary's eyes were flashing now with disobedience.

Zakia was wise enough to stop the conversation there. She could see there was no getting through to her daughter that day. The china cups were put away. The *kanaka* was washed of its coffee stains and polished before being placed back on the shelf. Zakia waited for the next proposal to turn up on her doorstep whilst Mary carefully looked over her shoulder whenever she took the tram to work.

Warsaw, POLAND, 2005

It was easy enough to look back on those years and laugh at her own determination to avoid marriage. What must her mother have thought, having a child so head-strong and disobedient?

It was difficult for Maman, Mary's reflective mood allowed that concession. The photographs, the long walks around the city that supposedly meant something to her husband were causing her to question her own past as much as his. Her mother, Mary decided, had been caught between a hard choice: ensure financial stability for her daughter on the one hand, whilst also knowing from her own experience that marriage was not a recipe for happiness. Perhaps witnessing the hardships of Zakia's life firsthand instilled a determination in Mary not to allow anyone to dictate her own life choices. Was that stubbornness on her part or merely self-preservation? In any case, it was a characteristic of hers that she couldn't change.

"I should never have insisted that we move to London." It was a statement that she had often thought but stopped short of saying out loud over the years. A self-criticism that she couldn't shake.

The city air had weakened Jozef. It had shortened his life. The move to Avignon had come to nothing and Mary recalled the despair she had felt on hearing that news in their cramped accommodation in the Masons' terraced house in Crewe. The rain had been pouring down, causing foul-smelling streams to run along the passageways and in and out of the outdoor latrines. The English weather had a habit of reflecting her dreary mood perfectly.

Many of their Polish friends had moved to Wales, filling the holes in the labour market created by the war. It was an option the couple gladly took. Anywhere to leave the tense atmosphere of their accommodation in Crewe. They found a cottage near to his employment on the edge of the Brecon Beacons. A school where Jozef found a job as a teacher. The cottage was a small affair with no running water, no electricity and no gas but there was no Mrs Mason.

"We move in on Saturday," Mary had decided for the both of them after a short amble around the empty building. They would have less than a week to pack.

"Mary!" Jozef had been horrified.

She'd have left the next day if she could.

The rolling, barren hills of the Welsh countryside had suited him. A sense of peace had settled on his soul and eased the lines of anxiety in his serious stare. It did not suit her. Nature was a haphazard host.

"Give me the clean lines of a city's streets any day! What am I to do with all this green? Am I to be a farmer now?"

It wasn't long before the couple and their young daughter found themselves moving again: this time to London.

"We should have stayed in Wales, perhaps Jozef's health would have…" A sentence she always started but never finished.

"We should have moved to London," he had insisted whenever she had questioned that decision. "We should have moved to London because we built a business here, we are comfortable and above all, you weren't happy and I needed you to be happy."

In the forests, in the countryside, that's when he came alive. His eyes were always looking for any hint of fungi on the forest floor, plucking an oyster mushroom here, a bolete there for the children to scrutinise. His enthusiasm for nature became infectious.

"I don't think the busy streets of a city life suited you." The thought brought a tear to her eye. Retrospection is a horrid curse.

"If you are talking about belonging, I don't think I belong anywhere. This forest reminds me of the camps," he had told her on the damp uneven folds of their picnic blanket, watching the children run in and out of the oaks and ash. "The woods, the work." His words had spilled out from a place he kept locked and hidden, tumbling towards her like the haul of mushrooms that had fallen over the edges of the handkerchief he had used for harvesting. "But even there, you could find something of life."

Harlesden,
ENGLAND,
1959

Eric was a delivery driver and builder that the Bekers got to know through the Rothbarts. A pleasing fellow who was London-bred and with a heart of gold. On his trips around London, he would sometimes stop off at Bramshill Road with a small paper bag full of wine gums. Having lost touch with his own children through his now ex-wife, he liked to spoil the children of his friends. Henry and Margarita would sit on the doorstep sucking the sweet juices from the little golden gems one after another whilst Eric was refreshed with a proper pot of tea and a cake in the Bekers' kitchen.

They talked of London and how it was changing. Fashion was getting bolder and brighter like the bright sunshine after a dense, thick fog. Demand for cloth belts was waning as plastic ones became all the rage. Pencil-thin ones, thick ones. They hugged the hips of the bright blonds and striking brunettes who strutted the streets with heavily made-up faces. The world was changing. Again.

"A day off today?" Eric asked. He noted that their house was quieter than normal with less of the energy that a large belt order created. Usually, they would have taken it in turns to pop in and out of the kitchen to keep him company whilst carrying on with production in the other room. But today, both Mary and Jozef had joined him for a cup of tea.

"We work too hard." Jozef smiled at his wife. "It's nice to have a day off."

"There are still plenty of things to do," she reminded him, placing the teapot on the table.

"I'm thinking of selling the business," Jozef confided in a wistful way, his fingers collecting the individual crumbs from the sweet *faworki* that had been on his plate.

They had talked about it before and with an increasing sense of urgency over the past few weeks. Mary had told him she was worried about his health: the pain in his shoulder, his breathlessness, the minor heart attacks that had crept up on him suddenly. As the belt orders slowed, he had had time to think, to breathe. A life of constant hard work was catching up with him and it was time to slow down.

"And what will you do with your time?" Eric asked automatically. As long as he had known the two of them, their hands had been busy with something.

"There's the garden."

"There's always the garden," Mary agreed, smiling.

"I'm done with working. We've always worked so hard, haven't we, Mary? It's time we took the time to enjoy life."

She nodded her agreement and he glimpsed the fine line her lips made in an effort not to show the worry he knew consumed her.

"If…" Jozef paused with his hand on the door to Eric's Ford Step van as he saw him off half an hour later. A quick pained look at the house but Mary and the children had already disappeared inside. "If anything should happen to me…"

"Don't be daft." It was a flippant comment which fizzled weakly against a tide of anguish that Eric was uncomfortable to witness.

"If anything should happen to me." Jozef's hand was raised with the importance of his words. "I'd like you to keep an eye on my family."

The words were wrenched out of him. Asking for help wasn't something that he was used to. Eric paused, his thick, hard-working hands on the steering wheel. Jozef was younger than him but even he noticed the gradual wearing of age, the telltale signs of a decline in health and the wearing down of a man whose life had been particularly hard.

"Of course, Jozef." Eric was an honest man who would not make a promise he was unable to keep. "You know I may not have the money, but I have these two hands and I will always do anything to help Mary and the children."

A fierce nod indicated that Jozef was happy with his answer, as if a weight had been released from his sagging shoulders.

"Thank you."

He closed the door with a satisfied thud.

"But you know." Eric leant out towards him. "It won't come to that."

Jozef said nothing. He merely tapped the van's side with his open palm in a final farewell before wandering back into the house.

Alexandria, EGYPT, 1937

"I don't know why you're still working there!" Therese, a friend of Mary's since their school days, exclaimed in exasperation. Mary had been recounting her previous day at the atelier and the conversations that she had been subjected to from her fellow work colleagues. They were sitting in a café sipping Turkish coffee by the window that overlooked a street where the Arab men with their *hookah* pipes smoked *shisha* and played backgammon on ancient boards. "Come and join me at L'Hôpital Européen d'Alexandrie. It is a much better way to earn a living."

It had not been the first time Therese had tried persuading her friend into a nursing career. She herself had gone into nursing once her time at L'Orphelinat de la Miséricorde had come to an end. Her place of work was a French Catholic hospital on Rue Cherif Pacha: a three-storey, white, nondescript building that was squat with flat roofs and rectangular windows that seemed otherwise out of place with the beautiful Italianate architecture of the shops that abutted it with their large awnings and wide pavements. It was a comfortable progression from their upbringing at the hands of the French nuns and more preferable than working in an Arab establishment, which was so at odds with Mary's Coptic background. Therese's proposal was starting to sound more and more attractive the longer she spent at the atelier and the culture it invited.

"You want to work as a nurse? *Ya Lahwi!*" Zakia's face fell and she immediately touched her forehead in repentance for her careless words. She had been plucking a chicken when Mary told her. It was a Saturday, and her mother was preparing the bird she had reared on the balcony ready for the Sunday family dinner. The chicken's lifeless head flopped on a snake-like neck over Zakia's skirts as she worked. The way it lolled and drooped with its half-closed eyes suggested it was as disapproving of the venture as her mother.

"I am not happy where I am," Mary explained, "I need a new job."

Mary was no longer a child waiting in trepidation for the sharp click of her mother's tongue. There was a woman now where a child had been. A tall, dignified woman who was capable of knowing her own mind. Zakia nodded and sighed.

"It is your decision, Mary," she said carefully. "If you must, you must. But your uncle will not be pleased."

Her mother was right; Iskandar was not at all pleased. They were visiting the family home in Luxor again. It was a few days before she was due to start in her role as a nurse in the dispensary at the Catholic hospital. She would be unable to take a holiday once the post had started so it seemed the right time for the family to visit.

"You are going to do what?"

His big bushy moustache twitched and flapped on his upper lip as rage emitted in little droplets of spittle from his mouth.

She repeated her plan and told him she was starting the following week. His eyebrows danced on a forehead drawn out with incredulity.

"A niece of mine is going into a job where she will be subjected to naked men! I think not!" he raged, his arms flapping wildly in the air.

Zakia thought to intervene but Mary was old enough and strong enough to fight her own battles. Nursing wasn't a profession most families in Egypt wanted their daughters to embark on. Charitable work was encouraged but dealing hands-on with the fleshy naked bodies of men and women, complete strangers all of them, was as unacceptable as prostitution.

"Are you going to keep me, then? Feed me? Clothe me?" Mary shouted back. "How else can I earn a living?"

Iskandar took a step back. His wife's hand slapped across her own mouth in a bid to stop the involuntary gasp from escaping. No one had dared answer Iskandar back before, let alone a female member of the family.

"Mary Hawash!" Iskandar thundered, his moustache threatening to escape his upper lip in incredulous rage.

"It is my life, not yours," Mary continued, buoyed with more confidence the longer the argument went on. "I shall do as I please."

"And you, Zakia? You are happy with this?"

"Mary will excel at whatever she puts her mind to." Her mother shrugged, trying hard not to show the internal pride she felt at her daughter's determination.

Iskandar's hands flew into the air one last time and he left the room. Mary couldn't help but smile.

The work was hard, the uniform practical. She smoothed the creases from the bright white A-line dress with its high collar, buttoned front and gathered waist: the garb of her new profession. Her dark hair was tamed back behind a white headdress that reminded her very much of the nuns at L'Orphelinat de la Miséricorde. She was embarking on a career in service to mankind, much like their own in many ways. What would Maman Ancette say if she could see her now?

Her first appointment at the hospital was in the outpatients clinic on the ground floor. It was light and airy with echoing stone walls and a cool stone floor. A steady stream of patients waited patiently on wooden seats by the hospital entrance. There were minor injuries that needed treating, nagging ailments to relieve. The busyness of the scene made her feel comfortable and eager to get stuck in. She was paired with a sister who seemed incapable of smiling. The young woman, who was only a few years older than herself, was constantly rushing around. Mary was under the impression that having a new nurse to train seemed more of a hindrance than a help. She found herself running to catch up as her mentor swept between the consulting rooms picking up and discarding instruments as she went. A hand was bandaged and then undone in order for Mary to replicate with eager anticipation. It was both lesson and exam, all rolled into one. She passed. Or at least, she thought she had. Her teacher had said nothing, done nothing and merely ushered her along to the next patient. At lease she hadn't shown her the exit.

It was the doctors that changed her companion's demeanour. A careful nod of reverent respect was always put their way as they reeled off orders and instructions that were obeyed to the letter.

"Sister, suture this wound."

"Sister, I will need morphine in room 3."

Mary was ignored. It was clear that in the stark white of the hospital building, she was going to have to work hard to earn her place.

Warsaw, POLAND, 1938

"It suits you."

A murmur of indignation as Szyja adjusted his cap in the mirror. It didn't suit him. They both knew that. Yesterday he had been wearing a tailored suit with a Fedora hat as he had started the new academic year as director of public school number 76 in Nowolipki Street, Warsaw. He had been promoted last July and the school was now in his sole charge. Today, he was trying on his new military uniform with its eagle cap of the Polish army. Universal military duty had become law on 9th April that year and that September it came into force. Szyja was now a cadet in the military reserves as well as a headmaster, father and husband. It was this new role that he found himself least adapted to.

"Perhaps you need to adjust it slightly…" Rozia's practised hands tweaked the edges of the peak of his cap, noticing how rough the material felt under her fingertips. That was slightly better. A smooth stroke down each shoulder and the material ceased to wrinkle on his unaccustomed shoulders. A pair of eyes were peeking through the crack in the door to their bedroom. Marysia was watching her father's transformation with a mixture of pride and keen interest.

"This isn't me," Szyja admitted with a sigh.

"It's still you underneath," Rozia snapped, repeating the strokes down the front of his jacket in a brusque manner that denied any further protestations. "Just keep your head down, play your manly war games and go back to your classroom with your head held high. The pupils need to see an example."

"An example of what?"

She shrugged.

"For the motherland!" Rozia smiled and Szyja was reminded of Mr and Mrs Sadlowski on Dzielna Street – elderly Jewish residents that the family helped with the shopping twice a week. A couple that had been born in Warsaw, grew up in Warsaw, saw its development from years of Russian oppression to its status as capital of the newly independent Poland of 1918. They were as much a part of the city as the buildings themselves. To them, there was no better place on earth. Life outside the city walls just simply did not exist.

Szyja didn't share his wife's flippancy. The *Warsaw Weekly* was full of the situation on the Czechoslovakian border with the sudden German occupation of the

Sudetenland. The thought of proper fighting filled him with dread.

"It won't come to that." His friend, Jan, was adamant as they learnt to fix bayonets on the parade ground.

"And how can you be so sure?" Szyja was more pragmatic than his friends on the situation. The rumblings in Germany, the unsteady situation with Lithuania, the rush on pacts between countries at the expense of their occupants, it was all leading to a general sense of unease.

"It just won't." Jan shrugged away the need for further explanation. "Besides, look at us all! Who would want to come up against this band of men?"

Szyja surveyed the men sticking sharpened knives into the sacks of sand dangling limply from the crossbars of hastily erected training frames. Their commanding officer, a rotund veteran from the Polish-Russian war with a telling limp, was following his men, shouting encouragement and obscenities as he pedalled furiously down the field on his bicycle.

Perhaps Szyja had misjudged his friend's sense of humour.

Alexandria, EGYPT, 1939

In the early part of 1939, Mary was learning something new. It had been six months since she'd embarked on her new career at the dispensary of the L'Hôpital Européen d'Alexandrie. Six months of constant bandaging and six months of attending to the doctors' every instruction. She could bandage a hand or an arm in her sleep. She had seen it all. Burns, scrapes, the unsightly diseases that accompanied any large city. The wounds did not faze her. The stories and the people behind them did. She could not adopt the cold, sterile detachment that the veteran nurses had hardened to over the years. She doubted that characteristic would ever come to her.

The stories of her patients followed her home, and her daily recounts were enough to persuade Alice to join the profession. For Mary, it helped having her kind and compassionate sister alongside her in the dispensary. Her gentleness was what she needed. It also meant she was able to keep a close eye on the younger sister she adored.

The work was endless. A long queue of fallen humanity shuffled into the outpatients clinic, below the cross of Jesus that hung on the waiting room wall. The latter was a huge depiction of Christ carved in wood at the final moments of His death. Wooden beads of blood cascaded over the cleverly crafted wounds in his hands, feet and side. Mary often caught herself musing on how quickly and efficiently every patient in the clinic was repaired whilst Jesus just stayed hanging there, bleeding. The blood of the worldly wounds captured in wood were beyond the hospital's capabilities.

She was restless, eager to carry on her learning, carry on progressing in her chosen career. It was in this last year of the 1930s that she learnt how to administer injections. It was amazing what could be cured, what illnesses could be prevented, what symptoms could be alleviated through the means of a small glass vial and a practised pair of hands. She learnt the names of the medicines and the appropriate doses she punctured into the arms of the wealthy and the not so well off. People were people. It didn't matter what their backgrounds were. Disease didn't care for money. She absorbed this humbling view of the world as she travelled across the city in her lunch break and into the fading evening light with her leather bag of vials and needles. The service wasn't free and allowed a supplement of between five and ten piastres a time to her nurse's wage. At some houses she would be plied with coffee and sweet, syrupy *basbousa* from a grateful family. At other houses she would be allowed across the doorstep long enough to carry out her work before being ushered out of the strangers' lives. Attitudes to nurses, she learned, varied from place to place (just like her family's).

The work was long and hard after being on her feet all day in the clinic, but she didn't mind. The bus and tram rides that she used to get from residence to residence allowed her a brief respite, a time to breathe as the city buzzed around her.

One such journey took her to the residence of the Turkish Ambassador – a palatial mansion that towered over a street in the eastern end of Alexandria. Here the Rolls-Royce cars swept down the wide boulevards. In the immaculate gardens, large-headed chrysanthemums leant towards the dazzling evening sun whilst lotus flowers bobbed upon the ponds designed to cool the intense summer heat. The undulating, echoing calls of the muezzin from the various domed mosques dotted around the city followed her footsteps as she alighted from the hot tin tram. It was a familiar sound that she heard everywhere and was a comfort in this alien part of the city, despite her difference of faith.

Mary clutched her bag of instruments to her and tried not to gawp as she pulled the doorbell on the wide stone steps. She had already navigated her way past the uniformed guards at the gated entrance to the estate and the sounds of the trams trundling down the street were distant as if she had been transported into another world.

The Turkish Ambassador's wife was a tall, elegant woman with long dark flowing hair and a chiselled nose which was softened by her heavily rouged cheeks. She lounged on a bright red sofa that matched her immaculately painted nails, close to the window of her study which was open to let in the cooling evening breeze. She had been unwell with a fever over the past week and the doctor had prescribed her two doses of penicillin to ease her symptoms. Mary was to deliver the last dose. The footman, with his bobbing head and exaggerated bow, left her at the door and she hesitated.

"I hope the journey wasn't too out of your way." The woman addressed Mary with a tired smile, the words in perfect Arabic tripping off her tongue.

Mary looked at her feet where her leather shoes had picked up the Alexandrian dust. It didn't seem right to bring the dirt from the streets into this elegant world. She rubbed the tips of her shoes onto the backs of her legs before tiptoeing carefully and almost apologetically over the wooden floor towards her client. She felt as if she should apologise for her appearance but was too embarrassed to mention it.

"*La mushkila.*" Mary rallied herself, placing her bag down by the woman's feet as she sank to her knees. "Not at all."

"Oh!" her client exclaimed. "No, no."

She looked up, embarrassed, fearful that she had done something wrong. Perhaps she was meant to address her with some sort of reverence and she searched her memory for the appropriate words.

The woman smiled and indicated a chair wrapped in padded red silk, similar to the one she was sitting on.

"Please do use a chair."

She flushed red and nodded. There was silence as the chair scraped across the polished floorboards, the strangled squeaks rebounding off the walls and high ceiling. The sudden assault on the silence brought the blood to Mary's cheeks again and she avoided the woman's gaze in a bid to calm her own embarrassment.

"Do you work at the hospital?" The woman laid her arm out on the arm rest between them. A long, slender arm that spoke of an easy life.

"*Na'am*, madam." Mary fumbled with the vial and then took a deep breath to calm her nerves.

"Ayeleen, please."

She responded with a smile but couldn't bring herself to be so overfamiliar in such a place as this. The needle ready, she placed it down on the table next to them.

"What is your name?" the ambassador's wife enquired with all manner of innocence.

"Mary."

She wished the lady would stop being so nice. It was quite off-putting.

"What a nice name," Ayeleen mused, her soft pink lips pursed together in thought. "Well, Mary, shall we set to work?"

"If I could just roll up your sleeve…" Focussing on the job in hand and the professionalism that came with it calmed Mary's nerves and she carefully rolled back the lady's cotton sleeve. She smelled of roses and a spice that she couldn't quite place. Mary was well aware of the stains on her own pinafore that she had hastily sponged clean before dashing to make this appointment. She wished she had had time to change. "Thank you. This might sting briefly." It was a phrase that tripped off her tongue. She automatically said this to all her clients in a bid to soften the unpleasantness of intentionally hurting another human being. Ayeleen winced ever so slightly, her dark eyes dreamily gazing out of the window as she avoided the sight of the needle entering her flesh.

"You must stay for dinner," Ayeleen said with some finality.

The invitation surprised Mary as she tidied away the instruments of her trade. She started a mumbled, clumsy protestation which was silenced by Ayeleen's slender fingertips.

"No, I insist. Unless… You haven't anywhere else you have to be?"

She thought of her mother and sister finishing their evening meal and leaving the leftovers to one side under a cover to ward off the flies.

"No, no. I'm finished for the day."

"That's settled then. Excuse me, whilst I get changed for dinner."

She wondered what her evening outfit might look like considering the tailored dress she was already wearing.

The study was austere and unwelcoming without Ayeleen's presence and Mary quickly gathered up her things and hurried down the corridor, rushing to find the exit. Despite the vastness of the ambassador's residence, Mary still found herself surprised at the number of servants that crowded into the parlour in the basement of the building. Cooks, maidservants, footmen and butlers bustled around with tasks that seemed never-ending. The chef, a kindly woman who was her mother's age, placed a plateful of cold meats and salads in front of her on the large oak table in the servants' dining room. She ate hungrily, having missed her usual lunch with a backlog of vaccinations to get through.

"Whatever are you doing, Mary?"

Mary was startled by a voice behind her. The other servants sprang to attention at someone who had just entered the room. Ayeleen was standing breathless and flushed in the doorway, her elegant evening gown of turquoise and blues flowing freely around her.

Mary dropped the flatbread she was holding and scrambled to her feet. Perhaps she had misheard the invitation and committed the most unredeemable *faux pas*.

"You invited me to dinner," she stumbled over the words, the colour fading from her cheeks.

"Yes." Ayeleen's hand clutched the doorframe to steady herself. "With me, upstairs in the dining room. Come, come."

The dining room? Mary's feet followed the lady of the house in incredulity to the sumptuous surroundings of the ambassador's eating quarters. A vast chandelier with twinkling glass dangled over the smooth lines of a mahogany table where the ambassador himself sat, flanked by his two children of school age. Her heart pounding, Mary took the offered seat next to Ayeleen and prayed that she wouldn't shame her mother with her lack of refinement. There was a variety of cutlery lined up as a challenge before her, more than she had been taught to use at the French school. At home they were all used to sitting on the floor and using their fingers. A man in a smooth white suit matched with white gloves placed a plate before her that was covered in a silver dome. He removed the dome with a flourish and a gesture that may well have asked for silent applause. Mary tried not to gawp at the buttered legumes, the crisp browned chips and the large hunk of meat that must have been a steak, although she had never been served one before. She could hardly concentrate on the pleasant talk the family exchanged with smiles and laughter as she savoured every mouthful of that delicious meal. She ate the steak first, carefully slicing the meat into small slivers that would easily fit between her waiting lips, which she moved carefully and steadily to show her manners. It was tender and buttery and smooth like nothing she had ever tasted. The chips came next with their crisp outer shell peppered with tiny flakes of sea salt that gave way to a smooth and fluffy interior. The legumes were fresh and full of flavour, unlike the bland and wilted greens they enjoyed at home. She ate every morsel of that dinner until her stomach hurt and her belt groaned. Just when she thought she had had her fill, her plate was whisked away by gloved hands and a delicate plate of sweet treats was laid before her; dainty pastries covered with honey and silky-smooth cream. *Oh, if my sister were here to taste this, instead of the dry bread, milk and cheese from the hospital canteen!*

She couldn't move. Her stomach was so full. She rested back in her cushioned seat like the Arab men outside the coffee shops at Ramleh, their rounded stomachs proclaiming the ease of a life in which they had no need to worry where the next meal was coming from.

"Did you enjoy dinner?" Ayeleen smiled, her dainty fingers lifting a delicate china *finjon* to her rouged lips.

"Oh yes." She was reliving every tasty mouthful in her mind. One of the children was playing the piano in the corner with a dexterity that Mary marvelled at due to his age. As well as the food, she had gorged herself with the stories the ambassador and his wife had shared, painting a life so at odds with her own. Their experiences had fascinated her.

She didn't want the evening to end.

The tram back home jolted and shook her out of the contented sleep that her body was trying to conjure. Her arm was knocked by a woman dressed head to toe in black as they all struggled to find space in the crowded tin vessel that clicked and whirred over the tracks of the city. Her sleepy eyes, still content with the pleasantness of such an evening, woke to the gentle clink of the cups dangling round the waist of a lemonade seller. She alighted from the tram with a lighter step as she returned to the narrowing streets of her home.

Her sister's jaw dropped open and her eyes widened in disbelief as Mary retold what had happened to her that evening. The meal was embellished into a banquet that was fit enough for a king. Their mother sat still and silent as she listened to her daughter's words. Mary knew what she was thinking.

"It's OK, Maman," she felt compelled to explain, "I didn't embarrass you."

That seemed to satisfy her. With a nod and a smile of satisfaction, she retired into herself and closed her eyes to the toil of the day. Perhaps she dreamt of the steak and chips her daughter had enjoyed? Mary wondered if she had ever tasted such luxury. Had those hard fingers and worn feet ever known a time when a meal shrouded in a silver dome had been brought to her as she rested on cushions of silk and cotton? As she settled down into her bed that night, Mary vowed that one day she would treat her mother to such a meal in one of the finest restaurants in Alexandria. A place where they would sip expensive wines and be addressed as if they were royalty.

The day would come. It was just a matter of believing.

Warsaw, POLAND, 1938

Most of Warsaw's residents seemed to be out for the weekend, making the most of the autumn weather before the winter set in. The previous winter had been harsh with snowstorms bringing the rail network to a halt. There was anticipation that this winter would welcome the same.

Rozia, Szyja, Arja and Marysia had taken a picnic to Saxon Gardens under the shadows of Saxon Palace, west of the Vistula River. It was a half-hour walk from their flat above the school. Marysia was running and ducking from her older brother's grasp as he reluctantly agreed to a game of chase whilst their parents walked arm in arm. There was no drill for Szyja that weekend – a rare break in their busy lives when they could concentrate on being a family without work or the troubles of the outside world getting in their way. Young couples were lounging by the Marconi Fountain tangled in their embraces as the water poured and spattered behind them. There were families, prams lined up by the nursemaids who fussed over their charges and young men on bicycles weaving in and out of the crowds. Rococo statues presided over them all, emulating an interpretation of the human concepts of justice, intelligence and glory. The sky was clear, the sun strong as it poured through the trees that were almost bare of leaves from the bright display of the fall.

It was easy to forget what was happening in the world on a day like that. Easy, but the feeling of uncertainty still remained below the surface. Nagging. Biting. Slowly, ever so slowly, gnawing away. Newsstands on their way to the park shrieked of the Polish 'victory' in Zaolzie (the land the Poles had annexed after the Nazis had carved up Czechoslovakia). The streets of Warsaw had been full of demonstrators only a few weeks before. Thousands of people had demanded the protection of their fellow Poles who called that land their home. The Bekers had avoided going out that day. Angry crowds with political messages created a natural fear in the minorities, the vulnerable.

They laid out a blanket in the sun and bought pretzels from a stand where the flies buzzed. Arja chose to flop on the grass, his arms and legs spread out as if he were making invisible snow angels. Marysia giggled as she licked the salt from her lips. She had her mother's hair. Dark, thick, long hair tamed into a ponytail that trickled down her back. Her face had adopted the stern and serious look of her father. Her cheeks were thinning as the soft roundness of her toddler years gradually disappeared. She was growing up. They both were. Arja was thirteen now. His voice was starting to deepen, and he fretted to tame his thick black hair into a position that satisfied his own self-awareness. That awkward age where he longed to become a man but was still caught in childhood. He was bright and argumentative. His young mind absorbed the world around him and he fired questions at his parents which they found hard to answer.

"Marysia! *Spadaj!*" Arja's little sister had finished her snack and had plopped herself down on her brother's stomach, taking the breath out of him.

"Children," Rozia's soft voice gently reprimanded them for breaking the peace of a beautiful afternoon.

"Marysia," Szyja playfully grabbed at his daughter and she hopped off her brother squealing. "Go, run and play and leave your brother to rest."

He watched her run amongst the damp grass, the moisture causing small droplets of dew to sparkle on the bows of her black leather shoes. He recalled the excitement she had expressed to him on returning from the shoe shop with the new purchase in her hands.

"They're ballerina shoes!" She had laughed happily. "They make me want to dance, to skip, to run!"

She twirled and laughed under his gaze, moving with childish abandonment through the park, the nursemaids with their prams, the young couples and families enjoying the sun.

"Leave her be." A hand on his arm and Rozia's soft voice kept him on the picnic blanket, restraining him from going after their daughter.

He could see her small frame stop and hesitate, her attention caught by a ball that had been carelessly kicked across her path to land at the feet of a girl of a similar age to her sitting motionless in the park.

"She ought not to stray so far." Szyja disentangled himself from the light touch of his wife, the crumbs of the pretzels and the sleepy body of his teenage son.

"*Tatuś.*" Marysia's hand had slotted into his, soft and warm, devoid of any blemish. "Why are her shoes so dull?"

He could see Marysia's toes ripple in her ballerina shoes as she stared intently at the child sitting on a wooden luggage box in front of them. The girl was clutching a ragged teddy bear, her eyes wide and scared. Behind her sat the rest of her family, all with drawn faces and worn clothes, luggage labels from their suitcases flapping in the breeze.

"Throw us the ball back!" The boys who were paused in their game were calling her out of her misery.

"*Ich verstehe nicht… ich verstehe nicht…*" She stared at them, unable to comprehend their meaning, not noticing the brown leather football looming before her.

"Throw us it!"

"*Tatuś*, what did she say?"

"Here, Marysia, take it to them." Szyja had picked up the ball and thrust it into his daughter's hands as if its removal would cure the girl of her wide staring eyes, her fear and her worn, dew-soaked shoes.

He hesitated in front of the girl, her family and their plight laid bare for all the world to see. He knew German, knew he could converse with this family but what good would words do? What could he possibly say in this moment, surrounded by children playing football amongst the chestnut trees that would go on to explode in colour this year and the next?

The man sitting with his wife and children and all that he possessed spoke for him, looked at him with his tired eyes, with his words steeped with the heaviness of those who had seen too much.

"Look after your daughter, *Mein Herr*," he said. "Just look after her."

Alexandria,
EGYPT,
1939

In Alexandria in 1939, the sun shone. The Europeans, enjoying a break in the sun from the frosts of Europe, strode the streets without care. Mary and her sister watched them from the tram as it trundled and shook them to and from their place of work. She could feel the hard, metallic clatter beneath her as the vehicle gripped the road. It was as if the tram was trying to remind her of her connection to this vibrant city that ran deeper than that of the tourists who wandered the streets.

The troops had become more noticeable. The British ones had always been there – remnants of the Egyptian pact with its former colonial ruler in 1936 which allowed some soldiers to remain under limitations. Alexandria was one of those designated places. Its position on the Mediterranean was important, vital even, in the continuation of supplies. But now there were more of them. The British stood out in their pith helmets as they accompanied the smartly dressed Egyptian soldiers that they were training. Red tarboosh next to the bright white of the British. They bobbed along like beacons on the broad Alexandrian streets.

It was payday and Mary's friends at the hospital had pleaded with her to use some of her earnings to accompany them on an evening out. It took some persuasion. She was careful with her money as most of it went straight back to Zakia who took control of the family's finances. It was a habit that she was loath to break but having watched her mother use some of last week's surplus to buy oranges and cigarettes for the poor at the hospital, she could no longer ignore her urge to enjoy the freedoms of a young, single woman. She and her sister, she decided, were going out.

She dressed in a mid-length, bias-cut, sea-green dress with puffy sleeves that crinkled softly as she moved. She had found it in a less than acceptable state of repair at the local market before lovingly restoring it using her skills with the needle. She was pleased with the result, although disappointed that her dull brown shoes with their thick buckle across the bridge of her slender foot didn't seem to go with her outfit as well as she'd hoped. She tamed her hair with a band that swept most of her frizzy curls back from her chiselled face. The last item to apply was the red lipstick she had bought and smuggled back to the house in case her mother didn't approve. She wasn't at home that evening, having disappeared round to a friend's for a night of cards and cigarettes. If she had been in, would Mary have been brave enough to wear it?

She handed the item to her sister and instructed her to do the same. Alice did so with a hesitation that spoke of her muted excitement at trying something new and perhaps forbidden.

"*Ya Lahwi!* You're not going out like that?"

The girls hadn't expected their brother to be home. He usually went out with his friends after his studies and it was this assumed lack of supervision that had finally persuaded Mary to agree to the rendezvous.

"What else would we do, looking like this?" Mary snapped, checking herself again in the mirror.

Alice baulked at her sister's bravado and quickly tried to calm the situation. Good Alice, sweet and dependable Alice. Always the peacemaker between brother and sister.

"We won't be long, Zaki." She smiled, stroking her elder brother's arm. "Just a few hours with friends to relax after a day on our feet."

"I think you've overdone the make-up."

A hand now on Mary's arm to calm her from the escalating argument. Alice smiled sweetly and kissed her brother on his cheek leaving a satisfyingly bright pink smear.

"Have a good evening, brother."

The warm Mediterranean air carried the girls to downtown Alexandria, to the open sea and the nightlife that littered the seafront. They clutched each other's arms as they lurched along the pavement, drunk with excitement. The seriousness of their lives was confined back to the day. The night had enveloped them in a carefree light-heartedness.

They talked of fashion, the latest film stars to adorn the billboards outside the Rex cinema and the patients that had kept them on their toes all day.

"He's following us, isn't he?" Mary asked the question in French through a laugh that had caught in her throat from their discussion over something that had happened on the ward.

"Huh?" The serious question hidden beneath such a light-hearted laugh was difficult for Alice to catch.

"Our brother," Mary persisted, gripping her sister's arm tighter in case her instinct to turn around would give them away. "He's following us."

Her finger pointed at the window of the shop they were passing where the figure of a man was highlighted pausing some way behind them. The suited figure stooped to light a cigarette, his eyes fixed on the two of them drifting down the road arm in arm. Mary tugged at her sister's arm.

"Pah," she scoffed. "*Laissez-le nous suivre!* Let him waste his evening hiding in the shadows if he so wishes. Let us give him something to worry about!"

"Mary!"

They met Therese and Laurens outside Athineos café on Safaya Zaghloul Street opposite Ramleh tram station. They greeted each other with hugs and a kiss on each cheek in the European way.

"Don't look now but our brother followed us here," Alice said worriedly.

"What on earth does he think you'll get up to?" Therese asked incredulously.

"We've not been out like this before." Alice worried.

Laurens put a comforting arm around her.

"*Alors*, you're in for a treat, then!"

The building was a large Greek café that was a popular meeting spot for an evening out. Its large arched windows spread out along its façade, which ran the length of a few buildings down the road. Smiling waiters in smart black suits greeted customers at the door and enticed others in as they walked along the pavement.

The waiter gave a formal bow in deference as the ladies entered, which sent the group into a fresh set of giggles. Zaki wouldn't follow them inside, they were sure of that. The confidence of that thought swept aside any fear of the lecture they would endure on their return home. The sisters were here to have fun and fun they would have.

Mary smiled as she caught Alice looking around in wonder at the high ceilings supported by a pristine white colonnade. The room was smoky and loud. People from every nationality lounged against the crisp white linen of tables strewn with Greek food. There was music playing from somewhere. The metallic, tinny sound plucked from the strings of the *bouzouki* carried across the room in direct competition with the male voices that accompanied it. A few dancers had already taken to the floor and were stamping their feet as the music upped its tempo.

Mary wanted to dance. The atmosphere was infectious. She forgot her tiredness from a day spent on her feet, rushing from patient to patient. She forgot that endless nagging feeling of needing to earn in order to keep her family afloat and ease the pressure on her mother whose feet seemed to drag more and more behind the cart she lumbered around the city. She forgot it all for a night of pure joy.

The women took a table by the empty floor space reserved for dancing, and flitted between the food, the retsina wines they had been persuaded to try and the dancing. Mary was exhaustedly happy.

"I could do this every evening."

"So could I," Therese agreed. They all felt light-headed with happiness.

The women were not short of dance partners. Their youthful looks and dark skin made them a target for the single men that occupied the bar. There were single men aplenty. French soldiers, British soldiers, the occasional Arab, men in suits with clipped ties. They all paid them attention. The food and drink flowed freely without them needing to dip into their purses. Therese had been right when she had predicted that it wouldn't be an expensive night.

Jean was tall, perhaps almost a head taller than Alice. He had a bristled moustache in the French style that hung onto his upper lip and gave him a sophisticated air. He held his uniform proudly, all dressed in white, a seaman from a French submarine. Mary found her stomach clenching as she saw the spark between them as they danced and chatted in French, her sister's head leaning into his so she could hear his words above the music.

How beautiful Alice had become with her soft smile and fun-loving nature!

Had Mary been so intent on guiding, on protecting her younger sister, that she had failed to see her growing up?

Jean was foreign and exotic, far different from the Arab men of their family who clung onto their long-held positions as the dominant sex. She recalled the man who had smelt of fish whose eyes had refused to look at her and whose intentions had been articulated through a rounded aunt with a slippery tongue. In contrast, Jean's eyes were devoted to her sister. They sparkled with pure joy as he drank her all in.

Don't you hurt her.

As the weeks passed, the relationship between Alice and Jean continued to develop. Her sister blossomed in his presence and blushed at the sound of his name. When he was deployed back to his ship, Mary feared his interest in her sister would wane, but he kept in contact through regular letters and soon it was clear there was an intention to marry.

Her younger sister might wed before her after all.

Sheerness, ENGLAND, 1959

Sheerness had become a favourite spot for the Bekers; a retreat from their hectic life in London. Holidays in the 1950s were a privilege only available to the few, but the belt-making business was comfortable and allowed for such luxuries. Their friends, the Smakowskis, had bought a small house in the town and persuaded the Bekers to do the same. Their holiday home became a small terraced house a few minutes' walk from the beach.

Sheerness itself was a traditional seaside town on the north-west corner of the Isle of Sheppey with ice cream parlours, amusements and shops selling buckets and spades. They decamped from London every year to rest on the long flat beach and enjoy some sun whenever the clouds would allow. It was a tradition that took them away from work and the stress of life. Mary felt they needed it now more than ever. Jozef was tired and still unwell from the minor heart attacks he had suffered over the previous years. The sea air gave him a peace that refreshed them all. It was no Alexandria. For a start it was cold and Mary hugged the blanket to her shoulders as she sat on the picnic rug looking out at the waves that gently washed over the shore and the sandcastle Henry was trying to make in between the shingle.

In, out, in, out. The calming motion was failing to soothe her this year and Margarita had gone to fetch her a cup of tea. She had seen the worry on her mother's face and felt it her responsibility to help.

Jozef wasn't with them.

The belt order had come in late that week and their carefully laid plans to get it delivered before their holiday were frustrated. Mary took the children on the long journey east via train whilst Jozef stayed behind to fulfil the order, promising to follow them later so their holiday could start properly.

But he hadn't come later. He was well over a few hours late. For a man as punctual as Jozef, that was a bit of a worry. Mary had tried calling the phone in their house on Bramshill Road but had received no answer and that had caused her to worry more. Only his actual arrival witnessed by her own eyes would calm the thoughts in her mind.

She had phoned Eric who had promised to pop round to the house during his afternoon break to check everything was OK.

She was passing the time on the beach, waiting for 3pm to arrive and the designated time Eric had promised to phone her at the red telephone box a few minutes' walk from their house. The house didn't feel the same this year without Jozef. The smell of damp from a property devoid of activity for a few months had lingered longer than normal. Their bedroom window had seized with the salt air and she had lacked the strength to force it. The place didn't feel the same as last year. The holiday didn't feel the same as last year.

"Pack up quickly, children," Mary demanded as she ushered them back into their tiny house, her face still as white as a sheet.

They were going home on the first train back. Eric had tried not to sound worried over the tinny line that crackled and hissed, but she knew he was thinking the same as her. He had duly popped by their house on Bramshill Road at the end of his shift and had received no answer at the door. The car was still there. *If the car was still there, then where on earth was he?*

She could stand it no longer. She was going to catch the first train back. She would find him and berate him for putting her through this misery.

"Why are we going back home now? We only just got here!"

Henry's protestations were quickly hushed by his elder sister. She had the experience of age to know when her mother meant business. There was no reasoning with her now.

The sun was not shining. It had disappeared behind the clouds as if it too was frightened by their mother's wrath. Mary's short heels clipped the pavement as the suitcases trundled and bounced over the uneven ground.

"Where on earth are you going?"

They had rounded the corner and almost collided with their father who was walking the opposite way.

Relief, anger, despair.

The emotions raced around Mary's mind and collided into angry words of Arabic that shot across the space between them.

"'*Ayn kunt?* Where on earth have you been?"

Two people on a pavement on a typical British summer's day when the sun refused to shine and the wind howled its resistance to any sudden change to the seasons. Two people from two different worlds speaking a language that belonged somewhere far from this quintessential seaside town, staring at each other in fear and in love.

"I was tired," Jozef replied quietly, drained with worry for his wife's pain. "I decided not to drive. I thought it best to take the train."

The suitcases were abandoned. She was in his arms, the worry turning into tears that cascaded down cheeks that had been carefully rouged that morning in anticipation of his arrival and the family time that was to come. In that grip of his safe arms, she felt the warm breeze of Alexandria, the feeling of home and her mother's smile. That dull, dark dampness of the British summer couldn't touch her.

"Don't ever do that to me again," she told him plainly, angrily.

Alexandria, EGYPT, 1939

Lucian was tall with dark skin. It was the first thing Mary had noticed about him when they met in 1939. Strange that she should notice this first and not the fact that he was lying horizontally in a hospital bed with his legs hoisted carefully above the mattress, heavily bandaged. Perhaps the years working in her chosen profession had numbed her to the sight of the bare wounds of the sick. Her mind chose not to notice the ailments but the human beings underneath it all.

She had moved from the hustle and bustle of the outpatients clinic to one of the wards with less serious health problems. It was quieter up here with less of the conveyor belt system of the dispensary. The quietness allowed more time with the patients. More time with people who fascinated her and opened her eyes to life.

She learned a lot about herself from her work on the ward. She was first and foremost a compassionate person to the broken human beings laid out before her. She felt their pain, listened to their stories, and offered a comforting hand to those that needed it.

Lucian's perfect French accent caught her attention. He had been admitted to the ward suffering from the effects of syphilis in his knees. A quietly spoken gentleman from Marseille who offered her a glimpse of a world she had only known through the textbooks and photographs the nuns had used to teach her French history. He wanted to talk. That was the only comfort he asked of her as he gritted his teeth against the pain in his knees whilst the antibiotics set to work.

She gave into his pleading eyes and chose to draw up a chair to his bedside rather than take her break in the nurse's room and the coffee and bread that called her. He settled as he talked, wistfully regaling a life on Marseille's fashionable coast. The food, the entertainment, the people. The exotic picture drew her in and she listened intently, completely losing track of time.

"*Chère Marie*," he told her, his hand gently brushing hers. "Your presence is more of a tonic to me than any medicine the doctors could prescribe."

Love. It had not been part of her plan. She had been so caught up in the need to work, to earn so that her mother would not be so overwhelmed with fatigue, that she had not seen it coming.

"So, you have found yourself a Frenchman too!" Alice announced with glee as her elder sister confided in her on the tram ride home. Her hands clapped together in happiness, desperate for her sister to feel the same excitement and contentedness her relationship with Jean had brought her.

The idea of marriage which Mary was so much against, was lurching towards her like a freight train. It had suddenly become a distinct possibility and for once in her life, Mary did not know what to think.

Warsaw,
POLAND,
2005

Mary hadn't thought of Lucian for a while. The memory of him was frozen in time so that his dark hair hadn't faded, his youthfulness of that moment in Alexandria had stuck with him and so had his infinite handsomeness.

I wonder where he is now, that man from France in his crisp white uniform?

He had propelled her down a path she was not expecting, touched her heart in a way she had not felt before. Her brother, Zaki, had not been happy and had made that abundantly clear.

"Tell me this, Mary, what kind of a brother would I be if I said I was happy with this?" Zaki's moustache had bounced up and down on his lip. She remembered an uncle with a moustache like that and her mind revolted at it. "In the absence of our father, it is up to me to ensure you are cared for, to find you suitable partners so that your future is secure."

"I will find my own partner and so will Alice, I do not need your lectures in love!"

She blanched now at the harshness of the tone she had used against a brother so overwhelmed with the responsibility of being thrust into a patriarchal position he had not asked for. It must have been hard for him to see both his sisters courting men who spoke a language he couldn't comprehend. Hard for him and ultimately hard for her.

The relationship with Lucian wasn't set to last.

Alexandria, EGYPT, 1939

"I'm going back to Marseille," Lucian said. It was a statement that cut harshly through a pleasant afternoon. He had taken her to the beach at Al Max with her sister and Jean. It was a favourite haunt dominated by the young where they could be away from the restrictions of life. Mary was brushing the sand from her toes, thinking about how the slim lines of her feet and painted toenails did not speak of the hours she spent on the wards, administering medicine, tucking in sheets and disposing of used bed pans.

"*Qu'est que tu dis?*" She blinked at him in the sun. Alice and Jean were spending a rare moment together paddling in the sea at the point where the gentle waves breached the shoreline. The cool electric blue of the water was lapping around their feet, and she couldn't help but be reminded of a painting depicting young love in all its beauty. How at peace they seemed together and how it contrasted with the seriousness of her own conversation with Lucian.

"Marseille. I need to return."

It was said matter-of-factly as if that was the end of the matter. The end of their relationship.

"That's it then? *C'est fini?* Done, just like that?"

There was fire in her eyes, her body stiffened as she felt an acute sense of wrongdoing.

"I was going to ask you to come with me."

Oh. She was taken aback. She had not thought this was where the conversation was heading. It had been just a few months since they had met. She was still getting to know him.

"Me? To France?"

He laughed at her naivety and rolled onto his stomach so that he could look directly at her.

"Why ever not?"

"Leave Egypt?"

"You could not do one without the other," he pointed out.

"I couldn't possibly... I mean, *Maman*, I..."

"Your sister is still here. You shouldn't take on all the responsibility yourself."

She was aware that her mother and Lucian did not share any form of rapport. He didn't speak Arabic and she didn't speak French. Their meeting was conducted with smiles and nods but progressed to nothing more. That pained her. She wanted the two most important people in her life to share the same bond.

"I don't know… I mean, I don't even have a passport!" The thoughts rushed frantically from her head.

"Apply for one." He shrugged simply. "Mary, for every barrier that you could possibly think of, I have a dozen solutions."

Was it that simple to him?

But then again, maybe it was? Perhaps his persuasion was just what she needed? Had she spent so long thinking about her family's needs that she was incapable of thinking of her own? He was opening up the prospect of a new life. A new life away from her current responsibilities at home. A new life in Marseille. The wife of a Frenchman settling in a country whose language and customs had been very much part of her without her ever visiting the place.

"Let's at least look at getting you a passport." Alice immediately took Lucian's role in persuading her. It was later that day and the sisters were alone and could freely voice their thoughts. It was of no harm, no consequence if they simply investigated the logistics of such a move, surely?

The thought did nothing to alleviate the guilt they both felt when they procured the relevant paperwork later that week. Guilt, since it was done without the knowledge of both their mother and brother. They tried to convince themselves that nothing had been decided, that nothing would come of such a move. The sisters were just looking into it for now, but they couldn't help but both worry…

"*Maa Hatha?* What's this?"

It was a Sunday. Mary was contentedly reeling in the fullness of her belly after the roasted chicken they had enjoyed with their *molokhia*. The coffee was brewing on the Primus stove and the shutters were open to the balcony. Zaki was out with friends and the women were left alone.

Zakia was holding the passport form in her hand. It was in French, but the seal of the French embassy was clearly visible at the top. Even though she couldn't read a word of it, it didn't take Zakia long to correlate its meaning with the fact that both her daughters had French partners, and neither were likely to settle here in Egypt. The chest in the corner, where Mary kept the material she used for her sewing, was open. The hiding place was discovered.

Alice had turned as white as a sheet. Mary's expression was full of remorse. The paper fluttered in Zakia's hands, and the girls flinched as if it were a loaded weapon.

"It was just a thought," Mary said. "Lucian is going back to Marseille so we were looking into options. It's nothing, Maman. A thought in the wind."

"*Lucian?*" The name was spat between them, bubbling, threatening. "You were planning on leaving us for him and you mention nothing to your mother?"

The remorse was unbearable. The look on Zakia's face was tearing her apart.

"She would not have done anything without first talking to you," her sister intervened from where she was standing, silhouetted in the window frame, half in the room, half out. Good Alice. Dependable Alice. Always the peacemaker.

"You!" Zakia turned on her youngest child with a venom that the two had not experienced since childhood. They saw the switch flip inside her, a rage borne out of love and longing. "She would not be thinking this if it hadn't been for you and your French man! How dare you take my daughter away from me!"

They were too big for the belt. Too grown up for the broom. The slipper on Zakia's foot was the only weapon left to her. It sailed across the space between them and caught the younger woman on the side of her face with a speed that prevented Alice from protecting herself. The soft cotton top glanced a blow that prepared her for the leather sole to come. The slap reverberated around the room. The slipper fell to the floor and bounced one, two, three times loudly in the silence.

Alice had a hand to her reddened cheek, her eyes smarting in pain and her mouth open in astonishment at the strength of her mother's fury. Zakia looked at her, unrepentant, teeth clenched, beside herself in disbelief at the disobedience of her daughters.

"*Maman!*"

Mary looked from her sister to her mother and back again. Alice was crying. Big childish tears were coursing over her shaking, womanly hands and puddling on the discarded slipper on the floor in front of her. No one moved. No one had a clue as to what should happen next.

The move to Marseille was called off before the possibility had properly begun. The paperwork for the passport was torn up and burnt on the Primus stove. Mary's relationship with Lucian was terminated. She had been the one to call it off. Seeing her mother so upset had made her re-evaluate what she wanted. She wasn't ready to leave her mother just yet. She needed her mother and her future partner to get along, a partner who could see Zakia in the same way that she saw her: a strong, intelligent woman, the rock in Mary's life.

She just hadn't met him yet.

Warsaw, POLAND, 1939

On 23rd August 1939, two men signed a pact. Two men in smart suits; one with a bristly moustache and glasses who cocked his head in a sincere way with an almost kindly manner; the other with a long-pointed nose and furrows in his brow that spoke of an intensity bordering on harshness. Two men from two different countries announcing publicly to the world their peaceful intentions towards each other whilst secretly carving up Europe between them.

It is easy enough to create a new world with just a pen and a map.

In Warsaw, the sense of unease was an undercurrent that was talked of in hushed voices on street corners and read by the inquisitive at the many newsagents. Szyja noticed a change in the atmosphere at the school where lessons continued unabated. His uniform of a Polish officer in the reserves hung ready in the wardrobe, to be worn at a moment's notice. The call would come. Nobody was quite sure when.

The teaching staff didn't stay long past the final bell of the day. Everyone wanted to get home, to scurry back to loved ones. Despite living above the school where he worked, Szyja decided to take a walk before seeing his family. He needed the space, the air to breathe.

The streets were crowded, full of women in small hats and wide furs and men in smart suits and fedoras. Only this time, the usual street traffic of the day was dotted with the dull brown uniform of Polish soldiers. Their smart caps that were emblazoned with the defiant Polish eagle, were replaced with tin ones as if only they knew what was due to be delivered from the skies.

There was a flower seller on the corner, the natural bawdiness of his produce flashing brightly against the backdrop of humanity that scuttled past him. Szyja bought a bunch of orange day lilies, their large buds opening out like trumpets. Not Rozia's favourite, but they would brighten up the living room.

His mother had written from South Africa. The factory she had set up was going strong. The weather was pleasing. Wouldn't it be nice if he could bring the family to visit? Perhaps during the school holidays or earlier if they could? He'd noticed that undertone of worry from the letter and he vaguely wondered if the news reaching her in that faraway country was more aligned to the truth than the information carefully censored by the Polish government.

In the gradual darkening of the skies, the brightly coloured lilies bounced against his shoulder, their reflection glittering freely in the shop windows he passed. How bright they were against the dull brown and greys of the clothes worn by the crowds of people he passed; nature fighting against the industry of man.

Something was different but everything was the same. It was unsettling and reassuring at the same time. A crowd on the corner of Nowolipki Street made him pause as people waited for a chance to cross the street once the trams had finished trundling past. He hovered from foot to foot, impatient for the people to disperse so that he could carry on with his journey.

The bakers had sold out of bread. A worried-looking man with gaunt cheeks teetered on the edge of a chair behind the glass of his shop front. He caught Szyja's eye and Szyja paused to observe the tiredness staring back at him. The man's gaze darted towards the bright bunch of flowers Szyja carried in his hand and then back towards the sealing tape he was sticking to the windows – criss-cross lines to defiantly stop any bombs damaging his empty display where *babka* and *makowiec* breads used to be.

As if tape would prevent a war.

"I think you should move back to your mother's in Skierniewice."

Rozia's hands paused on the vase she was preparing for the flowers her husband had brought her.

"Why?" she asked.

"Just for a while. Arja can stay here with me and continue his studies. You and Marysia should go. Just for a while."

There was no use in protestations. Despite her question, Rozia already knew the reason why. Warsaw seemed unsafe.

"I haven't visited Mother in ages. It would be good to spend some time with her," she conceded as if making up an ordinary reason was more palatable than the other thoughts on all their minds. "Just for a while."

A few days later, once the telegram reply had signalled Faiga's willingness to put up her daughter and granddaughter in her home in Skierniewice, Szyja and Arja saw them off at the train station on Jerusalem Avenue. There were no long goodbyes. They were running late and the platforms were busy with Polish soldiers having received the call to mobilise as the Polish Government realised the seriousness of the situation. One final hug and that was that. Marysia's bright eyes and dark hair were framed perfectly in the window as she leant out to blow raspberries at her brother as the train puffed down the tracks. Arja stood next to his father, waving back as they both watched them disappear in a cloud of steam.

"Will all this pass, *Tatuś*?"

What on earth was he to say to that?

***

Public school number 76 in Warsaw was all but empty when the *Luftwaffe* took to the skies above the city. There was no screaming. Szyja had installed a fierce attitude of calm amongst his staff and the remaining children (the ones whose parents were in denial or those who physically couldn't leave the city) were dispatched home swiftly and safely. School was closed. Nobody knew for how long.

It was with a nervousness of anticipation that Szyja donned the uniform in his wardrobe – the one he had hoped would succumb to the moths and the dust. The room was shaking with the vibrations of bombs already hitting the city and he wasn't sure if it was these vibrations or his own nerves that caused his fingers to shake and tremble. The buttons wouldn't slide into their holes and he cursed.

"*Tatuś*..."

Arja looked a lot younger than thirteen, standing in the doorway, his eyes wide with fear. Why hadn't he sent him to Skierniewice with Rozia and Marysia? Why had he kept him here to continue his studies amongst the fear and the bombs?

"You're to go to the basement and stay there until I come for you. Just like we practised. Quickly, Arja, quickly!"

They tumbled out onto the stairwell, Szyja half clutching, half dragging his son down towards safety. The widow, Mrs Wilsenka, appeared at her door, a shawl wrapped tightly around her as she steadied herself against the shaking walls.

"Arja, help Mrs Wilsenka." He shoved him towards her. "Get her to safety."

The task rallied his son and Szyja left the two of them heading down the stairs arm in arm.

It was the same passers-by on the streets outside. The same furs and fedora hats but they ran this time. The flower seller was still on the corner of Nowolipki Street, his flowers still blooming as he looked up at the clear skies. There was an expression of bewilderment on his face as he stood still, not knowing what to do as he watched the planes with their black and white crosses drop their bombs on the city.

Szyja hurried along, rushing down alleyways and dashing across streets. There was no time to panic. The whoosh of the bombs dropping from the unseen enemy in the sky and the splatter of breaking glass, splintering wood and crumbling bricks was met with a silent fear that caught in Polish throats. No one screamed. No one shouted. It was as if all this was inevitable. Expected.

He ran blindly, looking for his regiment – a task that gave him a purpose that focussed his mind and kept the anxiety at bay. In Mirowski Square a Polish soldier stopped the two young men in front of him as they rushed across the road. A shovel in each of their hands and they were pushed into the unnatural dip on the pavement to clear the rubble that spilled in waves across the street.

Two shovels in the face of all this carnage.

The soldier nodded at Szyja as he rushed past with the respect of a man in uniform, doing his bit running around the city not knowing where to turn. Loudspeakers were being erected on the sides of buildings and were already ringing out the pre-recorded monotonous tone of the prime minister, Felicjan Sławoj Składkowski, as he reminded Warsaw citizens of the might of the Polish army and the fight that they were all obliged to take part in. The government itself had already long gone, leaving Warsaw to its fate. His berating words fell on the deaf ears of the delivery driver who lay tangled and broken beside his horse and trap in a freshly made hole in the ground made by the German might.

Szyja was panting by the time he caught up with Jan and the rest of the reserves, his uniform dusty and damp from sweat.

"This is it, then."

There was a madness in Jan's eyes. A madness born not out of rage but out of the realisation that death was only a heartbeat away. They were going to face the power of the Nazi panzers with bicycles and revolvers and the willingness of madmen. They stood as the bombs crashed all around them as their commander detailed out their duties as if ticking off a register.

A man was sitting at a table outside a café in the square they were in. Szyja couldn't help but stare at him as he half listened to the orders their commander rattled out. The café was empty except for this one man who sat and drank his coffee, a napkin to his lips as the buildings shook and the tape in the café window peeled with the force of the blows a few streets away. Surely this was a place for the mad.

They built barricades out of bed frames, wooden doors and anything else that had fallen from the belly of the buildings whose skeletal remains clung to the earth that still shook and rumbled. They helped pull the dead and the living from the buildings they ransacked. Szyja noticed how the corpses all had that same look of surprise, frozen in death as if they couldn't quite believe it had happened to them.

They remained all night long amongst the broken furniture designed to stop any advancing army in its tracks. All night they waited to see the whites of the eyes of the German invaders passing by the perfumery, stockings and curtain shops that lined the road. But they never came. Frightened fingers tightened on their government-issued guns where they peeked precariously through the tangled wires of broken bedsprings. Watching. Waiting. And as they waited, civilians scurried in between the mouse-holed buildings carrying shopping over the dust and bricks. Szyja wanted to shout at them to get away; to go home and stay home before the Germans came. But the Germans didn't come. Instead, the enemy was the featherless birds in the sky that scattered their parcels of death amongst the streets, the shops, the homes. Fires burned and were left burning. The roads were peeled back by blasts that revealed the earth beneath. It was as if the Germans in the sky were trying to skin the heart out of Warsaw.

Szyja returned to Nowolipki Street in the early hours of the morning with his ears ringing and his uniform torn and dishevelled. To his relief, his home and the school remained standing. He stumbled into the basement, which was dark and damp and full of anxious eyes that stared at him.

"Arja!" He clutched at his son as the relief overwhelmed him. And then the tears came in a torrential flood that couldn't be stopped by the anonymous eyes that stared at them. He had left all sense of propriety under the rubble far above their heads and was too tired to draw it back. It was the first time he had ever remembered crying as a man.

"*Tatuś?*"

He held him against the tears, the sweat, the ugliness of a war that had fallen on them so suddenly. Just a boy. Only a boy.

Warsaw, POLAND, 2005

Why didn't Arja go to Skierniewice with your wife and daughter?

It wasn't a question Mary could ask out loud. It carried too much weight. The snippets of information Jozef knew about his family's fate came in droplets over the years like the raindrops before a storm that refused to properly start.

At first, in those early years of courtship, it had been a statement of fact. They were dead. They were all dead. Then, over the years, most often in the aftermath of the night-time terrors, a few details emerged from his dry, terrified lips. Words sobbed in self-loathing:

"She went with our daughter to her mother's. He stayed with me."

"And would it have made a difference if you'd decided

differently?" she had gently asked him.

The grief refused his answer.

The genealogist told them that a large contingent of army reserves was sent to Grodno. It was a town in the north-east of Poland that'd had a gradual build-up of soldiers in the mid-1930s as the Poles suspected the Russians of planning another attack. With the sudden German onslaught, those troops were dispatched eastwards and the gaps in Grodno were filled with volunteers, with police and young Girl Guides and Scouts.

Perhaps Jozef was sent there as a reserve officer? Perhaps he fled there with his son as a refugee when the defence of Warsaw seemed impossible? Perhaps he went there because his brother was already a resident there and there was nowhere else to run?

Whatever the reason, the decision had darkened his eyes, furrowed his brow and made him into the serious man she had fallen in love with.

It had made him into him.

Skierniewice/Grodno, POLAND, 1939

My darling husband,

I would write that you are not to worry about me and Marysia, but I know that is an instruction you could never bring yourself to obey. Instead, I shall tell you that Marysia is the centre of attention in my mother's house. It is almost as if the summer has come again this year and the family are together again… were it not for Arja's absence and you, of course.

You are not to send him here. I know what you must be thinking but my mind is quite made up on that. He shall be better off where he is – with you.

As for us? My elderly mother with her liquor store? Lenia with her baby? Me and little Marysia?

Hardly a threat to the might of the German army!
We shall be fine. I promise.
Keep well, my darling.
Rozia

***

Arja didn't say a word on the train journey from Warsaw to Grodno. He sat next to his father in total silence as Szyja stared blankly at the outline of his son's thin legs through the woollen trousers Rozia had bought him a few months previously.

"He's grown so much, Szyja!" He remembered his wife reaching up and ruffling their son's hair as he towered above her. "It won't be long until he'll need to start shaving. Where has the time gone?"

Yes, where had it gone? That time, so carefree. In every face he saw the unmistakeable sight of subdued fear. Where businessmen had once crammed into the train's corridors, there were now nothing but soldiers. Fresh-faced in their smart uniforms staring blankly at nothing as the gentle movement of the train rocked them this way and that.

My God, what was to become of them all?

***

"Well, you look like shit!" Morduch, Szyja's brother, met them at the station in Grodno and gripped their hands in welcome.

The comment was not mirrored by any sort of smile. The world had changed, their lives had changed.

"I left them." Szyja shrugged simply, allowing himself an uncharacteristic moment of hopelessness that came from deep within his soul. Even he was surprised at the depths of his despair.

"You did what you had to." Morduch shrugged. It was said quickly and without emotion. The events in the world were too overwhelming to show surprise at the actions of mere individuals. "You're no good to them dead."

So people kept telling him.

After the chaos in Warsaw, he half-expected some sort of peace in this eastern city but the *Luftwaffe* had even managed to reach here. The skyline still vomited smoke where the ammunition stores and factories had been. At least there were no tanks. Only the craters, dug in anticipation of their arrival, amongst the pleasant fields and allotments west of the Neman River.

Morduch's apartment, which was also home to Morduch's wife and sons, was small but comfortable, offering a view over the barren railway tracks which brought the refugees westwards, fleeing the Nazis in the east. The Jews here duly prayed in the city's synagogues. Prayed that the horrors the refugees brought with them, would not reach them here, whilst simultaneously disbelieving the accounts all the same.

There was news of a gathering of forces on the Russian border, carefully censored messages from the Soviets hinting at a call to arms to 'assist their Polish cousins'. Would the Poles of Grodno believe such an old foe? In response, the general commanding the Polish forces in Grodno fled. So did the mayor.

On 17th September the Russians entered Poland

from the east, like an actor entering the stage whilst the Germans held the audience's attention elsewhere. Within days, the Russian tanks were harassing the city's edges. If only they had prepared those trenches to the east of the city rather than the west, the earth would have swallowed up a few of those tanks and allowed the residents a brief respite of time.

"What do we do?"

Morduch's question lay heavily over the last of the vodka he had splashed into his brother's cup as they discussed their choices. As if choice came into it! There was only one answer.

"We join the fight." Szyja shrugged.

The defence of Grodno between 20th and 22nd September 1939 was conducted mostly by the reserves, the police and the young Girl Guides and Scouts. Rather than teach his son the intricacies of equations and geometry, Szyja found himself teaching him how to prepare and throw a Molotov cocktail at a T-26 light infantry tank.

For a while, it seemed to be working.

Abandoned burnt-out tanks lay haphazardly around the war-torn city in the streets that only a few months ago had been full of markets, children walking to school and the nondescript business of life. It became guerrilla warfare. Dirty, merciless, chaotic warfare.

Szyja continued to write to his wife when he could. He was well. Arja was well. She had no need to worry whilst she waited at her mother's house in a town now overrun with Germans. She was careful with what she wrote back but the sentiment was there. Life was continuing as normal, except it wasn't normal. Blue, six-sided stars against a backdrop of white were added to their coats, marking them out as different. Different from what? They rarely attended the synagogue these days; their lives were almost identical to any other Pole. Living, breathing human beings categorised by the beliefs and traditions of their ancestors. All the same underneath.

The Jews of Skierniewice were being herded together, neatly placed into a small section of the city 'for their own safety'. That was what the Germans had said. Szyja thought of his wife and child sharing his mother-in-law's house with his sister-in-law and her tiny baby and another niece. At least their residence was already within the confinement of the designated Jewish area. "*The shop is still open so we are fine for money*," Rozia's pen sought to reassure her husband. "*Everyone still has a taste for liquor. Especially the Germans.*"

Harlesden, ENGLAND, 1960

It was a few weeks before Christmas. The air was cold and bitter. People hurried down the pavements not wishing to remain long in the frost-filled streets. It was a busy few weeks of belt orders as the fashionable started to turn their thoughts to Christmas and the excesses the season would bring. Mary and Jozef were working flat out. They now employed over a dozen outworkers to assist them with the orders that came thick and fast. The whole family became involved in the sticking and the gluing and the fixing and the pressing. Their living room was cluttered with extra orders that would soon be shifted so that the space they occupied could be filled by the Christmas tree, the decorations and the presents they would all enjoy.

Mary felt lightheaded and tranquil as she held Jozef's arm. They were walking home after a night playing bridge at their friends, the Tippelts', house. It had been a good night with old friends. The wine had flowed, they had been plied with food and the conversation had come easily; an evening that satisfied both the soul and the belly. They huddled together weaving in and out of the streets they knew so well, their conversation switching between English, French and Arabic as naturally as the weather.

"Next year, we shall retire and spend every night playing bridge," Jozef decided, in a serious tone but with a smile on his face.

"As long as it's not for money. We may end up bankrupt otherwise!"

"As long as my stomach is full, I don't care."

A playful tap on his shoulder in gentle reprimand and they reached their house and their sleeping children within. Jozef collapsed that night into bed. His fuzzy head had forgotten the need to lay his day clothes out onto the chair next to him in preparation for whatever the night would bring. He was satisfied enough to crawl into the soft sheets and relax into a sleep induced by wine and a comforting arm around his wife. The night terrors were far away, back in a war that was nearly twenty years old.

He awoke in a hospital bed, his wife of fourteen years by his side, tearful, worried. It was a lesson in preparedness, and he had let his guard down. Just because there were no clothes laid out beside the bed, no escape route from the nightmares that reached out and grabbed him when he was least expecting it. This heart attack had come as a shock for both of them. Jozef's health of late had been good. He had been almost free of the breathlessness that had developed since his last tumble in health. He had almost found himself back with the energy and drive of his youth. Yet this latest heart attack had hit him hard when he was at his least guarded. His complacency had nearly killed him.

"If that wasn't a sign that we should retire, I don't know what is." Jozef tried to smile.

She held his hand, which was weak and pale. Lines of age bunched up in wrinkles across his skin where the diseased veins criss-crossed towards his fingers.

"You're not going back to work," Mary decided for them both.

"Are you angry with me?"

"No," she tutted. "Of course not, why would I be?"

"Because I almost left you."

"Almost but not quite yet. I'd never forgive you if you did."

"That's settled then."

"What is?"

"Our retirement. You and me. Perhaps we should go to France after all."

She allowed herself a smile.

"A chateau in the country. Wine on the veranda whilst our grandchildren play amongst the grapevines far below?"

"Of course. I already have the tickets."

"Good. We need to be prepared."

"Always best to be prepared."

The smile stayed on his lips as he gently fell asleep. Her hand in his and his hand in hers.

Grodno,
POLAND (now in modern-day BELARUS),
1939/1940

Grodno succumbed to the Russian invasion on 22nd
September 1939. There was only so long that single-shot
rifles and bottles of turpentine could ward off the tanks
that kept on coming. In Morduch's flat on Jagiellonska
Street, Szyja made his son and nephews strip to their pants
and burn their uniform that identified them as Scouts. A
few hours before, Morduch's wife had returned home in a
panic. She had been searching for what food supplies she
could amongst the stores covered in rubble in the market
square when she had witnessed a column of Scouts being
marched at the run by a group of Russians with fixed
bayonets.

"They were just boys, only boys!" she sobbed into her
husband's shoulder. A group of boys with terrified eyes

all led to their deaths in a hail of bullets. The mothers' screams had carried with her all the way home. Arja and his cousins stood shivering as the khaki shirts and black ties disappeared into the flames.

"What now?" Morduch raised his hands in despair.

For now, nothing.

A relative peace descended on the city amongst the burnt-out tanks, the crumpled buildings and empty shops. Students returned to school and everyone returned to work. Szyja remained uneasy. The news from the west was harrowing and his days were absorbed with thoughts of Rozia in the middle of it all. More refugees staggered out of the train station with barely any luggage. At first, he thought this was the speed with which they had fled their homes, but he later found out that it was because most of their possessions remained in the no-man's land between the Germans and the Russians, having been first looted by the Nazis and then afterwards by the Poles.

He had to find a job. This became the key to his survival. There was no place in the Soviet system for those who were unemployed. Everyone worked. If you didn't, the Russians found you work deep in the heart of Mother Russia and from there, there was no going back.

As a carpenter, Morduch had the right hands for socialism. Good solid, working hands, completely at odds with Szyja's soft intellectual fingers that had spent his working days deep in the recesses of books.

Soon a new fear gripped the residents of Grodno. Whilst the Germans categorised the people they conquered into two groups (the Jews and the non-Jews), the Russians had their lists. These were the less-desirables, the ones to be held with suspicion as assumed enemies of socialism: lawyers, doctors, intellectuals, bourgeoisie, the new refugees from German-held Poland. They were all ear-marked as targets of correction long before the Russians stepped foot on Polish soil.

The cleansing started.

In the early hours of the morning when the sun had yet to burn their fears away, the residents of Grodno were awakened by the hammering of rifle butts on their doors. The occupants were dragged from their beds whilst their names were checked against the lists. Half an hour to pack before sending them to God knows where. Why bother with the lists when it was well known that if the names the Russians sought were not in the beds they ransacked, they took the occupants anyway? Anything to make up the quotas demanded by Moscow.

"Can't sleep?"

Morduch hadn't been to bed. His clothes were still tainted by the tiny strands of sawdust from his daily trade.

"No. You?"

"It's those damned Russians. They make so much noise." The purges had been getting closer to where they lived as the nights wore on. The noise was unsettling in its regularity.

"You know I can't continue to stay here."

The words that had been rolling around Szyja's head now tumbled out of his mouth into the void that they both had been afraid to acknowledge.

"Arja must stay with us," Morduch decided.

It was an impossible decision. Staying here amongst the Russians was dangerous but being on the run was even more so.

"Thank you. I couldn't… if… if anything…"

Morduch held up a hand to stop any further words. They weren't needed. The words they kept hidden inside tired minds were far more telling. Despite the protestations from the fleeing Polish government, their insistence that, with the British and the French now involved in the war, it would only be a matter of time, they all knew where this was heading.

***

He didn't have much to pack. In the light of the day, amongst the ruined allotments where the craters still waited for the German tanks that never came, he buried his papers: the official documents that portrayed his pre-war profession, the fact that he was a refugee and his rank as an officer in the reserves. In that hole went his identity and his name. He would no longer go by the name of *Szyja*. He would now be known as *Jozef* – an ordinary name plucked out of the air in desperation. If he was captured by the Russians, it would be better to be just an ordinary Pole. If he was captured by the Nazis… Well, it would be better to be anything but Jewish.

He buried the lot. Buried them in his only act of defiance against a world he couldn't control. There was the possibility of returning someday; returning to pick up his life where he had left it, in the darkness of the muddy earth, ready to pop up like the flowers of spring.

"Where will you go?" It was Arja's tears this time. Big boyish tears that cascaded unheeded down his sunken cheeks.

"Best you don't know." The truth was he wasn't even sure himself.

"And what am I to do?"

"Do?" Szyja asked, trying to keep his voice from breaking. "You keep your head down; you do what your uncle says and you keep on studying. There's no better gift than the gift of learning."

"You will come back, won't you?"

Szyja's hand pulled the back of his son's neck so that their forehead's touched. So warm. He closed his eyes. A Warsaw spring. The sound of the trams with their gentle rhythm, the pedlars with their wares in open suitcases. The children in the school on Nowolipki Street with their eager eyes and fresh faces. The smell of the *Cholent* stew simmering on the stove for hour upon hour so that by lunchtime on Shabbat all of their mouths were salivating in anticipation.

He broke away and planted a kiss on Arja's forehead. Morduch saw him to the door.

"Mother had the right idea getting out when she did."

A nod of agreement. When they had gathered together to see their mother off on her long journey to Johannesburg, there had been feasting and dancing and a happiness for better things to come. There had been none of that this time.

"I'll write when I get…" Szyja thought hard. "I'll write when I'm settled."

Another nod but this time they both knew that it was an empty promise. Szyja could not write for fear of giving away his hiding place and who knew when he'd be safe enough to enjoy the freedom of writing to let his family know he was safe.

He left no trace of his presence in the home he had found shelter in for the last few months. No indication that he had ever been there, taking with him everything he had arrived in – except his son. A firm shake of his brother's hand by the rear entrance to the flats and he slipped away into the shadows on a warm summer's afternoon. He was on his own. No family to accompany him to whatever lay ahead. Just another goodbye.

Life seemed to be full of goodbyes these days.

Harlesden, ENGLAND, 1960

Jozef's health wasn't improving. An overnight's stay in the hospital turned into a week, which then turned into two. Mary wrote to her mother and sister. She yearned to speak to them. Her mother's voice would bring her home to Alexandria, to the comfort of a mother's love. But there was no easy way to connect with them. They didn't have telephones. She would have to rely on the slow passage of her hurried letters and wait for the comfort of a few scratched notes in return. Only her mother could understand her fear. The last years of Hawash's life came back to haunt his daughter and now, Mary could feel the understanding Zakia warned her she would come to know. But the immeasurable pain was more acute. She knew she loved Jozef in a way that Zakia had never felt towards her own husband.

But her mother was too far away...

No, there was nothing left to do but persevere until Jozef was well enough to come home. That was the only thing that could be done.

Their Polish friends rallied round. In the absence of their regular nights playing bridge, they busied themselves cooking extra meals that would be left on the Bekers' doorstep. Warm, hearty meals of stews and sweet cakes designed to comfort and calm. A small gesture in a world that seemed to be breaking down all around her.

She carried on with the belt-making business, relying more and more on the outworkers that had become their friends over time. Eric was there. He popped round in between his shifts and even during his shifts when time would allow. He brought her shopping when it was needed and a friendly ear when she needed it the most.

Jozef came home after two weeks. The doctors were not hopeful but they both felt he would be better off at home in familiar surroundings and with the help of family and friends. For a time, these home comforts rallied him and he was able to sit up and read in bed. A few paragraphs at a time but the pleasure of absorbing those words on the page put a smile on his tired lips and Mary was happy. Margarita went back and forth to the library each Saturday and added to the pile that grew on his bedside table. He started learning Swedish to pass the time. Even with his fading health, he had not lost his love of learning and, in particular, his love of languages.

Mary slept fitfully next to him, waking in the night to check he was still breathing, fearful that she could lose him if she wasn't vigilant. She envied the peaceful way the covers rose and fell over his chest, rhythmically and steadily, his hands clasped over the covers. She was not ready yet. Neither was he. Their time together had been steadily leading to a crescendo of happiness that she felt they had not yet reached. *We're always working too hard*, Jozef would say. *No time to be still and just be.*

He died on 21st December 1960.

Passed away in his sleep.

She found him peaceful yet gone, his hands still clasped over the covers. The undertakers took him with gloved hands, carefully, respectfully. Their breath fogged up the air in front of them as they carried him on a stretcher down the stairs and out to the blacked-out van that reminded her too much of Eric's. Mary couldn't help comparing the undertakers' warm, steaming bodies to that of the body shrouded on the stretcher between them.

The world continued.

The Christmas lights twinkled on Oxford Street (a tradition that had come into practice only a year before). The butchers were starting to stock the Christmas turkeys ready for the Christmas Eve rush. The markets were full of trinkets for the stockings hung in anticipation on the mantelpiece.

Mary didn't have anything to wear to the funeral. Her wardrobe was full of greens, pale pinks and mauves but no black to shroud her skin to reflect the feelings of her soul beneath.

"Are we not having a turkey this year?"

Henry's eyes were wide with innocence. He'd only just turned nine and already lost his father. She reprimanded herself for wallowing in her own self-pity. She had a family to support. It was Christmas Eve. *Treat yourself. What good is this doing to you all?*

She took the children to Shepherd's Bush Market and, with the feeling of Jozef by her side, she bought the biggest turkey she could find. A turkey and a tree that would fit perfectly in the corner of the living room in that space by Jozef's empty chair and the fireplace. The chair he liked to sit in with a glass of Krupnik listening to Max Bygraves on the gramophone with that contented smile lifting up the corners of his cheeks.

She did Jozef's job of putting up the small flower-shaped lights on the prickly branches and tried hard not to cry. They dressed the tree with baubles of bright pinks, purples and blues and then placed the presents the family had prepared weeks ago on the floor beside it. Small packages all wrapped in brown paper and string with carefully written labels so that they all had something to open as the music continued on the record player. It was a dull and muted atmosphere with none of the joy of the previous years.

Margarita handed her mother the last remaining present from underneath the tree; a soft package that crinkled as she held it. She stared at the label that faced her. *To Mary, Happy Christmas, Love from Jozef.*

"Open it," Margarita urged her.

She couldn't. Her hands were stiff. Reluctant.

The children helped her carefully unfold the paper and untie the string. A package in tissue paper flopped onto her knees. She held it up against the muted lights of the tree. A simple yet elegant velvet shift dress all in black that finished just above the knee with slimline sleeves and a rounded neckline.

Oh, Jozef. My Jozef…

PART THREE

Warsaw, POLAND, 2005

I found out what happened to your brother today. Nothing of your son, but your brother and the two nephews...

Mary felt the need to tell him, to involve Jozef on this journey of which he could not be a part. Had he known about the fate of Morduch and his two beautiful nephews? He had never said, never bothered her with the details. He had known they were dead, but had he ever filled in the gaps of the where and how? Perhaps the knowledge was more painful than the silence and that was why he had chosen to leave the details blank.

"They were shot in the street sometime in 1941," the genealogist had told her, her mouth drawn in a fine line of apology. "Shot by the Germans once they'd pushed back the Russians under Operation Barbarossa."

The facts stared emotionless at her from the innocent pieces of paper lying amongst the coffee and sour-cream cakes.

"Why?"

A shrug reflected the matter-of-fact attitude that came from researching too many tragedies. What was one more in the whole scheme of things?

"Because they were Jewish," the apologetic reply.

No. Both you and I know, Jozef, that they were far more than that.

Somewhere in Russia, 1940

Dear Rozia,

A short note, I am sorry for my scrawl but I find myself with little time and too much to say. You must not worry about me for I am well. I am on a train but I do not know where it is heading. Somewhere eastwards no doubt. One of my companions thought we may have entered Kazakhstan yesterday but…

The guards treat us well.

I have my coat and boots but would be grateful of some more gloves and possibly a better hat. When we have reached our destination, I will write to you again to let you know the address. There is already concern for the cold and we have not yet reached winter.

It is difficult not knowing how you are, how you all are. The news we get from the Russians is scarce…

Your mother, is she well? And Lenia's little baby?
Please write soon. When you can. News from you is all I crave.
Hugs to Marysia and to you, my darling,
Your loving husband

He couldn't bring himself to ask after Arja. Morduch had promised to get word to her that their son was safe and he had to assume she had received the news by now. He worried about the Russian censors too much. Worried that even a hint of a family member behind Russian lines would mean a visit in the dead of night, an empty bed and another passenger on this train of misery. No, better to stay ignorant and hope for the best; protect his family as much as he could across the growing miles of their forced separation. He would have prayed like a good Jewish boy, but any religious thoughts had been burnt out of him.

There was no God.

How could there be?

Alexandria, EGYPT, 1940

Jean, Alice's fiancé, was killed when the submarine he was in was torpedoed. The news came in a letter from his mother, which took two weeks to reach Alexandria from Jean's hometown in France. The war, which had started in a faraway country in Europe where the sun didn't shine so much, had now reached them. Its tentacled fronds of destruction were creeping over the world and affecting all those in it.

The British presence in Egypt, and in Alexandria in particular, was on the increase. The Allies feared for the supply chains of oil and goods via the Suez Canal and King Farouk was worried by the Italian presence in North Africa and what might happen to his borders.

Alice was devastated. Mary held her in her arms, the

letter with its black news dangling limply from Alice's numb fingers. In the space of a year, both sisters had lost the men they had loved and their dreams of settling in France. Zaki, intelligent and hardworking Zaki, had finished his university degree in engineering with a first and their mother revelled in her son's achievement whilst her two daughters wept.

Work was increasingly arduous and tough with little pay to redeem it. A friend of Mary's suggested that she apply for a position at a military hospital just outside of Alexandria called L'Hôpital Anglo-Suisse. The pay was better there and, being a military hospital, there was that unfounded assumption that she would be better looked after. Whilst her sister carried on at the Catholic hospital, Mary transferred out in the summer of 1940.

The change was a shock.

She saw the effects of war first-hand; missing limbs, burns that covered grown men from head to foot as they cried pitifully for their mothers from the soft mattresses that exacerbated their painful sores. Their minds turned to madness.

Man's inhumanity to man.

She patched up their wounds and helped the doctors sew them back together, much like the dolls she had repaired in childhood. Patched-up dolls held together by thread to play once more. The soldiers returned back to the fight in the desert and she returned to her mother's flat, numb and quiet, trying to blot out their mangled bodies and their tortured souls. As the casualties rolled in, her heart hardened. Hardened, but not hard enough. The stories of the men and the lives they longed to return to before the guns had started, touched her soul and she pitied them and cried for them and cursed herself for it.

Gabriel was a young Frenchman of twenty. Just three years younger than herself. A pale boy with an anxious look in his eye and perspiration on his upper lip where a gentleman's moustache should have been. He sought out her kindness and gripped her hand as she fussed over his bed sheets and held a glass of water to his parched lips. He had no legs. He'd left them on the sandy battlefield along with most of his friends. His war was over but so was any hope of returning to his mother and the country he was fighting for.

Life was so fragile. So precarious.

She refused to disentangle herself from his grasp. It didn't seem right to leave the dying alone.

He had a locket that he'd worn around his neck and his fumbling fingers showed her the picture inside of his mother: a proud woman with strong cheekbones and a fierce but kindly smile. He insisted Mary keep it. He knew what was waiting for him and he'd have no need for the trinket there. It only remained for him to ensure that this treasured possession would not get lost.

He died during the night whilst she was sleeping at home. He was too weak to scream. She, in turn, lay still, wrapped up in the exhaustion from another draining shift. She'd placed the locket by her bedside. When she'd learnt the news of his death, she felt guilty for that. It didn't seem right that the object he had held so dear lay discarded on that drab wooden table whilst he fought for breath. She immediately paid for the small package's return to his mother in France with a note that aimed to allay her fears of her son's last moments. A little lie as one last favour to the dead.

"I don't think I can continue working there," she confided in her friend Tamile over coffee one afternoon in the Ramleh district of a city distanced from the horrors. "The patients… to hear their stories…"

"You take it too much to heart. It's a job. You can only do the best you can. Try not to get involved."

"That's easier said than done…"

"You know," Tamile thought out loud, "they are crying out for nurses back at L'Hôpital Européen d'Alexandrie. Come back and join us. It'll be like old times!"

She was back again, busying herself in A&E and handing the instruments to the doctors in the operating theatres. Back with old friends and her sister in a familiar environment where the patients were just patients and she didn't have the time to become involved in their stories. This life suited her better even though it remained physically just as hard.

"There is no break!" Eva complained, kicking off her shoes in the nurse's room after a morning of rushing from one patient to the next. "The same days, week in, week out. If only we could take some holiday, my feet wouldn't end up so sore!"

There was no such thing as a paid holiday for nurses in Egypt. Any amount of time off, even for a doctor's or dentist's appointment, had to be taken unpaid. Mary had taken just two weeks off in the last two years to be with her family in Luxor and even then, she'd had to continue her side business of repairing uniforms during her stay to ensure she had enough money to share with her mother at the end of the month. There must be a better way to live than this.

"Why don't you start a union?" Vincente was a friend from her teaching years at L'Orphelinat de la Miséricorde. They met one evening when the heat of the day was starting to cool and the lights of the vibrant Alexandria twinkled invitingly to the young, enticing them out with thoughts of the night to come.

"A union?" Mary hadn't heard of such a thing.

"It's where a group of you get together with a spokesperson to ensure your concerns are heard by your employer. There is surely more power in numbers! You know, Mary, if there's to be a spokesperson for such a group, it should be you."

"Me!" She thought of Sister Angelique with her fierce reputation and the thought of standing in front of her demanding the rights of her fellow nurses. "Why me?!"

"Because you have guts, Mary," Vincente said simply, matter-of-factly. "You are good with people and you have the benefit of instinct. I surely can't think of any other better candidate."

She laughed nervously, unable to believe her friend, but stopped when she saw she was serious.

"If you want something badly, Mary," Vincente continued, "you just have to go ahead and do it yourself."

An idea had been planted in her head that manifested itself into action, which was surely Vincente's intention. Over breakfast in the staff canteen, before the start of their shift, Mary explained her plan to the rest of the nurses. It was agreed that it was an excellent idea and they looked at each other with that expression of wonder as to why they hadn't thought of it before.

Each nurse contributed a few piastres from their monthly wage and Mary collated it with a system whereby each nurse could have the same amount of time off a year and receive a substitute pay. Buoyed by their success, they urged Mary to act as their champion in liaising with the administration, doctors and senior nurses at the hospital. There were other changes in the workplace that also needed addressing. The number of breaks the nurses received between their shifts on the wards. The number of staff on a ward at any one time.

She found herself standing in the Matron's office, feeling as if she was twelve again, standing up to Maman Ancette, preparing herself for the consequences of another misdemeanour. Only this time, she wasn't twelve. She was an adult now. And not only that, but she had the hopes of the rest of the nurses balancing on her shoulders.

"What is it you want, Mary Goued?"

"I represent the nurses, Matron."

The eyebrows of her superior rose above the level of her glasses and the pen was quietly returned to the inkpot.

"You do?"

Mary's cheeks flushed red before she collected herself.

"Yes," she said firmly. "There are some things that need addressing. We wish to improve our situation for the benefit of the hospital."

"Oh?"

The matron's question wasn't said with the challenge she thought it might initiate. She felt buoyed despite the churning feelings inside her.

"A week's paid holiday for each nurse," the words tumbled out, bouncing around on the whitewashed walls. "Each year," she added.

The matron seemed surprised but not angry. Mary felt it best to leave the other demands until later. There was a tense silence before a slight nod of her head and her hand picked up her pen again.

"I shall take your concerns to the administrators."

And that was that. There was an anxious wait over the next few days. Mary feared she had overstepped the mark but the smiles and nods from the other nurses kept her spirits up. She was called back into the same office the following Thursday.

"One week with 75% pay," the matron stated before she'd had a chance to catch her breath. "But only after the first year of full service."

Mary caught herself before her jaw could drop. Not quite what she had asked for but more of a concession then she was anticipating. The nurses were ecstatic. Vincente had been right, there was power in numbers.

A month later and Mary plucked up the courage to ask the matron for her first paid week off work. There she was, standing back in that same office with its plain walls and immaculately tidy furniture. But her spirits were raised this time.

"I wish to take next week off."

The matron raised an incredulous eyebrow.

"The whole of next week?"

"Yes."

"And what will you do with yourself with a whole week off?" The matron seemed to be horrified at the prospect of there being any pleasure in life outside of their place of work. She lived the hospital, lived and breathed its bleach-smelling corridors.

"Oh, I'm not sure, Matron." The question surprised her.

A sharp noise indicated her disapproval and her superior went on to look at the paperwork that was piling up on her desk through her spectacled eyes.

"Very well."

Mary spent the week redecorating her mother's flat. The paintbrush flew lightly across the walls as she sang to herself in the knowledge that she was being paid for her time off and it was she who had made it this way.

Warsaw, POLAND, 2005

Standing in the leafy Nowolipki Street in Warsaw amongst the orange and grey blocks of flat with bicycles perched on the balconies, it was hard to picture the horrors of the Warsaw Ghetto. The school where Jozef had taught, the apartment where he and Rozia had lived were all gone. Mary understood now why he insisted on never returning. It was the same reason why her own short holiday to Alexandria back in the eighties had been such a disaster.

Things are never as you remembered them to be. The cruelty of time and its constant changes have such a devastating effect on our memories.

Instead, she felt that she was standing for him on the street that he used to know, near the site of his last Polish residence. Standing where he couldn't be.

Rozia had returned to Warsaw just before the Skierniewice Ghetto had been cleared. Returned with her daughter to the flat where they had lived along with her mother, two of her sisters and two of their nieces. The flat that was comfortable enough for the four of them before the war now housed their extended family of seven. But not just them. A family of strangers had also been given space in their apartment.

How cramped it must have been for all those people!

And then what?

Mary had seen pictures of the barbed wire, seen the high walls that had been erected, looking out of place in the black and white photographs of the crowded streets. All those people with stars pinned to their jackets forced into a small area of the city and Jozef's apartment and his wife and child trapped inside it.

Had he known then? As he sat on that train on that long hellish journey northwards, had he known where his family now found themselves? And Rozia? At home, in a place where she should have felt safe, had she known?

How did you cope, Jozef? Cope with all those years of not knowing...

Arkhangelsk Oblast, RUSSIA, 1940

It took them well over a week to reach their final destination by train through the depths of northern Russia. A train full of families of men, women and children. It was the height of summer and the mosquitos hit them with more force than the Russian troops ever could as they stepped off the carriages onto Soviet land. Jozef had been captured fleeing northwards in a bid to outrun the Russians and their efforts to scoop up all the 'undesirables'. It helped that he spoke the language fluently. The power of words could not be overstated when one had to bargain for one's own life. He was just another Pole. There would be some use for him yet.

He wasn't actually sure where he was, but with some preliminary enquiries amongst the other inmates, he gathered it to be somewhere in the Arkhangelsk region of Northern Russia. So very far away from home. There was nothing but woods here. Great pine forests that harboured the flies in the summer and bristled with the biting cold of the north winds and endless snow in the winter. The soldiers herded them into the wooden log buildings that offered little protection whatever the Russian weather. They counted them and counted them again. They had to ensure their quota was still valid.

The crimes of this pathetic mass of people, the reason for their banishment to this godforsaken place, was their beliefs, their jobs or just suspicion of their feelings towards socialism. For some it was mere association. All sentenced to labour in the vast expanses of the Russian countryside working in logging, farming cotton or in the mines. The camp that Jozef found himself in revolved around the logging industry. On meagre rations that would barely keep a fly alive, they were to cut down the trees by hand and prep them before their final journey into the depths of Mother Russia. Trees for houses, trees for bridges, trees for fuel, trees helping the war effort. Life expectancy was just a few months. The lack of food, the harsh winters and the endless toil was too much for any man. They were all just waiting for the alleviation of death to free them from this place. Nowhere to run – the nearest town was miles away. Nature would kill you even if the camp didn't.

Jozef found himself billeted with a young family with a sickly child who cried all night. They fashioned a wall between them using a threadbare curtain. The initial primary concern had been preservation of modesty but that soon came to be the least of their worries. What did it matter what they looked like when they were all just skin and bone underneath?

They were given a straw mattress each with one woollen blanket that harboured the lice and flies that ate you alive when you tried to sleep. There was no pillow. Jozef lay on that hard, lumpy bed that first night fully clothed, listening to the crying child and praying for sleep to overtake him.

At 4am in the morning they were woken and counted. A lengthy affair in the cool of the morning, swaying figures fatigued through lack of sleep all standing in zombie rows as the soldiers paced up and down with clipboards. Counting and re-counting. Jozef could see the nervousness with which they strode through the pathetic crowd of prisoners. It would be on their heads if the numbers didn't tally. The prisoners and the soldiers seemed to be aligned in their fear of that unseen authority that held power over them all and had the final say over life and death. There was always someone more in charge, more deadly in his socialist beliefs.

"Why must we stand for so long…"

"You get used to it, Comrade," the man to his left replied.

That was another thing he couldn't understand. The endless reference to each other as *comrade*; prisoner to prisoner, guard to guard, guard to prisoner and vice versa; as if all this mutual suffering was an essential part of the socialist state. Russia needed suffering to exist. Red, the colour of blood, the colour of communism.

He thought of nothing but his family that day. As they trudged in line to receive the watered-down coffee and stale bread for breakfast, he thought of Rozia cooking at the stove, a smile on her face and her hair pinned back. The smell of her was as close to him here as the smell of pine in the forests that dominated their waking hours. As they dragged their weary feet further through the dense trees, he thought of his walks in the woods to find mushrooms with Arja, the boy jumping and running by his side with the boundless energy of the young. Smiling, laughing, running. As he lay in bed, restless in his sleep, he thought of Marysia curled up on his lap with the gramophone playing in the corner. Home, sweet home. Thousands of miles away from here. A lifetime away.

He would not give up hope of returning there. Whether it took a year or two or even longer. That morsel of hope would keep him going; keep the frost in the winters from biting off his fingers and toes and keep the disease and starvation from his wasting frame.

When we have nothing, there is nothing left to do but hope.

Alexandria, EGYPT, 1941

Home for Mary was hot and vibrant. The cloud of war was still far off in the desert. Near enough to warrant daily reports in the *Al-Ahram* of the fighting along Egypt's borders, but not near enough to warrant panic in Alexandria's streets. There were more soldiers; that was very much evident. Their eyes were bright with wonder as they sampled a world they would otherwise never have seen. British, Australian, New Zealanders, French. The port was full of Allied ships and the natural harbour occasionally rocked with the mines that exploded far offshore, spraying metal and the twisted guts of the navy across the Mediterranean Sea.

There was talk of a German man named Rommel and his tanks which burned through Libyan soil. Mary thought of the casualties lining up in those military hospitals on the outskirts of the city. Lines upon lines of stretchers carrying the wounded, the diseased, the dying. Her friends and family had not seen what she had seen and she was thankful for it. That image remained in the sands and hospitals of the desert and she tried hard to keep it that way.

She was making a name for herself at the Catholic hospital where she worked; a tireless worker with a keen sense of what injustice was and a willing pair of hands to comfort those that needed it. She remembered a time when she had walked the hospital corridors unnoticed and invisible to the doctors and the consultants that hurried this way and that with their air of mysticism. Now she would receive a respectful nod here and a kind word there. The hospital was as much part of her blood as the blood that was spilled from the patients she attended to.

There had been no one since Lucian. Her life had settled into a routine which suited her. A routine of work, of friends, of quiet evenings playing cards with her mother in their flat on Harah Mussa. They talked about the past, the future, but never about the man that had caused the hardships of earlier years. Hawash, Mary's father, was a distant memory who stayed locked up in her mind with his ruddy complexion and pleasing smile; a fleeting thought of comfort that she couldn't share with anyone else. Her mother would not have listened. Zakia's memory of him was full of pain and sorrow; of a life misjudged, misled.

Then he turned up at Mary's place of work one day in May. Or rather, that bitter memory of his death and the hardships it caused turned up at the hospital asking for help that was undeserved. Mary had been seeing to the patients in the dispensary. It was unusually busy with no place left to stand in the waiting room. Tempers were running high as relatives sought assistance for their loved ones from one complaint or another. She had no time to finish her break, no time to sit and rest her legs, which throbbed and ached from the constant rushing.

Her uncle, Goued, caught her arm as she helped her next patient towards the consulting area. She hadn't seen him at first. The waiting room was a mass of humankind that melded into one melting pot of illness that she was trying to alleviate. She had no time that day to lose herself in the stories of the injured. She just saw the daunting task of fixing people as quickly as possible.

Goued had grown older over the years. The onslaught of time had faded his physical similarities with her father. Hawash was still stuck in the image of youth whilst Goued had had the privilege of sauntering through the passage of time.

She withdrew her arm, irritated and annoyed.

"What is it?"

He frowned, mistaking her frosty question with a lack of recollection as to who he was.

"It's your uncle, Goued."

"I know who you are. What is it you want?"

He was no longer the tall, daunting figure of her childhood. She was no longer the little girl afraid of her elders and the fear they created.

He fumbled with his words, his reassurance gone. She knew his predicament had exposed his vulnerability and the coolness of her reception exploited that.

"My son, your cousin." He stepped back, his arm pointing limply at a man she had once known as a young boy who had taunted her appearance, her mended clothes, her faded shoes. He was slumped in a chair, shivering despite the heat. "He is unwell and needs medicine."

"He'll have to wait."

She almost mirrored her uncle's height. Where had the time gone? The giant that had haunted her through her mother's degradation had vanished. He'd almost become a figment of her childhood imagination.

"But Mary…"

"*Nurse*," she had the pleasure of correcting him.

"Nurse." The word didn't sit right on his tongue. "My son is unwell and needs assistance."

"Everyone here needs assistance," she snapped, "why would you think you have the right to be first in the queue?"

She didn't allow him time to answer, her feet already taking her sharply away. Clip clop down the corridor. She imagined a small girl, picking up the pieces of her mother's despair. She remembered her mother's pleas for assistance even though she knew it wouldn't come. Not from a man like that.

He asked for her mother's current address. It was asked awkwardly as his hand hesitated to take the medicine the doctor had prescribed. His son was one of the last patients to be seen in the morning clinic and Mary wanted to get back home for lunch. She felt a betrayal of her mother's trust that she had had to help such a man. She wanted to get back home to make it up to her.

"Why would I give you her address?"

"I…" A shrug of the shoulders and a flush of red in his cheeks. Was he trying to match her father's complexion?

"You were never there to help her. She asked you for help and you didn't give her any. And yet, here you are asking for help for your son and I have helped you, only because my job dictates that I must."

She left him standing there, her face hot with indignation. She had missed the tram she'd wanted to catch to get her back home for lunch. She walked the rest of the way with her soles hurting from being on her feet for so long and her pride knocked by the chance meeting with her uncle.

There, outside their small apartment on the dusty street of an Alexandrian side road, was her mother's cart. She stopped to notice how worn the wheels were, the wood cracked and chipped. It had always been a monstrous thing, but now seemed small and pitiful. How many years had her mother dragged that thing around? A burden she alone had had to bear for the sake of her children and the lack of a husband to provide for her.

She wanted to throw her arms around her, suddenly overcome by guilt and a thankfulness she couldn't hope to convey. But her mother was sleeping soundly in the comfort of her chair, her slender neck tilted to one side as her chest rose and fell, still shrouded in the dark clothes of mourning that propriety forced her to wear.

Mary wanted to wake her, wanted to tell her about the uncle that she had always been afraid of, always hated without knowing why. How he had turned up at work asking for help and how she had reprimanded him on her mother's behalf, for her mother's sake. How in that moment she had felt a small pleasure in making him feel so small. But now that she was in the warmth of their flat with the worn, empty cart outside watching her mother sleep through her exhaustion, she realised that whatever that small moment of satisfaction had given her, it had still not changed a thing.

Harlesden, ENGLAND, 1961

There was a lightness of spirit in the air as the winter frosts began to thaw and the first few flowers of spring tiptoed through the hardened earth. London was awakening.

Mary took a deep breath and opened Jozef's wardrobe for the first time in four months. A gentle waft of his Aqua Velva Ice Blue mixed with the musty smell of abandoned neglect enveloped her. She wanted to cry but forced herself not to. She had done enough of that.

The demob suit he had received from the army when they had left Crewe still held the creases spiralling out from the lower button where he had forced it to fit. Its brown pinstripes were now faded like everything else that remained from their short time together. He had not thrown anything away. It was a habit he had got used to from the war when everything held a value no matter how broken or how worn.

She carefully packed everything into the bags waiting on the bed, ready to take to the church to help another family in need. She considered everything she touched, mulling over its sentimental value before placing it carefully in the bags. She kept his watch and a tie Henry had bought him last Christmas. The rest she collected together and immediately took it to Our Lady of Willesden Church before she could change her mind.

"That's very kind of you, Mrs Beker." Father Keegan with his kindly eyes opened the door to the vicarage. She could see the look of sympathy spread across his face. "Can I ask how you and the children are doing?"

Of course you can ask. The question is, what answer am I supposed to give?

"Fine, thank you, Father."

She wanted to leave quickly before she risked another long goodbye to her husband through his possessions which hung between her and the priest, encompassed in brown paper.

"Oh, Mrs Beker," he seemed to suddenly remember something as they stood awkwardly, "I have something for you. Something the women put together. Just give me a moment."

He discarded her act of charity beside the door as he disappeared off. She stared blankly at Jozef's brown flannel trousers, wishing to be anywhere else but there.

"Here." He presented her with a large brown paper bag which bulged from the soft contents held inside. "Some clothes for the children. We thought you might…"

The offering dangled between them. She didn't raise her hand to take it.

"Thank you." She felt insulted. "But we are not in need of anything."

She cleaned the house from top to bottom and set about preparing the spare bedroom in the attic for the arrival of lodgers. Two young gentlemen she had been introduced to via the Tippelts who promised to be both reliable and hard-working.

The room had been barely used except to store clothes that the children had outgrown. The practical work of clearing, dusting and cleaning gave her purpose that kept her mourning at bay. She kept herself busy, not allowing herself to pause her hands on the objects around her that immediately made her think of Jozef.

A spare small chest of drawers from their bedroom would be adequate enough for the lodgers' bits and pieces. It took her a while to haul it up the stairs and she took a moment to pause on the landing to congratulate herself on her progress. The bottom drawer had slipped open, digging into her hip. It was stuck on something that prevented it from closing. Her hand reached inside and she pulled out an envelope from the empty drawer.

No.

Not now.

She cursed him with a spontaneous cry and immediately shielded her offending lips with a repentant hand. The tears streamed unabated down her face. Why hadn't he said?

In her hand she held four tickets. Plane tickets. One for each of them: Jozef, Mary, Margarita and Henry. The date was two months into the future. Six months since Jozef had passed. She knew the destination before her eyes saw it screaming out at her in bold type.

Egypt.

Their first trip on a plane was to take them back to her country of birth. She longed for the hustle and bustle of the markets, the smell of spices in the air, the resonating sounds of the street musicians with their *Ouds* playing to the heat of the warm Mediterranean sun.

Why don't you visit? The tickets are already booked and it would be a shame to waste them. Maman and I have not seen you in so long...

Alice's reply to her last letter offered her the reasons to make the journey across continents to reach them. Her heart was torn. She could not get the tickets and the possibilities they presented out of her mind.

"I am unsure what to do." Mary sat down heavily opposite Eric in the kitchen at Bramshill Road and stirred the froth on her coffee. She had told him of Jozef's planned surprise. "If I go, it will be harder for me to come back."

"Do you need to come back?" Eric asked her carefully, slowly.

The question halted her spoon and paused the breath on her lips. It was a thought that had been rolling around in her mind looking for purchase. Now that thought had been spoken out loud, it seemed more of a possibility.

"I mean," Eric added quickly, "I would be devastated to see you go... but your happiness. That would have been what Jozef would have wanted."

"It's not as simple as that," she said harshly, almost angrily. "Oh, Eric, I have no idea what to do..."

"Then it's simple. You take a piece of paper and you write down all the arguments *for* moving back to Egypt and all the arguments *against*. Then you'll know what path is the better one for you."

A practical solution for a practical problem.

She sat in Jozef's chair that evening with the radio on, her pen hesitant over the piece of paper that held just two columns: for and against. Where to start? Normally this would have been the type of decision she would have made with Jozef. He would have listened and then together, the most viable option would have been chosen. There was no Jozef now. Just her.

A creak upstairs as Henry stirred in his bed. She was not alone in this decision. Her children were relying on her. What sort of opportunities would be open to them if they all moved back to Alexandria?

That settles it then.

She tore up the piece of paper and told herself that self-pity was not getting her anywhere. She would do what she always did – gather herself together and with sheer perseverance she would carry on. England was her home now. For the sake of the children, she would stay.

Arkhangelsk Oblast, RUSSIA, 1941

It was possible to survive in the Russian camps if one had the inclination to. When the will to survive went, the body soon followed. Those close to death stumbled around the camp with the vacant, haunted look of the living dead, the *dokhodyagi* – beings who had lost any human resemblance. Their teeth would fall out and they would lose any control over their bodily functions. The other inmates would give these comrades a wide berth. There was nothing to be done. No amount of help through an extra bit of bread there or the lending of an extra layer of newspaper in their Valenki boots would save them from their fate. Inmates were unable to help each other for the real risk of becoming *dokhodyagi* themselves.

Jozef bore his Russian guards no ill will. He watched them stamping their feet and clapping their sides in the freezing dawn as the monotony of the roll call played out in the inhospitable climate of the Great White Bear. The guards' rations were just as meagre as theirs, their protection against the forces of nature just as inadequate. The enemy was the state and its assault on the minds of the individuals living under it.

Those in the camp received no news from Europe. They were cocooned in the Siberian winter that blanketed their lives against the outside world physically and mentally. There was no word from Rozia, no word from Morduch or his son. All he could do was live in the hope that they were surviving better than he, that the horror of war had sidestepped their lives and they were carrying on in the shadows waiting patiently for it all to end.

His knowledge of the Russian language was excellent. He used it to try and glean as much information as possible from the guards, who talked in hushed tones when time would allow. But he found out nothing. They were as much in the dark as he, and young, so young to be marching around playing war. He caught a boy of seventeen dressed in a Russian soldier's uniform that he would never grow into, eyeing up the watch Jozef kept religiously on his wrist. It was the one thing left of value in a place where the rest of his possessions were either gone or in tatters.

"How much for the watch?"

He could see the boy eyeing it greedily as if it were a piece of jewellery of the most precious stones. His eyes twinkled as he followed the hands ticking around its dark face. Watches in Russia were very scarce. A watch was an indication of superiority, only available to the very few. A symbol at odds with the supposedly non-hierarchical system of socialism.

"What's your name?"

"Wasilei," he replied, his eyes not leaving Jozef's wrist.

Jozef saw an opportunity to practise his teaching instincts. The boy was young and intellectually malleable. He would do well to use the opportunity to help him in life.

"Well, Wasilei," he decided. They were in the canteen, queuing for the meagre lunch of watery soup that was supposed to sustain them until supper. It would have been easy to supplement his ration with an extra piece of stale bread or another bowlful of the soup, but that would only result in a momentary satisfaction that would be forgotten once the pangs of hunger crept over his aching bones and reminded him of his endless predicament. No, much better to achieve a moral victory of lasting consequence. "I will give you my watch if you promise me and give me your word of honour that for the period of one week you refrain from your Russian curses."

Wasilei's eyes shone with pleasure and a boyish determination to keep his end of the deal. He couldn't. He lasted all of five days before he came to him with tears in his eyes and the revelation that he had tried so hard, but the words had just slipped from his lips.

The watch stayed on Jozef's wrist and ticked off the time in manageable minutes that were broken down into manageable seconds when life in the camp became too much.

Alexandria,
EGYPT,
1941

Mary found herself in the market on the wrong day at the wrong time. The tram she was taking to visit a client in the east of the city had derailed leaving her with no choice but to walk the last remaining mile on already exhausted feet from a hard morning at the hospital. The market was awash with limbs and arms that jerked angrily in their movements. Before she realised what was happening, she was caught in the swell, her face dribbling with the spittle from the men that shouted and cursed. This was no place for her, here in this bubbling pot of retribution.

On the crest of the mob that rippled and surged like the waves that crashed against the Citadel of Qaitbay was the reason for this outpouring of hate. The woman's eyes caught Mary's in a split second of despair. Large bulbous terrified eyes that pleaded for any sense of humanity. Mary gasped. She couldn't help. No amount of her nurse's training could save this woman from the punishment about to be bestowed on her: death by stoning for the crime of adultery as dictated by the laws of Islam.

She hurried away before the first rock could be thrown, before the first screams of the terrified woman could carry across the crowd to enter her ears and be imprinted on her memory. She felt the urge to throw up in fear and revulsion.

So cruel, so cruel.

Mary fought her way free of the crowd, her heart pounding in her chest and her uniform creased and dishevelled. It was not a place for her. Her feet took her on to her appointment, keen to put order into her day that had suddenly turned so dark, so brutal. Surely the positive act of administering an injection, of attending the sick and making them better, would overturn that awful deed and restore her faith in humanity?

It was a poor suburb where the children were shoeless and the houses unkept. She knew that there would be no *basbousa* and coffee after her task was complete. That much was evident by the furtive way the couple ushered her in from the landing where the paint peeled. She was a necessary evil, dressed in her nurse's uniform. The prejudices here were as deeply rooted as the diseases that her trade was designed to improve.

The injection was completed quickly and efficiently. She had barely packed away her instruments before she was back on the landing with the few piastres required for her services pressed into the palm of her hand. She was glad of the excuse to hurry away, craving the love of her mother after the trauma of that morning, which still sat heavily on her mind.

Her purse was missing by the time she arrived hurriedly at the junction, waiting for her tram. She remembered the client, ushering her into the room of his sick mother, insisting he take her bag so that she could get on with the job in the confined space.

How stupid she had been!

The piastres (now warmed in the palm of her hand where the son had left them) were not enough to see her home. That luxury was in her purse, which was now in the hands of the couple she had been asked to help.

The walk across the city as the evening air crept from the sinking sun was enough to flame her indignation and remind her of the poor woman in the market with her pitiful cries for help.

"Why would they do such a thing?" she asked her mother. Zakia's concern was one of tenderness as she wiped the tears from her daughter's eyes.

"That is just the way of the world, Mary," was all she could say.

Mary clutched at her, her eyes screwed shut as she forced the sounds of the woman screaming in the market and the couple with their thieving hands from her mind. It wasn't fair.

The world wasn't fair.

Harlesden, ENGLAND, 1961

Winter was coming again. The world had almost completed a full cycle since Jozef's death. He had missed the beauty of spring, the warm lull of summer and now the mushrooms he had always loved to pick were sprouting again in the Surrey woods. His memory remained everywhere. Mary found it both a comfort and a curse. Just when the thought of him lightened her spirit, his very absence became a crushing blow on her senses.

And now, in the darkness, she was burning his memories.

In their garden, by the vegetable patch with its wilted tomatoes – a testament to Henry's efforts to keep his father's habits alive. The flickering flames from the metal drum licked high into the night as she pulled her woollen, fur-lined coat closer to her body.

What are you doing? he would have said if he were here now, smiling, the corners of his mouth rising slightly in love and wonder.

Yes, what am I doing?

She was doing what was necessary to keep the memory of him pure and untainted; an impulsive action of hers brought on by the events she had witnessed earlier that day. She could still hear the young, cackling laughter of strangers in her ears – so inappropriate after the funeral service they had attended with all its solemnity.

The Polish friends the Bekers had known for years all seemed to be exiting the world simultaneously. Dying one after the other so that Mary had found herself in that black dress of mourning more than a few times over the past year.

That horrid sound of laughter had drawn her away from the wake with its dignified remembrance to the dining room in that little semi in Harlesden. She had been curious and appalled all at the same time.

"Oh look! Another one," the laughter had declared.

"How many letters did they write to each other? What does this one say?"

Through the crack in the door, she had watched the daughters of her recently deceased friend poring over the private correspondence of the dead, carefully kept in shoeboxes. A whole lifetime laid bare.

I didn't want that happening to us, she felt compelled to explain later, to the quietness of the evening air, the dying tomatoes and Jozef's handwritten notes and letters as she placed them one after the other into the fire. *I didn't want anyone laughing at us. At you. At what you'd been through.*

Jozef had once attempted to document what had happened to him in the Russian camp, to articulate all the tragedy and horror in words. It was at the suggestion of a doctor friend. An idea to try to keep the nightmares at bay. She remembered him sitting alone amongst the half-made belts, scratching down in painful detail all that he was trying hard to forget. Handwritten sheets of A4, trying to make sense of it all. She hadn't asked to read it. She had felt that knowing all those details would change the way she behaved towards him, make the sympathy spill over, and that wasn't how he wanted her to be. She was his reason for forgetting; his reason for moving on. So, they had folded up his memories and put them in a shoebox and now she was placing them on a fire to be destroyed for good.

They smouldered and crackled in the flames. All those experiences, thoughts and feelings hidden permanently from the world in the silence Jozef had created all those years ago.

Forgive me, Jozef. Forgive me.

Arkhangelsk Oblast, RUSSIA, 1941

The work in the forest was back-breaking but to allow the body to stay still against the inhospitableness of the Russian winter was far more dangerous. They worked in groups, sawing, felling, chopping. At the start of their shift, before the sun could tantalise the workers with the promise of a few degrees of warmth, they built a fire in the snow which remained well stocked until break time. By then, a pit had appeared as the heat from the fire melted a patch in the deep white snow that was wide enough to fit eight men in a circle around what little warmth remained from the dying embers. With the lack of any comfort in their life at the camp, they embraced any solace that made their situation more bearable.

During the warmer autumn months, Jozef supplemented his bland diet with edible fungus that grew hidden amongst the foliage in the forest. Boletes were plucked from the ground and dropped whole into his watery soup to give his body some of the sustenance that it so desperately craved. Nothing was wasted. A group of inmates once captured a dog and roasted it on the fire. Jozef couldn't bring himself to eat that meat no matter how much his stomach ached and groaned.

And then came the day he found a chicken.

It was summer and the flies were at their most ferocious; humming, buzzing things that settled on anything that moved and bit the inmates to pieces. The guards had a chicken coop attached to their quarters on the edge of the camp. A small affair with seven measly birds that seemed to suffer as much from communism as the humans that cared for them. They produced eggs that were few and far between and were as precious as gold. The guards either shared them out between themselves or bartered them depending on their needs. Only once the hen had invariably stopped laying was it destined for the chop.

Jozef was trudging back from his work detail when he came across one such bird that had made a pathetic attempt at a break for freedom. As it had squeezed through the wire that surrounded its coop, it must have damaged its leg. It hopped on one foot, its scrawny body wobbling from side to side. It was so small that it was difficult to see it amongst the bushes by the side of the road and when the guards weren't looking, he grabbed it by the leg and stuffed it under his shirt, holding it tight to stop it struggling.

He broke its neck once he was back in his room, the child from the family that shared his space watching eagerly and with fascination as the creature went limp and lifeless. He hung it under a pile of coats on the wall and could hardly sleep that night for fear of it being discovered. There was expectation from the couple, Mr and Mrs Wiśniewski, as they awoke that morning. A yearning look of hunger in their eyes as they furtively glanced at the coats and the contraband beneath. Mrs Wiśniewski plucked it and gutted it and they carefully tipped both feathers and guts into the toilet to minimise the risk of discovery.

It felt cold and scaly next to his skin as they smuggled it into the forest the next day. Jozef could feel the perspiration on his forehead and was thankful for the warmth of the sun that acted as his excuse for the sweat that may have given him away. They lit a fire on the pretence of making a tea from the nettles that stung their bodies as they wielded their axes in the forest. The chicken was left boiling in the pot whilst they worked and they were all worried that the smell of it would give them away. It tasted like heaven. Small morsels of flesh were shared out amongst the workers in their tin cups which were filled with the boiling liquid and a layer of fat that bubbled on top.

They had all mostly had their fill when the guards discovered the remains of the chicken in the pot. The taste of that heavenly dinner faded just as soon as it settled on Jozef's stomach as he fretted over the punishment that would surely follow.

"Who has done this?" The soldier tipped the remains of the fatty liquid complete with chicken bones out onto the fire and it fizzled and spat as if mirroring the soldier's rage. The workers were all silently looking at their feet, their faces white as if the snow had fallen again early this year.

"If no one owns up, the whole camp will be punished!"

Jozef felt sick, his breath halting in gasps as he waited for someone to say his name. Nobody did. It was as if the threat of the punishment hanging over them was worth it for the feeling of a full belly the stolen chicken had brought. He watched the spitting fat on the fire as the smoke billowed up around the soldier's face. So young to have so much responsibility over who lived and who died. Jozef remained silent, unable to speak, looking at the floor at his feet.

Dinner was cancelled for the whole camp that evening. They all went to bed, still tasting the delicious bird on their tongues, but that did nothing to alleviate the hunger that crept back with a vengeance.

Warsaw, POLAND, 2005

Mary was remembering the chickens they had kept in that small garden on Bramshill Road. Noisy, smelly things which always seemed to be plumper than the specimens her mother reared on her balcony in that searing Alexandrian heat.

"You spoil those chickens," she'd once told her husband. "They eat better than we do!"

"Ah, but Mary," he'd said with that glint in his eye, "when they're fresh out of the oven, stuffed and with their skin salted and crisp, you'll understand why."

When the first of those birds had stopped laying, she'd suggested they take it to market and see what price it would fetch. The china in their kitchen cupboards was cracked, their best tablecloth had ripped and was past repair. The extra money would be useful.

He had point-blank refused.

"What's the good in money if our stomachs are empty?" He'd shrugged.

The evidence for such an argument had been burned in that oil drum a year after his death. Painful truths of the harsh year he'd spent at the hands of the Russians scratched out in pen and tossed on the fire when she was too wrapped up in mourning and overprotective of the man she'd loved. She still wasn't sure if the world had now reached a better understanding or whether the judgement of a generation protected from war still found it easy to laugh at the desperation of the desperate.

It was still hard for her to let go. It was still difficult to allow all those awful things to be openly talked about.

Arkhangelsk Oblast, RUSSIA, 1941

The Germans retracted on the promises they had signed with the Russians when they implemented Operation Barbarossa in 1941. Suddenly, and with ruthless efficiency, the Nazis ploughed into Russian lands with the aim of taking Moscow. As they went, they looted, they killed, and they ravaged the houses and burnt the land. The Russians, in the view of the Nazis, were subhuman; not the blight on humanity they perceived the Jews to be, but subhuman, nonetheless. The bodies piled up with the falling leaves, as summer turned to autumn before winter swept in. There was no love lost between the Nazis and the Russians.

It was because of this that a new alliance formed between the Russians and the Allies. Russia was now, in theory, on the same side as the Poles. The thousands of

Poles that had been taken prisoner by the Russians at the start of the war were now a nuisance in the theatre of this new and uneasy peace.

Something had to be done.

The exiled Polish government, which had found a temporary home in England, pushed for the release of its citizens on Russian soil. The soldiers and their families that had worked the timber, the mines, the cotton fields and the farms of the Soviet machine were now offered the chance to form a new army to aid the Allies against the Nazi forces. There would be no Russian apology, no reckoning for the crimes committed against the Polish people by this new ally. The Russians simply opened the gates of the camps and let the inmates go.

It was a warm day in September 1941 when Jozef walked out of the hell that had confined him for just over a year. He was a few stone lighter than when he had arrived. There was stubble on his chin that he had fought to keep clean-shaven in a desperate bid to maintain his dignity. His eyes were gaunt and sunken into cheeks that spelt out the overwork and hunger he had endured. He was free but trapped at the same time. The Russians gave the inmates no money, no food, no provisions. They had promised to set their Polish prisoners free, but they had stopped short of helping them on their journey.

The flies were buzzing around him as he hesitated on the threshold of the camp. In his hand he held a single piece of paper that had been given to him by the guards as they relieved themselves of their responsibility over him. A piece of paper in lieu of a passport, which acted as his permit to travel.

The wave of humanity that stood with him, hesitating, varied in ages and in stages of degradation. There was talk of a Polish army gathering in Uzbekistan nearly 4,000km away. There was no other choice but to somehow reach this place if he was to eventually find his way home.

He walked, took up the offer of lifts from farmers, sitting on the backs of trucks and on carts pulled by donkeys as emaciated as he and sometimes found himself on a train with other refugees on the same mission. They avoided the Russian secret police, the feared NKVD. They were released prisoners but prisoners still in this inhospitable land.

The warmth of the autumn gave way to the biting winds of winter and he had no choice but to offer his labour on collective farms in order to survive the long nights on straw in the barns with the animals he looked after. If you didn't work, you didn't get your ration of food and you simply starved to death. Jozef saw it everywhere he went. The young melted away before his eyes. The old collapsed and were buried where they stood. Everyone was suffering and no one batted an eyelid. Compassion was for the weak and vulnerable.

Winter turned into spring, and he found a frozen onion in the thawing earth. Its silver skin touched his worn *valenki* boots, which had been bolstered by newspapers and any other material he had scavenged in a bid to keep out the frostbite that threatened his toes. A hasty, furtive look around him as an animal might search for any threats to a freshly made kill. It was small and not much of a meal on its own, but next to it he found (and here his stomach somersaulted with joy) the remnants of a stale piece of bread no bigger than the palm of his hand. He pounced on it and held it under his padded vatnik coat to allow the warmth of his body to heat it.

The bread's last owner could still be seen in the teeth marks over its jagged edges. Small bite marks that probably belonged to a child who had nibbled each salivating mouthful before carelessness had caused its loss in the frozen snow.

His teeth sank into its deliciously crumbly, yeasty goodness, his tongue tingling from all the taste sensations that assaulted his mouth. He alternated from the onion to the bread and wasted nothing.

He enjoyed his meal sitting on the hard earth with his back against a tree looking up at the heavens. He smiled bitterly as his mind turned to the supposed godly salvation that was meant to be there giving hope to those on earth. He had seen little of God in his time at the camp and even less on his journey. He begrudged no one their hold on faith. Everyone dealt with survival in their own unique way. But it was not for him.

When he reached Tashkent in Uzbekistan in the spring of 1942, there was already a camp set up. A camp teaming with the half-starved remnants of the Poles who had been spread across the Soviet Union in their thousands. Men, women and children hoping to join General Anders and his army as a way to escape the inhospitable Russian soil. It was their best chance of survival.

There were faces that he recognised in this sea of Polish people. Friends from his youth that he greeted with warm hugs and tears in his eyes.

"Szyja? Is that you?"

He was standing in a queue waiting for his morning allowance of bread and coffee from the Polish officials, with the NKVD looking on in despair at the assistance granted to these non-Russian exiles. The verbalisation of a name he had buried thousands of miles from here made him turn. The man that addressed him was bearded and shrouded by layers of clothes designed to keep out the dawn cold. He was used to greeting people with frowns of stumbled slow recognition as he struggled to decode the frail figures of the camp with the people he had known before the war. They all looked different, devoid of their smart clothes and their health.

It was a cousin of his from his mother's side of the family. A man named Mozes Montag who had shared the flat she'd owned in Łódź before she'd emigrated to South Africa in the late 1920s. A man of the same age as Jozef but with whispers of grey in his hair from a hard year in the Russian forests. A plight mirroring his own.

The frown turned into a smile and they embraced, feeling each other's bony shoulders under their ill-fitting coats. They asked after each other and the conversation turned into the usual inquisitions on whether they knew of the whereabouts of family and friends.

News was just as precious as food these days.

"Rozia and Marysia? Our son, Arja?"

Mozes's expression turned to one of pain as he realised the ignorance in his cousin's question. "I'm sorry, Szyja, but the last I heard your home was flattened. Warsaw has gone, cousin. You cannot count on any family back home. There is nothing left. No Warsaw. No family."

There was a frown of denial, a sharp look of pain.

"You must be mistaken?" It was a plea for hope.

"I'm sorry, cousin…"

He walked from the queue. Stumbling. Tripping. His ears shut to the people around him. There was not a cloud in the sky as the sun rose over the tents. No birds either. Just the broken sounds of humanity amongst the Polish mass of people, all of them nearly 3,000 miles from home.

And into the silence, he howled.

Warsaw, POLAND, 2005

We couldn't find any trace of what happened to them. No clues as to the fate of Rozia, your little daughter and the son you had together.

It was the one gap in Jozef's past that couldn't be plugged in their visit to the city that had sprung up anew after the catastrophe of the war. There was no document, no list, nor oral history to give any indication of the family's fate at the hands of the Nazis.

Rozia's and Marysia's future had been sealed as soon as they had entered the gates of the Warsaw Ghetto. Their home destroyed. A mother and her daughter either killed in the rubble of their former city or in the camps that followed.

"I'm sorry," the genealogist offered as an afterthought.

And what of Arja? That still remained a mystery. A mystery that haunted Jozef every day and in the darkness of the nightmares that enveloped him. He had not died with his uncle Morduch and his cousins. In February 1942 he had still been alive, but alive in the confines of the Bergen-Belsen camp in Germany that went on to hold thousands of Jews in appalling conditions but, at the time Arja was there, was still a prisoner-of-war camp mainly for Soviet soldiers. Had the Russian language lessons Arja had taken as a child helped him meld into their ranks as the Germans advanced? How long had he survived? Where had he died? There was no record, no document, no scrap of information.

And what about the survivors? The ones left behind. The Jozefs.

In this journey, this trip to Warsaw, Mary found herself with a new connection to the man she had married and lost all those years ago. His past, the constant searching for information and the all-consuming not knowing had shaped him as much as her past had shaped her. It had brought them together and, in some respects, drove them apart and now, in the Warsaw that bore little resemblance to the one he once knew, she was loving him and understanding him all over again.

Tashkent, UZBEKHISTAN, 1942

Jozef spent his days blindly wandering around the foreign city of Tashkent in Uzbekistan, a constant ache in the pit of his stomach which had nothing to do with the hunger that clung to him but more with the all-consuming grief of his wife and daughter, the constant worry of a son out of his reach.

Tashkent was a bland, dreary place overrun by the Soviet will and made more dreary by the hastily erected tents and yurts designed to rally the wandering Poles in their never-ending trek to salvation. It was a relatively deserted place with half of its former glory lying in the ruins of crumbling ornamental arches and fanciful buildings reduced to dust. The high street was dominated by Communist shops and numerous cafes selling tea which the Uzbeks sipped sitting on woven mats. There was a constant soup kitchen at the train station that filled the refugees' bellies with a watery broth as they stepped off the trains. Its empty calories reminded him of the camps. He found his feet shuffling across the hard, frosted ground with the similar purpose to the *dokhodyagi*. He tried to rally himself. He tried to maintain his mission. If he were not to survive, then what had been the point of it all?

"It will do you no good moping in the past," Jan Stroynsky's words were harsh in their directness. A no-nonsense but jovial fellow; a captain in the Polish army who had spent the last year and a half working the mines in the Czelabinskaja Oblosc region north of Kazakhstan. He too had known loss. They all had. Whether it was loved ones, their homes, or their humanity.

He took Jan's advice and began searching for a way out of the tents, the soup kitchens, and the day-to-day drudgery. Polish recruits were beginning to be evacuated from the grips of the USSR, southwest of where he now found himself, around the barren hills surrounding Samarkand. He would need his travel permit validated. The NKVD held sway everywhere and were particularly interested in the Polish refugees. Those that could not prove their worth as potential recruits to the new Polish army were under the very real threat of being deported all the way back from where they had fled: into the grip of the Great White Bear.

His situation was becoming precarious. He needed to consolidate his acceptance into the large swathe of Catholic Poles trudging through this inhospitable country. He could not afford to invite any suspicion to his former life with his Jewish sounding name. To the Russians, how could a Jew possibly fit into an army of Poles?

He would need to validate his documents for travel, have his identity confirmed in print. He needed to prove his worth, achieve his acceptance, in order to escape this country and the uncertain future it held.

Jan introduced him to a Polish officer, a kindly fellow who willingly carved the seal of the *kompostirovka* expertly and swiftly out of a potato. A stamp carved out of a vegetable to fool the NKVD of his own legitimacy. The officer had the permit card waiting and agreed to forge it for him without a fee. No questions asked.

"Name?" he asked, the pen hovering.

"Beker." And then Jozef paused for a moment. The name he had buried in Poland came back to haunt him. It connected him with Rozia, with Warsaw, the job he had loved and left all those months ago. To have a document without that name seemed as if he was shutting the door on his past. "Jozef," he said.

A new identity for a new life.

PART FOUR

Alexandria, EGYPT, 1942

In 1942 a possible suitor was put forward as a potential husband for Alice. A cousin of the family. Tired of waiting for Zakia to secure his nieces' futures, Iskandar put forward his own son, Saadalla, as the perfect match. Alice didn't complain. He was a man she knew well, had grown up with during their long trips to Luxor and whereas her sister scoffed at the very idea of settling down with an Egyptian man, Alice was happy to go along with the family's wishes.

"So that is it, then?" Mary sat next to her sister on the tram on their way to work. It was early in the morning and the city was waking. Her nurse's uniform was tight against her knees and her hat wasn't straight. She was tired and cross and unforgiving of her sister's decision. "You would

347

throw away your career and become nothing more than a slave to a man you don't love?"

"Oh, Mary." Alice's voice was soft and calming. "I was always going to settle down at some point. Besides, it will be such a relief for Maman to not have to worry about me."

"But I shall. I shall worry about you very much when you are gone far away from us, from *me*."

Saadalla was a carpenter working for the British army in Suez. To think that Alice would give up the relative freedoms of their lives in Alexandria for a place like Suez was beyond anything Mary could ever imagine.

"Don't worry yourself, Mary. I shall be fine. I will always be fine."

Mary resisted the urge to tell her that she was only fine because she had always been there looking out for her sister even when Alice hadn't seen it. It was Mary who had looked after her at school, acting like a surrogate mother when Zakia wasn't there. It was Mary who had got her a position at the hospital and guided her through her career as a nurse. It was Mary who had integrated her sister into their group of nurse friends and shown her all that Alexandria had to offer.

"If it's what you really want, Alice, then so be it. But if he mistreats you in any way, he'll have me to answer to."

"I don't doubt it, Mary," she said with a smile. "I don't doubt it at all."

Harlesden, ENGLAND, 1971

Bad news always seemed to arrive on the doorstep of Bramshill Road on small bits of paper with impersonal typescript. The telegram arrived in April. The days were lengthening with tantalising glimpses of a summer yet to come.

It was two short lines of script that rocked Mary's world.

MAMAN HAS DIED SUDDENLY.
WILL SEND MORE INFORMATION BY LETTER.

It took more than three weeks for the letter to reach her. Three agonising weeks.

Ma soeur,

I am so sorry to tell you this and my heart is aching as I write. Maman passed away this morning. It was a shock to us all. She was standing on the balcony of a friend's flat when it gave way beneath her feet. She was taken to hospital but insisted that we bring her home. We have been caring for her for the past few weeks and I was sick with worry whether I should tell you or not, but the delay in the post… I didn't want to tell you of her condition until we knew for sure.

I know this must come as a dreadful shock to you and I am sorry that I am not there to wrap my arms around you as I tell you all this.

It will be hard for you without us there and I am sure, if you wish to come to the funeral, arrangements can be made. We plan to hold it this Thursday in the church where you and Jozef were married. She would have liked that. A chance to celebrate her life in the place where she had fond memories of that happy day you were wed.

We are otherwise all well and I don't want you to worry about us.

Look after yourself, my love,
Alice

Mary was alone in the house when she received it and she wept openly over its contents as she read it again and again. She had received the news too late to attend the funeral, which by now had already happened. She wouldn't have wanted to go anyway. What was the point in visiting when her mother was already dead? There would be no warm arms to comfort her, none of the familiarity of her perfume. Just her undeniable absence. Why travel all that way to remind herself of that?

The last time she had seen her mother had been at the docks in Port Said as they had waited for the ship to be ready. They had stood at the dock, bustled by the crowds of passengers around them, seeking a new life in Europe. Her mother had been in her late forties. That was younger than Mary now found herself as she held the letter in her numb, damp hands, collapsed in grief in Jozef's chair in the empty lounge of their family home.

She closed her eyes to remember the feel of her mother's touch. How she'd had to reach up to kiss her on the cheek as age had yet to stoop her stance and her skin had been smooth and supple. It did not make sense that that woman was now gone. Just like Jozef. The two people who had been so important in her life, both now vanished and leaving her with a hardened heart that ached with the pain of their separation.

Zakia had helped her pack when she'd left Egypt. She had stood in Mary and Jozef's apartment, cradling her granddaughter in her arms as Mary folded their clothes and wrapped their few possessions carefully in newspaper. She had packed as the two of them had sought to reminisce about happier times to keep the tears and fear of the future from saddening their last few days together. They talked of chasing the chickens around the balcony as they sought to prepare for Epiphany or walking on the promenade arm in arm, people-watching against the backdrop of a vibrant city.

"It was hard at times." Mary had felt compelled to confide in her as the last suitcase was closed and the clasp tightened shut. "Growing up."

The smiles dropped slightly in saddened agreement. Zakia nodded and placed Margarita down on the floor, watching her crawl about on writhing legs.

"I didn't know any better," Zakia said carefully, sincerely.

It was the most she would allow herself in apology for all the beatings and the punishments she had laid out on her children.

"I know," Mary agreed, her expression pained but understanding.

"When I…" Zakia's hand waved at the unspoken words that refused to come out of her mouth. "I was too young to have a family. I wasn't ready. I didn't have a mother to ask. I didn't have the security of a husband to have the patience... It was hard…"

"It was hard for all of us," her daughter agreed, before clutching her to her body in an intense hug. "And I don't forgive you as there is nothing to forgive. I can only tell you that now that I am older, I understand. I understand, Maman, I understand."

Harlesden, ENGLAND, 1974

Mary invited her sister to England. The years since Jozef's death had ticked by and she was missing the calming influence of family. She had set out her plan in a letter that she knew would take weeks to reach her sister in Egypt and waited patiently for the reply. A visit would be just what she needed to reignite old times. Just the two of them. Two sisters now in their fifties who used to dance together in the cafes and casinos of Alexandria. Two sisters with their dark Mediterranean features and lust for life, attracting the attention of the young men around them. Mary was looking forward to it with a yearning in her heart. She needed Alice's soothing touch.

"I don't feel it's right that I come and visit you before our brother."

The line was crackly. To Mary's delight, Alice had recently had a phone installed and she had looked forward to hearing her voice with as much excitement as hearing the answer to her question. But the quality of the line was poor and they'd had to ask the operator to reconnect their call a couple of times before their conversation could really get started. Mary could feel the disappointment sink into the pit of her stomach.

"Why ever not?" she snapped. She was looking out of the window at the blossoming British trees and thinking of how Egypt would have looked this time of year. Spring there followed the same pattern as England; the start of the warmer months would have seen the Mediterranean flowers bloom but with more vibrancy than those in her garden, in her little piece of England.

"It's just not right. Zaki would want to visit you first…"

The years of being married to an Egyptian man had enforced in Alice the attitude that men were above women. Mary was not pleased.

"Oh, *viens maintenant!* What on earth has that got to do with anything? If you want to come, then you come."

"Mary…"

Alice would not relent. Zaki arrived two months later leaving his wife and children at home. He looked smart in his beige suit and clipped moustache but hesitated on the steps of the plane as the cool British air hit him. To Mary he looked out of place amongst the different attitudes of the country she had come to know as home. She greeted him with an all-encompassing hug that transported her back to Alexandria and the family she had left behind.

"You've put on weight," she told him plainly, stamping on any ideas he may have had about asserting his manly authority. She was his big sister and she didn't want him to forget that.

They took the bus back to Mary's house in Harlesden and she smiled when she saw him trying to hide his amazement as he gazed at her large and tidy home with its neat rose bushes and clipped lawn.

He had brought a large suitcase and made himself comfortable in the spare room overlooking the road and the England he had wanted to see. The suitcase was big enough to worry her into wondering exactly how long he was expecting to stay, but still lacked the jewellery their mother had promised her in her will. The necklace of gold with bright studded opals and topaz which Mary had remembered disappearing in those early days of her childhood. Disappearing for days on end before reappearing from the pawn shop when the family's financial worries had eased.

"Oh." Zaki waved a hand dismissively when she asked its whereabouts. "They were confiscated at customs," he offered by way of an explanation with no apology to follow.

She was fuming.

It was not so easy to forgive when life had thrown you out on your own for so long and with so many challenges. Having her brother around stifled her. She was in the kitchen, cooking and cleaning up after him as if she was in her teens again.

"I can see why you moved here, Mary," he announced one day, sipping on the coffee she had brought him and skimming through the newspaper he was using to brush up on his English skills. "I have always thought of moving here myself at some point—"

"Here? Not in my house." Her temper was quick and fierce, suspecting her generosity was being taken advantage of.

"Just until we find a house to live. We'd need a sponsor—"

Ah, that was the reason she had been forced to invite her brother over and he had happily come to visit.

"No, no and no." She fumed. She could see where this was heading. Memories of all those years where she had been expected to wait on her brother came flooding back to haunt her. She would not spend the latter half of her life in the same predicament as her first. "You want to move here, you do it on your own back, not on mine."

Did her refusal surprise him? If it did, he didn't show it.

She took him to see the sights of London and they laughed and reminisced about happier times. For a while she was content to feel the temporary warmth of family close by her. To her joy, his presence brought the memories of her mother alive. But it was only temporary. Zaki's attempts to resettle in the UK came to nothing and after a while, Mary saw her brother off at the airport with a sigh and a pride in what she had achieved. This life in London thousands of miles from the place of her birth had all been achieved through her and Jozef's own determination. Now that she was on her own, she was only reliant on herself, and she was determined not to forget that.

Luxor, EGYPT, 1942

Alice and Saadalla married in Zakia's home city of Luxor in 1942 after a short courtship. An engagement long enough to give both sides time to get used to the idea of spending the rest of their lives together. Mary travelled with her mother and brother on the train from Alexandria to the wedding, which was attended by hundreds of well-wishers.

Zakia wept with relief and happiness as the responsibility of her youngest daughter's future was passed onto her new husband. Alice looked radiantly beautiful in a long gown of pure white adorned with the red-jewelled cape the priest placed carefully on her and her husband's shoulders. The crowns they wore symbolised their position as rulers of their new household. They glinted in the light of the candles in the church the family had attended for generations. As the ceremony concluded and the two young people were declared man and wife, Zakia had no problem in joining in the undulating cry of the *Zaghareet* with the rest of the women, the shrill sound echoing off the walls in a brief moment of unadulterated joy.

A tent was erected outside the Ghali family home over which Iskandar (Alice's uncle and new father-in-law) ruled. The caterers roasted a whole sheep and had to conduct three sittings to feed the hundreds of well-wishers that had descended on the couple.

Her belly full of lamb, falafel, rice, lentils and *macaroni bechamel*, Mary travelled back on the train to Alexandria with her brother the next day. She needed to get back to work having only secured a few days off. Zakia chose to stay on, wrapped up in the comforts of family whilst overseeing her daughter's impending move to Suez.

"This marriage business," Zaki wondered, stroking his chin in a move that he was prone to do whilst deep in thought. The stark scenery of desert interspersed with the occasional populated settlement rattled past the window of their train carriage. "It doesn't seem all that bad."

Mary looked up from her daydream. She was still picturing her sister in her wedding dress – young and beautiful and apprehensive on the crest of her new life. Mary knew that things would be different at the hospital and their home without her.

"Marriage?" she asked lazily.

"I think it might suit me," Zaki continued. "What are your thoughts on Ernesta?"

"Ernesta?"

She was another cousin of theirs, a daughter of one of their mother's sisters. A small quiet woman with ordinary looks. She remembered how, when they were younger, her brother had been keen on Ernesta's older sister, Matilda. That was until a childhood accident had taken one of her eyes.

Mary's cheeks flushed with indignation. It surprised her how she could still find herself astonished by men's attitude to finding a suitable mate; bartering over women as if they were at a market.

"Yes." Zaki was still musing out of the window, half in thought, half in conversation with his sister. "She seems pleasant enough and will make a suitable wife, don't you think?"

"I think it is as much a matter for Ernesta as it is for you," she clipped. "And what about Maman and your duty to her?"

"Mother?" Zaki's eyebrows rose as if the thought had never occurred to him. "I think she would much rather see me happy. Besides, you're still at home."

The brakes of the train heaved as it squeaked and rolled into the next station. The bustle on the platform carried through the open window as passengers began to get on and off. Two water sellers were vying for custom, their animal skins full of fresh water stooping their backs as they deftly dispensed their cups through the train's open windows. Mary glared at her brother, wanting to shout at him, her temper getting the better of her.

"Yes," Zaki continued, oblivious to his sister's rising temper. "I think that would be the right thing to do."

He had pulled his suitcase down from the rack above his head without a single glance at her and promptly stepped off the train.

"Where are you going?" she called out to him.

"Back to Luxor to ask my uncle for Ernesta's hand in marriage."

Mary's mouth opened silently in astonishment and then he was lost in the steam of the train and the bustle of the crowd. Surrounded by strangers but alone in the carriage, Mary fumed at the insensibility of it all. As practical a person as she thought she was, she couldn't fathom the idea of wanting to spend the rest of your life with someone just because it was expected, because it seemed the most sensible solution. When she found someone, it would be for the right reasons. It would be for love, for respect and an understanding that would intertwine the important pieces of both their lives.

Harlesden, ENGLAND, 1961

With the help of her daughter, Mary gradually wound up the belt-making business, selling the machines that punched and glued and stamped to a buyer Margarita had found. It was a relief to hand it over. Business was slowing with the ever-changing fashion trends, but the truth of the matter was that it just didn't seem the same without Jozef.

She was content. The lodgers in the spare room in the attic brought in a fair income and she enjoyed the extra company it provided. Mary thrived on social interaction. People fascinated her. Their stories, their experiences in the world; she would willingly listen to it all.

The money from the sale of the business was put to good use purchasing another property in the area with the intention of letting it out. Their bank manager guided her on the purchase that would secure her family's future. It was a large property with four bedrooms which she was able to let to individual tenants in order to secure a steady income.

She was waiting at the bus stop one day for her son to return from school when she noticed an advertisement advising of a closing-down sale for a local hotel. Henry had barely stepped down onto the pavement before they had both turned around and caught the next bus to the vacant property on the Victoria Road. She purchased six beds and four wardrobes as well as a table and chairs to furnish the rental property she had just secured. They took what they could carry (which included three lamp shades and a coat stand) and caught the bus back home, sitting with the purchases bouncing on their laps as the passengers squeezed around the coat stand swaying in the aisle.

"Thank you for your help, Henry," Mary said with satisfaction as her son slumped down into his seat to avoid the curious stares.

Eric was procured to ferry the beds and larger pieces of furniture in his van once he'd finished work for the day.

"Well, I give you this, Mrs Beker." His eyes glinted as he manhandled the final bed frame into the back of his van under her watchful eye. "You certainly do have an eye for a bargain."

"Jozef always told me that," she agreed.

She frowned. She had said his name out loud as easily as if she was referring to the weather. It had tripped off her tongue and for the first time in as long as she could remember, there was no deep intake of breath, no quiet sob in her soul; only a satisfyingly subtle happiness.

"I don't think I'm going to have room for any passengers with all that in there," Eric said apologetically, as he surveyed his van.

"Oh, don't worry, Eric." She smiled. A broad, contented smile that mirrored her soul. "I'll get the bus. There'll be another one in a minute. I'm in no hurry. It's a nice day to just stand here."

"Isn't it just," he agreed.

She stood, feeling the warm breeze on her face in a perfect place of satisfaction. The traffic was rushing by and the street was vibrant with the smiles and laughs of people going about their day.

"With all this rushing about, isn't it nice to stop and just be?" she added.

Wasn't that something that Jozef would say?

Alexandria, EGYPT, 1943

Jozef was used to the heat of the Mediterranean by the time he arrived in Alexandria in the last week of February 1943. After joining the Polish II Corps in Uzbekistan, his journey had taken him through Iran, Iraq, Palestine, Jerusalem and finally onto Egypt. He had covered more miles than he'd ever thought possible, treading the earth on a winding route through the USSR and the Middle East, alone, but with new friends, continually thinking of his family and their fate. There was no closure for him in that respect. The unanswered questions as to their final moments, when exactly they had died, was a continuous assault on his senses, a cruelty that gave him hope that seemed impossible to sustain.

How do you mourn when there is no body? How do you find closure when all the facts are missing?

He bore these questions alone.

What good would it do to voice these thoughts?

The world seemed lost and broken. Every other man in his battalion had a similar story of loss. There was no space for sympathy, just an unspoken, quiet empathy and a will to move on, to pick up the pieces of whatever was left of their lives. The silence descended and was embraced by them all since the alternative was too painful to bear.

They all had scars.

The hard work of the camp, the malnourishment, was easily fixed by the British army rations, but the mental hardships would always be there in the seriousness of his eyes and the determination in his smile. He had accepted what life threw at him day by day and took nothing for granted. Each meal could be his last and he treated it as such. There was no point saving anything as it may be gone in the blink of an eye.

The streets of Alexandria hit his senses and he felt a warmth of feeling as he compared it to the city he had left in haste three years ago. It felt closer to home than the poverty of Russia, more westernised than the streets of Iran and Iraq.

He was now a 2nd Lieutenant attached to the British forces in the Middle East. His proficiency in languages had propelled him into a position of worth. Whereas the Russians had viewed his academic achievements with suspicion, the British had seen them as an asset. As the rest of Anders' army headed onto Italy and the mountains of Monte Cassino, Jozef remained in Alexandria, stationed at the British headquarters in the city, acting as an interpreter and free to sample the cultures of a new country that provided tantalising glimpses of home.

The headquarters of the British forces was a large building on Rue St LeToille. Through the window of his office, he could just about see the white, stark building of L'Hôpital Européen d'Alexandrie. He walked past it every day on the way from the tram junction in Ramleh that brought him in from his billet in Cleopatra. He walked past it and saw the locals queuing up for treatment in the outpatients clinic and the nurses scurrying in and out. Perhaps he had even caught a glimpse of Mary before he even properly met her in late 1943. Perhaps he had seen this dark-skinned nurse that his military colleagues would have referred to as exotic, long before any type of attraction between them had grown. In any case, he finally stepped into the hospital building early one morning before he was due to report to work for the day. He had been bitten on the back of his hand by one of the many mosquitos that plagued the city and, as the days passed, the bite had become infected, bubbling up into an unsightly boil that domed his hand and made writing difficult. A friend had told him that he ought to get it seen to and rather than wait in the medical orderly's office, he decided to pop into the outpatients clinic on a whim that morning.

Mary had just finished her breakfast of milk, bread and cheese, remembering how she and her sister used to halve their rations so that some food could be saved for their brother. Her stomach full, she had smoothed down her uniform and headed upstairs to work. Matron had stationed her in the outpatients clinic that morning, suturing wounds and repairing bodies damaged in the course of life. The large effigy of the dying Jesus on the cross still hung over the patients that waited expectantly on chairs, waiting for pain relief. Amongst the Arabs and street traders who had wandered into the clinic in the hope of getting seen before the day called them to the markets, a man in military uniform sat with a cap in his hands. He was next on the list and her patient to fix. A short man, with dark hair and serious eyes.

"Jozef Beker? *Viens avec moi*," she demanded with her usual smile of efficiency.

He hopped to it, but not in a way she expected someone from the army to. His demeanour was relaxed with none of the stiffness the uniform brought with it. He followed her dutifully into a side room where curtains separated three distinct seating zones which were each used as consultation areas.

The wound was easy, a bite that had turned into a boil which, on brief inspection, would need to be burst, cleaned and dressed.

"That will need lancing. I will give you a shot of morphine to numb the pain." His hand was hot and soft in hers as she scrutinised the wound.

"No need," he replied. His accent was different to the high-clipped British officers she had seen in the cafes and bars; one that she couldn't place.

"Where are you from?" The curious question crept out of her before she could stop it. It was not her place to ask but she couldn't help herself.

"Originally from Poland," he answered. "But, if you are talking more recently, I would say I've just come back from hell."

She looked up from her work, her hand still holding his. She saw the weariness of war that brought her thoughts back to the military hospital and the tired and weary men recovering inside it. They all held the same guarded look that feared the release of all those horrific memories they were trying so hard to conceal beneath.

"Oh?" She was drawn in. Curious. Sympathetic.

"I'm sorry," he said brusquely, moving his hand away from her compassion in embarrassment. Why had he said that? "I shouldn't have…"

"*Non… s'il te plaît.*" Her other hand rested on the top of his, sandwiching it between her dark Mediterranean fingers.

"It was wrong of me…"

Perhaps finding himself in a situation of vulnerability, asking for the help of another human being and submitting to their capable hands, released the bitterness holed up inside him.

"You speak very good French." Mary decided to change the subject, picking up her tools to begin repairing him.

"Yes. Language is a habit of mine."

"There are worse habits to have," she noted, her back turned to him as she busied herself.

He was intrigued by her; curious about the way she held herself and the ease with which she switched from the business at hand to a sympathy fuelled by compassion.

"Are you from Alexandria?" he found himself asking, wondering whether the French she spoke pointed at a history of displacement from her country of origin. Perhaps she was a refugee like himself?

She nodded but made no oral reply, her mind now lost in the task of lancing the wound.

"This may sting…" she warned.

"It's a beautiful city," he said, wincing, before turning his head towards the window as if the act of refusing to look would numb the pain.

"Yes, it is." A slight smile as she agreed, a sparkle in her eye as she couldn't help but recall the night she had spent in a café in Ramleh with Theresa and Tamile earlier that week.

"Would you show me?"

Her hand paused with the swab she held pressed onto his wound. She was confused, startled by his question.

"Show you?" She repeated the words as if she had misheard them at first. His tone was blank, there was no smile, no warmth in his question.

"Yes." He almost sounded irritated at having to repeat himself. "I would like you to show me Alexandria."

"But we don't know each other!" she spluttered. Her voice was clipped and reminded her of the matron that oversaw the nurses, a no-nonsense woman who found fault with everything.

"That is why I want to take you out," he stated, "to get to know you."

She blushed, taken completely by surprise. Who did he think he was with his cool presumption? Did he assume that just because he was a foreigner, she would willingly bend to his every command?

"No."

"Why not?"

"Because…" Flustered, her fingers slipped with the bandage and the end rolled onto the floor. She cursed in

Arabic and he smiled and asked her to dinner in her native tongue.

She seemed irritated and he worried he had gone too far. And then he thought of the work camp, the need to live hour by hour because the next day was so uncertain. The joy of a piece of extra bread smuggled in thinning, cold hands. The grabbing of any momentary feel of satisfaction before it was gone in a blink of an eye.

"When do you take your lunch? Perhaps I could take you to lunch if you'd rather?"

"I hardly think it appropriate!"

"Why ever not?"

She finished bandaging his hand without another word, her face still flushed with indignation.

"There, you are done," she declared when she had finished. "That should not cause you any further trouble."

"Let's hope it does," he replied ruefully, "and then perhaps we could continue this conversation."

"The door is that way, Mr Beker."

"Jozef, please." He turned back towards her in the waiting area. "I don't know your name?"

"No, you don't," she agreed before turning on her heel and away from the curious stares of the other patients.

"He seemed nice." Theresa nudged her friend.

"Don't they all," she huffed, determined to shake the shade of red that gave away her discomfort, her anger, her embarrassment.

Who on earth did he think he was?

***

He was back a few days later. The bandage needed changing and he secretly delighted at the chance to meet the curious nurse again. It was his day off and he travelled into the city from his billet in Cleopatra even though there were nearer clinics to his digs than the Catholic hospital near his place of work.

"He's back," Theresa whispered to her friend with a conspiratorial nudge.

The same flush of red and a fierce cloud of outrage immediately enveloped her and she dropped the pan of discarded swabs and bandages with a clatter on the floor. Too late. The noise had drawn his attention and they exchanged glances across the corridor; his, a smile of relief that his visit was not to be disappointing and hers, a glare of anger that dared him to repeat his previous performance.

She picked up her scattered tools and looked back at her friend, flustered.

"You deal with him." It was a demand. She didn't relish the opportunity of speaking to him again.

Theresa looked at the man in uniform and back at Mary.

"I'm sorry, Mary, but he's your patient." She skipped off to the nurses' room before her friend could protest.

So, this was how it was going to be.

"Well, you'd better come through." Her tone was brusque and she avoided looking directly at him.

"Whatever you wish." He was smiling. She could tell.

"You haven't been looking after this wound," she tutted as she engaged herself in scrutinising the bandage that was dirty and the pus that had seeped into its folds.

"No, I suppose I haven't," he agreed. "I don't mean to upset you, Mary."

Her hands paused in her work and she looked up, startled.

"How do you know my name?"

"I asked your friend."

"She had no right to say!"

He winced as her anger tugged at the last strands of the discarded bandage with less carefulness than was needed. The move stirred a moment of compassion that she quickly brushed aside.

"This is going all wrong again…" he admitted quietly.

"Yes, it is," she snapped. "At least we agree on something."

"What will it take for you to give me a chance and let me take you out?"

Her breath escaped her open lips in one long movement of exasperation. She glared at him but found his stare unwavering as it met hers. She was angered by his determination.

"Mr Beker, if you care for your wound in the way you should so that there is no further need to clutter up my waiting room, I will go out for coffee with you."

She surprised herself with her snap decision. Where had that come from? Did she expect the challenge not to be met? Was she confident that she could avoid a further meeting?

"OK." His face beamed with triumph and she immediately felt her promise was misplaced. "I have my orders and I will follow them to the letter."

***

"Why are you hiding, Mary?"

Theresa looked on in amusement as her friend stood, half concealed, clutching the fraying edges of one of the partition curtains from the consulting area.

"He's back again," she whispered, frantically waving her hand at her friend in a wordless order to conceal herself before Jozef saw her.

Jozef was indeed standing, cap scrunched in his hands behind his back, under the cross of Jesus, rocking back and forth on his heels with pursed lips as his eyes flitted across the ceiling. The man was stubborn. She'd allow him that.

Theresa giggled in an excitement that she immediately quashed as she saw the look on her friend's face.

"What's the harm, Mary?"

"I can't just go out with a man I don't know."

"Why not?" Theresa shrugged.

"Because..." She failed to find the words. "Maman for starters!"

"If he's a decent man, then what's the harm? Looking at him, I think he's more the decent sort."

"All I see is a man in uniform."

"And what's wrong with that? Half the men in Alexandria seem to be in uniform!" Theresa lowered her voice and placed a hand on her arm. "He'll keep coming back until you say yes. What's the harm with just one coffee?"

***

They drank Turkish coffee in a café just beside the Ramleh tram terminal a short walk from the hospital. It was late in the afternoon. Mary had agreed on one drink on the understanding it was after her lunch and their meeting took place in the light of day. Meeting in the evening on her own with a man she hardly knew was out of the question. She told nothing of her plans to her mother and brother and secretly wished her sister was at hand to confide in.

Their table was one by the window with faded green leather chairs and a table top made of tinted glass and wood. Mary could see the fuzzy outline of her stockinged legs through the glass as she crossed and re-crossed them underneath her stiff uniform. Her gaze alternated between the table and her cup of thick, sweet coffee and the foam that she stirred constantly with her spoon.

"I get the impression that you don't want to be here?"

The directness of Jozef's question startled her, and she immediately put down her spoon. She thought of the nuns at her old school, her mother and felt guilty that she had let slip on those lessons of good manners that they had all drummed into her.

"Not at all."

"You're a mystery, Mary."

"I'm a mystery?" she scoffed at that. "And what about you, Mr Beker? You turn up at my surgery and ask me out and I don't know the first thing about you!"

"You know that I'm currently in the army and that I have an injured hand. That's a start. But you…?"

"You know that I'm a nurse and that I was born and raised here in Alexandria, but you…?" Her tone was almost mocking as she copied his words.

"So now we know each other." Jozef smiled, choosing to ignore her subtleties. "What shall we talk about?"

"Oh!" Mary said involuntarily in frustration and she sat back and folded her arms. "If my mother saw this…" She mumbled to herself.

"Ah, so you have a mother." He nodded. "See I'm getting to know you more and more with each passing minute."

"Everyone has a mother, Mr Beker."

"Please call me Jozef. Yes, but mine is thousands of miles away. They all are. All my family, either that or…" He stopped abruptly, his brow furrowing in confusion as he remembered Rozia, Marysia and Arja. Their dark hair and calming voices. The feeling of love they sparked inside him. To his dismay, he realised that he hadn't thought of them that morning. He thought of them every morning but today the only thought in his mind was the excitement of spending time with this mysterious lady. It had given him a buoyancy that had recently been lacking.

"Jozef?" She had spoken his name softly, delicately, gently bringing him back to this moment, in this café, in this city. The disinterested look had gone from her eyes and she had muttered his name hesitantly and with such care that he recognised that deep compassion inside her again that made him want to tell her everything.

"It's nothing." He was annoyed with himself that the mood had turned. "Is it always so hot in this country?"

A fly landed on his hand and circled the scar that indicated the invisible spot where the boil had been. The boil that had brought them together; an abhorrent thing that resulted in their meeting, much like the war that had brought him across seven countries to this spot, in Alexandria. With her.

"You've been looking after yourself better than the last time we met," she pointed out, her fingers stroking the place where the wound had healed with medical satisfaction. "Oh, sorry, I apologise. Habit." She withdrew her hand, frowning that her work had crept into this social scene.

"No, don't apologise, please. I find your care and sincerity refreshing. We could all do with a bit more humanity at the moment. Don't you agree?"

She nodded. Unsure what to say.

"Another coffee, perhaps?" He had asked her before she had even placed her current cup to her lips. It made her smile. This serious man, stumbling over small talk in a bid to keep her there, with him, in this small café by a busy tram station with the roar of the street in both their ears.

"No, this will do me quite well, Mr Beker." And then she smiled again. "I mean, Jozef."

***

It was a week since their first outing together. Mary had looked up at the imposing classical building of the British Army Headquarters as she passed and wondered which window was his and immediately reproached herself for being so sentimental. She exited the tram on her way to work, looking over her shoulder, scanning the crowds, looking out for the man in uniform with the serious stare. Theresa teased her about it. She had been right, she'd said. The man had piqued her interest in a way that none of the others could.

"It was just the one outing. I must have bored him," she confided, quite matter-of-factly. Perhaps she was trying to convince herself in a bid to still her feelings.

"Now, I hardly think that possible, Mary!"

She thought no more of it until she came home one day to find him sitting on the sofa in her mother's living room, sipping coffee and looking quite at peace and at home. Mary's jaw nearly dropped to the floor.

"What on earth are you doing here?"

"Mary! That's no way to treat our guest," Zakia said swiftly. She mirrored Jozef's relaxed manner as she sat comfortably in her chair, in her slippers, the coffee cup and saucer on her lap.

"I hope you don't mind, Mary," Jozef said, "but I was passing and I thought I'd pay you a visit."

"Pay me a visit? But I never told you where I lived!" He had spoken to her in stilted Arabic but she had replied in French, knowing full well that her mother would not have understood what she'd said. The embarrassment was palpable.

He shrugged as if it was of no consequence.

"Jozef brought me some gifts." Zakia was smiling. Mary couldn't recall her smiling like that before.

"Brought you some gifts?" she repeated.

Then she saw the eggs, flour, onions and vegetables laid out on the coffee table before them. They had 'fallen out' of the NAAFI supply van that Jozef had been asked to drive on an errand that day. He thought it wise not to divulge this fact to them in Mary's current state of shock.

"You must stay for dinner, Jozef," Zakia decided.

He looked for Mary's approval before answering. She just stared, open-mouthed.

"I don't want to put you to any trouble," he said hesitantly.

"No trouble at all," Zakia decided before scooping up the goods and hurrying to the kitchenette to prepare something worthy for their guest.

"I can't believe it!"

"It's nothing really."

"Not the food, the fact that you invite yourself here…"

"Technically, your mother did."

"…and how on earth did you know where I lived?"

"I followed you the other day."

"You followed me? Jozef, you are so frustrating!"

"I've upset you and I'm sorry for that. That is not what I intended."

She was silenced by his sincerity. He genuinely wanted to please her. But what on earth for?

"Let me make it up to you." Jozef stood up. "Let me take you out for dinner."

"Well, I…"

"I had no intention of causing a scene so I will leave you now but please say I can see you again?"

She stared at him, this serious man with his ill-fitting military uniform, shrouded in mystery. *What was it about him?*

"OK, then." Her subconscious decided for her. "But you'll have to stay for dinner now," she added as an afterthought. "For the risk of upsetting my Maman, you understand?"

"Absolutely."

They ate a small feast and when it was over, Mary sat back and watched whilst her mother and Jozef talked for hours about nothing and everything. She smiled as she looked on that scene. As much as she fought with the feelings inside her, she was drawn to him without knowing the slightest reason why.

***

The music in *Athineos* caused a pleasing dizziness in her mind which made her forget the wards with the work that toughened her hands. The food that filled her stomach and tantalised her taste buds made her forget the war that was causing so much wanting, so much suffering. Her cup that Jozef kept on filling even made her forget about her mother's cart and the need that kept it laden day-in, day-out.

"Does he make you happy?" Her mother asked in the light of day, when she had swapped the red dress that hugged her waist for the practical uniform of a nurse at the Catholic Hospital.

The smile that she had been wearing since Jozef had twirled her about the dance floor faltered a minute, paused in slight confusion at the question her mother asked. The last few weeks had been unexpected. Life was moving in such a way that she hadn't the time to think, to acknowledge her own feelings.

She looked at Zakia in her widow's clothes that hadn't aged even if the woman they shrouded had aged underneath. There were fine lines appearing around eyes that were less bright, grey streaks in her otherwise deep black hair. Her life had revolved solely around children and work. Circumstance had caused the hardships that stooped her stance and created the bitterness that thinned her lips into a permanent thoughtfulness.

And here was her daughter with a chance of something different.

"Yes," Mary had to admit. "I guess he does make me happy."

"Good." She smiled, the anxiety gone. "Because he makes me happy too."

.

Warsaw,
POLAND,
2005

Mary sat in the airport departure lounge contemplating how easy it was to travel the world these days. That trip from Egypt to England for the first time, all those years ago in 1948 would have been a much more palatable experience without those endless weeks at the mercy of that boat and the waves that constantly tossed it.

Now it was just a case of hopping on a plane.

Their time in Poland had come to an end. They had vigorously searched every resource, every location they could to explore Jozef's Polish life; a fitting tribute to the man who would have celebrated his 100th birthday today. Now, at the end of it all, Mary found her body relaxing, her mind at peace with the bustle of the world around her.

Henry and Margarita had gone in search of coffee. One of those instant kinds, no doubt. Not the thick, strong, velvety Turkish coffee she really craved. Her children had left her alone with her thoughts, perhaps worrying that she was tired, assuming her age was exhausting her.

Why did a number matter so much?

The seats were filling up as the time of their departure crept forward. Families, couples, men in business suits. A variety of different languages and accents. Such a noise around her and still the peace descended, filling her, comforting her.

"That's a pretty piece."

The young couple opposite her, entwined across their separate seats, had both their hands on the woman's slender finger where their touch caressed the ring that dazzled in the harsh glare of the airport's lighting.

The woman blushed, the man catching her embarrassment with a smile.

"Thank you."

"Look after that one." Mary winked at him. "Love is just so precious."

Another smile as she watched them, seeing how the woman's hair cascaded tenderly over his shoulders and how his whole body turned subtly towards her.

"Your coffee, Mum." Margarita had returned with a steaming cardboard cup.

It was hot and tasteless. The seat she was sitting on was hard and uncomfortable, just like the one in the Warsaw University library with its vast glass ceiling and echoing corridors, but for the first time that week her hands were not tense, her feet were not sore and there was a calmness in her soul that seemed to cover and caress her.

Ah, I know now, Jozef. She smiled. *I know where this peace has come from.*

"You know," she said dreamily, placing the unfinished coffee beside her, "he never lied to me - my Jozef - not once. I couldn't have asked for more than that."

Alexandria, EGYPT, 1946

"Nurse?"

Mary was on one of the wards that day, looking after patients recovering from burns, changing dressings, administering pain relief, cleaning wounds and generally caring.

"Nurse!"

She was on her own. Her friend, a sister of the same age, was on her break and she was dashing back and forth, trying to get through her list of jobs.

"Nurse!"

Two patients were sitting up in bed staring out of the window and calling her over.

"What is it?" she demanded.

The one with a bandage over his arm and chest raised a finger to point out of the window that was open to let in the fresh, warm air. Then she heard it. The sharp, shrill sound of an accordion that scratched and squeaked its way along a tune that she didn't recognise, sung by an Italian tongue.

"*Oj Mari… Oj Mari…*"

She pulled down the window and told the music player to go away at once. The window was shut with a thud. The musician didn't pause and sang more loudly and more persistently towards the closed window on the second floor.

"*Arápete fenesta, famme affacciá a Maria…*"

"Nurse?"

Her indignation rising by the minute, she strode back to the window.

"Stop this nonsense at once!" Her voice carried down to the player and his squeaky instrument. Her angry words reverberated across the street and back again.

The man looked up and hesitated and then seemed to look towards something in the shadows.

"Mary!"

Her mouth dropped open in shock as she saw Jozef emerge. A wave of his hand and the man was playing again, loudly, in words that dripped like sugar on his Italian tongue.

"*… ca stóngo 'mmiez'â via speruto d' 'a vedé…*"

"What are you doing here?" She had to shout to get herself heard.

"I came to see you."

"We agreed to meet later," she scolded him. "I'm at work. You're disturbing the patients!"

"I needed to get your attention."

"Whatever for?"

"Because I want you to marry me!"

Heart beating loudly in her chest; the music bumping against her ears so that she couldn't think.

"Jozef Beker!" she exclaimed, exasperated and she withdrew her head back into the ward.

All the patients were looking at her now, smiles on their faces that were sometimes barely visible beneath the bandages that shrouded them. The smell of disinfectant was heavy in the air. There were splashes of bodily fluids all over her uniform from a hard morning's shift. Her hair was out of place and she had not had time to put her make-up on that morning.

This was unexpected.

"Mary!"

She could hear him shouting again over the music. The tune of one drowning out the shouts of the other.

She reappeared at the window.

"Shhh! People will hear!" she shouted down to him. She was sure the matron would appear any minute, her face flushed and red, demanding what all the noise was about.

"Well, Mary, what's your answer?"

There he was, cap in hand just like the first day he had met her, a fleeting look of anxiety in amongst his serious smile. Waiting. Expecting.

"If I give you your answer, will you tell your friend to stop his music so I can get on with my day?"

"Of course."

"OK, then." She briefly looked out over the rooftops of Alexandria. Even in war it was beautiful, the architecture of man in all its intricacies. The city seemed to buzz under the afternoon sun. In the distance, the first calls to prayer were being sung by the muezzin, which were soon picked up by others across all the mosques in the city. The Italian singer was still proclaiming his song of love. In this cacophony of sound, she looked down at Jozef, at this man from Poland who had been on a journey crossing continents before arriving at her door with a wounded hand and tantalising glimpses into an alternative future. The man who was asking for *her* hand in marriage.

"Yes," she said.

AUTHOR'S NOTE

The lives of Jozef and Mary as outlined in this book are as close to the truth as possible. A truth built on faded memories, document scraps and a few photographs that brought their lives alive in black and white. There has been artistic licence in some places to fill the void where there was simply no memory or no paperwork of truth to embellish.

I was fortunate enough to spend time with Mary during the last six weeks of her life as she recalled the life she had led in Alexandria and the life she had known with Jozef. Her childhood had been incredibly hard with the untimely death of her father effectively leaving the family penniless. Egyptian women had few rights. Her mother, Zakia, was not entitled to any of her late husband's wealth. There was an expectation that she would become a servant in her husband's family home in return for food and shelter. This was an acceptable practice at the time. However,

Zakia was not a woman to comply with expectations – a trait her daughter, Mary, soon copied.

Mary chose a profession that was frowned upon and, despite her family's horror, she truly excelled at being a nurse. She was hard-working, compassionate and conscientious in her work. She set up a union for nurses in the hospital where she was employed – a testament to her strong sense of fairness. It was this work that eventually led her to that meeting with Jozef in 1943. She was on duty that day to administer medical care to a Polish officer with a painful boil on his hand. After a stilted first meeting, Jozef persevered in winning her affections. They planned to settle in Alexandria but events in Egypt decided otherwise. Alexandria, like other cities in the country, was becoming too dangerous for foreigners, particularly those in uniform and those associated with the British (Egypt's previous colonial ruler). Jozef once again found himself an outsider in a country he was starting to see as home.

What must it have been like for Mary to leave her home and travel to a country where she stood out and didn't speak a word of the language? The separation from Zakia was clearly painful for her (even in her later years of life) and the stories she told of the prejudice both she and Jozef endured as foreigners went some way towards explaining those feelings.

And the feelings she had for Jozef? These were very much evident in the interviews I had with her – the smile that crept over her lips at the mention of his name, the sad glint that followed in her eyes. They were devoted to each other, despite their time together being so short.

And what of Jozef?

Jozef was much harder to interpret. He had died long ago and with no family left from his earlier life in Poland. He had left his country of birth (forcibly and not of his own will) with just the clothes on his back. The few photographs he cherished later in life were obtained from his mother in Johannesburg. There were no photographs of Rozia; no indication of his life with her, other than a couple of photographs of their children. Marysia was only five when she died either at the hands of the Nazis in the Warsaw Ghetto or in a subsequent extermination camp with her mother, then aged about thirty-eight years old. It was originally assumed that Arja had died with his sister and mother, but subsequent research unearthed a previously unknown family survivor in the USA who had been living with Rozia and her daughter in the Warsaw Ghetto under Nazi occupation. June Feinsilver (Jozef and Rozia's niece by one of Rozia's sisters) had escaped the Ghetto before it was liquidated, leaving her family behind.[1] In her documented memories of the Holocaust, she recalled that Arja, like his father (Jozef), was *somewhere else* in 1940. Subsequent research revealed that in amongst the various advertisements Jozef had placed in newspapers seeking information on his family, he had contacted the International Tracing Service run by the Red Cross in the immediate years after the war.[2] It was the only central service at the time set up to reunite families separated

---

1   Her testimony is available at the Midwest Centre for Holocaust Education in Kansas, USA https://mchekc.org/testimonial/june-feinsilver/. She also provided a more in-depth testimony to the USC Shoah Foundation, which is where snippets of information regarding Rozia and Jozef's whereabouts at the start of the war were obtained.

2   These records are held by the Arolsen Archives in Germany: https://arolsen-archives.org/en/

by World War Two. In the details he provided in his application, he lists Arja's address at a property in Grodno (now part of Belarus) and that the last he had heard of his son was that he was in the Bergen-Belsen Concentration Camp in February 1942. There were rumours in the family that during the war, Arja was a member of the resistance movement acting as a runner, which is highly likely as Grodno had an active resistance movement during the war years (first against the Russians and then against the invading German forces). The city itself was largely defended by army reserves and youths recruited from the Scout movement at the Battle of Grodno between 20th and 22nd September 1939. We know that Jozef was in Grodno with his brother at the start of the war. Could he have taken his son there with him?

If Arja was indeed later incarcerated in Bergen-Belsen in February 1942, he was possibly there as a prisoner of war as the camp did not officially become a concentration camp for Jews and other persecuted minorities until 1943.

Arja was only sixteen when he went missing.

Of Jozef's time in the work camp in Siberia, only a few handwritten pages of his memories remained. Over a few pages of paper, he documented the horror and hardships he had endured at the hands of the Russian system. It is thought that he may have written down more recollections after the war but, if he had, it was assumed that Mary had destroyed them. In the aftermath of all that pain and destruction, Mary maintained a real fear that her husband would be judged if these memories were read. Talking about experiences of the war was not common in the years after the guns had stopped. Some never talked about their experiences at all but, the nightmares and night sweats were no less real. Those sheets of paper were the only record of the direct voice of Jozef that has survived through time. That is, the only voice apart from the love of an extraordinary woman that outlived him for nearly fifty years.

This book is printed on paper from sustainable sources managed under the Forest Stewardship Council (FSC) scheme.

It has been printed in the UK to reduce transportation miles and their impact upon the environment.

For every new title that Troubador publishes, we plant a tree to offset CO_2, partnering with the More Trees scheme.

For more about how Troubador offsets its environmental impact, see www.troubador.co.uk/sustainability-and-community